Bandun Gate

Miriam Van Scott

[signature]

"A modern-day Charleston ghost story that
will haunt you well after you finish it."
Christian Senger, *Holy City Sinner*

www.darkstroke.com

Discover us online:
www.darkstroke.com

Find us on instagram:
www.instagram.com/darkstrokebooks

Include **#darkstroke** in a photo of yourself
holding this book on Instagram and
something nice will happen.

Acknowledgements

I would like to thank the following for providing expertise, consultation, or other input to this project:

The Gullah Geechee Cultural Heritage Corridor Commission
Lilly Ashwell
Daniel Deitch
The Staff of Wando Mount Pleasant Library
South Carolina Picture Project
Horror Writers Association
Shining Sol Candle Company
Wrong Element Productions
South Carolina Writers Association
The Corcorans

About the Author

Miriam Van Scott was born in Washington, D.C. and attended George Washington University and George Mason, earning a B.A. in Journalism. During her early career, she was a public information representative for government agencies and worked as a photojournalist for a variety of publications in the Metro area.

Van Scott's first book, *Encyclopedia of Hell* (Macmillan) was published in 1998. Since that time her articles and photos have appeared in over thirty publications ranging from *Good Housekeeping Magazine* to the *Chicken Soup for the Soul* franchise. She has also provided content to *The History Channel, Sy-Fy, The Learning Channel, ABC News, Paramount Entertainment Group, Media General* and many others. Van Scott's published works include the books *Song of Old: An Advent Calendar for the Spirit*, the *Shakespeare Goes Pop!* series and the children's picture book *Boomer's Criss-Cross Christmas*.

Bandun Gate

Prologue

I was a biographer of demons in a city of ghosts; nothing that happened in Charleston's moss-veiled marshlands should've come as a shock. Sharing the story of Bandun Gate is especially difficult because I know I'm twice-guilty — once when I shrugged off the demonologist's warning, then again when my daughter paid the price for my recklessness.

"You're opening a door you'll never be able to close," the old priest had told me back in 1996, when Abby was just a baby, and I was writing a book about Hell. "While you're poking around the abyss, the damned are eyeing *you*. Sooner or later, some vile thing is going to poke back."

Sure enough, twenty years later, along South Carolina's haunted shores, some vile thing did.

Chapter One
Aside the Holy City

I almost told Abby about my nightmare that first morning she visited our new house in South Carolina. It had been years since I'd dreamed of Hell, and I wanted to spill the details, hear my daughter's reaction. She was still in the cradle when I'd been researching *Encyclopedia of Hell*, and dark visions muddied my sleep on a regular basis. Obviously I never told Abby or her two brothers about those nightmares at the time; I rarely shared them with my husband, Dan. But Abby was just a few weeks shy of twenty-one now, about to start her senior year in college majoring in criminology. She read Stephen King between lectures, and thumbed through serial killer bios while slasher flicks played in the background. I figured there wasn't much she hadn't been exposed to, horror-wise.

We were cresting the Ravenel Bridge into Charleston as I prepared my summary, the city laid out before us like a postcard photo. Church spires, too many to count as the minivan zipped along, stretched their way into the blue morning sky while a scattering of boats dotted the harbor below. The late-August sun was already well above the horizon, illuminating a sea of pink rooftops and emerald palmetto trees lining the Holy City's cobblestone streets. Even with the windows up and the A/C blasting, I could smell the ocean air.

"Bridge songs!" Abby shouted just as I was about to begin my tale. "I'll start. *Bridge Over Trouble Water*."

This game was a family favorite — impromptu 'Round Robin' trivia. Someone would call out a subject, then we'd take turns naming things that fit the category until we got stumped and had to drop out. Last one standing was the winner.

"Does it have to be 'bridge' in the title, or just mention bridges somewhere in the song?"

5

Victory often hinged on technicalities, and it was best to nail down the rules upfront.

"Just in the lyrics. I'll throw you a bone."

"Okay, let's see," I said, shifting focus to this new endeavor. "*London Bridge is Falling Down.*"

"*Graffiti Bridge.*"

"*Ode to Billy Joe.*"

Abby shot me a questioning look.

"It's a 70s tune about a boy who jumps off a bridge."

"Wow. Sounds like a great wedding song. Um, *Under the Bridge* — Red Hot Chili Peppers."

"*Seen the Lights Go Out on Broadway.* Pretty sure there's something in there about blowing up bridges."

"Well, keeping with the destruction theme, Paramore *That's What You Get*, cause it's all about burning bridges."

"Okay, lemme see. Oh! *Love Can Build A Bridge.*"

"*We Didn't Start the Fire.* 'Bridge on the River Kwai.'" Abby sang that last part.

I wracked my brain, but couldn't come up with another. "You're queen of the bridge songs, Abs."

Abby flung a triumphant fist into the air as I turned left onto East Bay Street. We rode past the Cooper River docks where metal cargo containers, stacked like Lego bricks, were loaded onto westbound trains. Further along, the mingled architecture offered a rolling tutorial of Charleston's blended history. Antebellum houses sporting white columns and wrap-around porches shared the block with glass-front office buildings and repurposed military quarters. Downtown, churches dominated the skyline: modest chapels, elegant temples, magnificent cathedrals. I took a right on Pinckney and headed towards the market district.

"Wow, there really *are* a lot of churches here!" Abby observed.

"That's why Charleston's called the Holy City."

Traffic was thick even on a Wednesday — August is peak tourist season — and navigating the narrow streets required my full attention. Dan and I had only moved to the lowcountry a few months earlier, and I still struggled with Charleston's maze of one ways and through-streets that suddenly became 'right turn only' lanes or parking spaces. It didn't seem a good time to bring up my Hell dream, so I pivoted to something breezier.

"You wanna stop anywhere before Grandpa's?" I asked my daughter. "We're near the Sheds, if you're up for some shopping."

"Perfect!" Abby said while I slowed to let a horse-drawn carriage cross in front of us. "I promised Sarah I'd get her a sweetgrass basket."

Sweetgrass baskets are an iconic part of Charleston's history. The containers are hand-woven with green-gold grasses gathered from local marshes, then shaped via a technique called coiling. They're the signature craft of the Gullah, a people who forged a unique culture along Carolina's Sea Islands and coastal plains.

And though the baskets themselves are beautiful, their history is anything but. Coiling was brought to the region in the 1600s by Africans snatched from Sierra Leone, Senegal, and the Gambia. Slavers targeted rice farmers along West Africa's 'Windward Coast' because their growing conditions were nearly identical to those in the Carolina lowcountry. It was the agricultural expertise of these stolen Mendi and Temne tribesmen that ensured flourishing rice harvests along the salt marshes around Charleston, and African coiling skills came in handy for making baskets to collect, sift and transport the grains.

European plantation owners, however, found the tidal plains unlivable. The wetlands were filled with alligators, poisonous snakes and mosquitoes that carried malaria and yellow fever. During hurricane season the areas often flooded, and even a storm-free summer was marred by sweltering heat and oppressive humidity. The white aristocrats couldn't cope, so they moved inland, leaving their African captives to manage farm operations themselves.

Isolated from European influences, the enslaved laborers not only produced Colonial America's largest cash crop, they also developed a culture rooted in their West African heritage. In addition to cultivation and basketry techniques, Gullah included a unique language which blended African dialects with Creole and English. The people enjoyed a rich spirituality, too, with white magic, hymns, spells, conjurings, potions, curses, and cures.

Like other Gullah customs, the art of basket coiling has been passed down through the generations. Our family had been vacationing in Charleston since Abby and her brothers Roman and Charles were all preschoolers, and everyone always loved visiting the Historic City Market (nicknamed 'the Sheds') to watch the 'pullers' work. The artisans would sing folk songs as they produced their goods, or share traditional Gullah fables. On one such trip, I asked about the time required to generate such lovely works.

"How long does it take to make one of these?" I said, pointing to a basket the size of a serving bowl.

The craftswoman glanced over and gave me a smile.

"A thousand years."

"A thousand years?" I repeated, eyebrows raised. "That seems kinda long."

"Well, it is centuries back to Africa, to my ancestors who had to teach themselves the craft before they could hand it down to their children. Learning to gather grass, weave patterns, coil reeds using a bit of bone as a forming tool. To master their art.

"Then a long, bitter age for that terrible journey away from their shore to this new one, where they would have to start building a different life, something once again their own. Decades spent learning to weave with unfamiliar grasses and perfect the methods once more.

"And then ages on past my own, to my grandchildren's grandchildren, who will take their place in the long line that connects future to past in the coiling of a basket."

"A thousand years," I whispered, humbled. "That sounds about right."

Abby and I arrived at The Sheds an hour before we were due at my dad's place for lunch. Parking was a debacle — the area was jammed with tourists — but we snagged a spot just a few streets away. In addition to the sweetgrass basket sellers, there were boutiques and open-air kiosks which stretched on for blocks, offering everything from saltwater taffy to hand-tooled leather goods. A woman in a yellow sundress was trying on beach hats while her toddler fidgeted with a toy car, two elderly ladies were debating what flavor fudge to buy. I led Abby through the crowd, past vendors peddling souvenir T-shirts, pecan pralines, sterling charms shaped like palmetto trees, watercolor paintings of the historic houses on Rainbow Row. After quite a bit of jostling we finally arrived at the sweetgrass display.

"Those flat ones are called fanners," the proprietor said as Abby examined the baskets. "They're good for holding bread, fruit, candy, whatever you like."

The puller was an older man, in his mid-eighties I'd guess, around my dad's age, and a master at his craft. He continued to coil as Abby looked over the various designs, his fingers twisting the reeds into treasure like Rumpelstiltskin spinning straw into gold. We chatted as Abby browsed. He complimented my daughter's long auburn hair and lovely green eyes, and I praised his beautiful woven works. Abby examined just about every basket in his collection, then went back and selected a fanner. She paid the man, and when he gave her the change, he also handed her a miniature basket. It was a tiny twin of the one Abby had just purchased, about the size of a silver dollar, with a loop of red satin ribbon tied through its rim.

"Put this on your tree at Christmas," he told her, smiling. "It'll bring you a blessing."

As Abby and I headed back to the van, we passed a rack of touristy brochures outside a sandwich shop. In addition to being famous for its Southern charm, Charleston has a reputation as being one of the most haunted places in America. Apparitions in the Holy City are so common that locals don't ask, "have you ever seen a ghost?" but rather, "*how many* ghosts have you seen, and did any of them speak to you?" The Old Jail, where America's first female serial killer was executed, is said to be a veritable hub of paranormal activity, likewise the Dock Street Theatre and Provost Dungeon. Another favorite hotspot is the

Unitarian Cemetery, where the restless spirit of Poe's *Annabel Lee* supposedly wanders the grounds, searching for her lost love. Intriguing, sure, but I never took any of these claims seriously.

Not then.

One particular flyer caught my attention. Nestled between ads for jet ski rentals and two-for-one miniature golf coupons was a leaflet advertising 'Charleston Ghost & Graveyard Tours.' The picture showed a shadowy figure hovering above the tombstones, its tagline promising 'bone-chilling haunts that defy earthly explanation.' I considered pointing it out then segueing to my nightmare, but quickly dismissed the idea. Abby and I would have plenty of opportunity over the next few days to discuss the subject.

At least I thought so at the time.

We left the city and drove north to Blue Heron Manor, the seniors' community where my father was living. (He'd moved to South Carolina earlier that year, prompting me and Dan to relocate from Northern Virginia, while Roman, Abby and Charles remained in the D.C. area attending college.) The Heron's main building looked like a set from *Gone with the Wind,* with its lavish pillars and two-story balconies that overlooked a landscaped courtyard. Dad met us at the door and gave Abby a big hug.

"Abigail! Welcome to Charleston!" he said, sweeping her into his arms. "So good to see you! Are your brothers here too?"

"Just me today, Grandpa."

"Roman's wrapping up a summer internship," I explained. "He'll be here Saturday. He's bringing Charles down with him."

"Mom and I are having some 'girl time' before the boys get here."

"What about your father?"

Abby shrugged and looked over to me; even *I* wasn't sure of my husband's exact schedule. I relayed it as best I could remember.

"Dan left yesterday for Phoenix. Then it's Vegas, Sacramento and finally Seattle, I think. All I know for sure is that he won't be home until Monday night."

"That's quite an itinerary. Almost a week. I guess business is going well."

Dan's business dealings *were* going well. Fantastic even. He sold digital security-software for an international company and was consistently ranked among its top salesmen. The downside was that the work kept him on the road almost constantly. In the ten months since we'd moved down from Virginia, Dan had spent twice as much time away as he had in Charleston. Product demonstrations, sales seminars, computer expos, corporate events. But he'd promised to fly home immediately after his last meeting this trip and take the rest of the week off. All three kids were going to be in South Carolina, and between their college classes and Dan's work schedule, this would be the last time the whole family would be together until Christmas, at least.

Dad gave Abby a quick tour of the Blue Heron's main level, concluding in the grand dining room. Once he was through pointing out the cut-crystal chandeliers and ocean-themed oil paintings, we sat down to eat. The last of the lunch crowd was ebbing away; a few white-haired retirees were finishing off club sandwiches or Cobb salads, but the spacious room was mostly empty. A heavenly aroma of warm peaches and butter-crust hung in the air, letting us know there'd be fresh cobbler for dessert. Dad recommended Abby and I order the Heron's Wednesday special — shrimp and grits, a Charleston favorite — and we took his advice. He was right, it was delicious.

"So, what have you ladies done so far?" Grandpa asked as we dabbed our plates with homemade cornbread.

"Well, I just got in late last night, so really just some shopping this morning," Abby replied. "Remember my friend Sarah? I got her a basket."

She fished the miniature from her purse and held it out on her open palm. "The man gave me this, too, It's a Christmas ornament!"

"Why, it's marvelous! You should show that to Bernadette. I think she's a sweetgrass coiler herself."

Bernadette Aubelle was the Blue Heron's activities director. She was about mid-thirties, with a muscular build and coppery skin, and seemed to truly delight in organizing Bingo games and bus trips for the seniors. Bernadette was Gullah, born and raised in a tight-knit community a few miles away off route seventeen, and fluent in the language and culture of her people.

The first time I met Bernadette we'd been discussing her heritage when she confidently proclaimed, "You know, Miriam, you already speak some Gullah yourself."

"I do?" I asked, surprised.

"Yes, yes! You know the song *Kumbaya*, don't you? That is Gullah for 'come by here.'"

Bernadette sang then, replacing the familiar lyric with its English translation.

"'Someone's singing Lord, come by here! Someone's crying Lord, come by here!' See, you speak Gullah, and you didn't even know it!"

Dad and I kept an eye out for Bernadette as we ate, hoping to show off Abby's new ornament, but she never showed up in the dining hall. When the three of us had finished lunch, we relocated to the Blue Heron's main parlor. The room was splashed with sunlight from its half dozen floor-to-ceiling windows that showcased the back courtyard's three-tiered fountain and crepe Myrtle trees. We sank into a trio of overstuffed wingback chairs and savored the view.

"So, what do you two have planned for the rest of the day?" Dad asked.

"I'm going to try to find that creepy gate I told you about," I responded. "I think Abby would love it!"

"Oh, yes. I think you showed me pictures."

I took out my phone and swiped through photos until I came to several showing a mysterious construction Dan and I had discovered a few months earlier. We'd stumbled upon it after getting lost in the Wadmalaw River marshes, but I was pretty sure I could find it again. The fence was made of wooden posts strung together with wire mesh, running alongside a dirt road deep in the woods. It had an opening bounded on either side by metal columns at least twelve feet tall, and spanning them was a welded-on arch made from highway guardrail. Underneath the archway, an overgrown path disappeared into a tangle of shrubs and trees. The entire thing was painted a drab grayish-white and speckled with rust and mildew.

Such a massive makeshift creation in the middle of nowhere was odd enough, but what made the structure truly bizarre was the way the thing was decorated. Hundreds, maybe thousands, of various items with no apparent similarity had been attached to the fence and columns via twine or wire ties: screwdrivers, VHS tapes, silk flowers, plastic dinosaurs, scrub brushes, knitting needles. A pair of deer antlers wrapped in Mardi Gras beads poked out from the mesh a few inches off the ground. Serving spoons and baby shoes dangled down from the overhead arch. A telephone headset, vintage 1960, was tied to the left column by its cord. And every last one of these 'decorations' had been painted the same blah color as the framework. It was a truly captivating piece of work.

I had taken a few close-ups of particularly creepy ornamentations, like a hubcap with a scowling face scratched into the metal, and a headless porcelain doll lashed to a post, its moldy arms reaching out as if asking for a hug. Then there was the strange mask...

"Oh, there's Bernadette!" Dad called out, rising to his feet and waving her over. "Bernadette, come meet my granddaughter, Abigail. She has something to show you!"

The smiling woman joined us in the parlor. Dad did a quick round of introductions, then Abby shared the tale of our morning shopping adventure.

"Show Bernadette what the man gave you," my father prompted.

Abby produced the mini fanner and handed it to her.

"It's beautiful!" Bernadette said, examining it closely.

"Don't you make these yourself?" Dad asked.

Bernadette chuckled. "Well, Granny taught me to coil, but I don't keep up with it like I should. This is wonderful, though. A real gem." She handed back the ornament.

The four of us chatted a little more in the charming room.

"Well, it was nice to see you again Bernadette," I said as we prepared to leave. "Abby and I better get going. I want to show her something out near your neck of the woods."

"Oh, where're you headed?"

I handed her my phone opened to a picture of the unusual structure. "It's a weird fence and gate thing, out by the Wadmalaw marshes."

When Bernadette saw the photo, her smile evaporated. "You're going to Bandun Gate?" she asked, voice dropping to a whisper.

"I didn't know it had a name!" I exclaimed, excited at this new information. "Bandun. Is that the family who owns the property?"

The woman stared down at the picture in silence. Abby gave me a quizzical look, intrigued by Bernadette's reaction. "No," she said at last. "Bandun is Gullah for 'abandon.' The name comes from a sign described in an old story."

"Abandon all hope ye who enter here?" I interrupted.

She looked up at me, eyes wide. "Yes, yes. That's it."

"From the *Inferno*?" chimed Abby. "Isn't that what Dante says is written over the gates of Hell?"

Bernadette nodded solemnly. "I wouldn't go there if I were you. I wouldn't go anywhere *near* there."

Dad smiled. "Surely you don't think there's a portal to the underworld here in the lowcountry, do you? Charleston is more like paradise!"

"All I know is, we stay away from there. It's a bad place. A woman died there not long ago. And she wasn't the first."

"Died how?" I asked. "Murdered?"

"Well, the police said it was an accident, but my people say a haint got her."

"What's a haint?" Abby inquired. I glanced over at my dad, who was grinning. He'd obviously heard the term before and found it rather amusing.

"A haint is a restless spirit that won't depart this world, like a ghost," Bernadette said, again in a hushed tone. "Only very angry, very mean. Vengeful. They can do dreadful things to the living. *Dreadful* things. I've heard stories…" her voice trailed

14

off as she shook her head. "If I were you, I'd stay away."

Abby's eyes lit up as Bernadette spoke; there was no way she was going to pass up visiting a haunted gate tucked away in the murky, mute swamplands. Abby was a September baby, a child of autumn, lover of all things dark and mysterious. Her first-ever job was 'professional zombie' at a big amusement park outside Richmond. She'd absolutely devoured the role, creating a backstory for her character complete with details on how she became infected with the 'undead virus,' and which loved ones she'd eaten after 'turning.' Abby was so adept at ghoul-craft, she was quickly promoted to Talent Coach, and created bios for all her fellow creatures at Zombie High. Her co-workers affectionately referred to her as 'Mombie.' When the park closed at the end of the season, Abby was recognized as 'Monster of the Year' and given a commendation from none other than 'zombified President Ronald Reagan.' We were *going* to Bandun Gate.

Abby and I thanked Bernadette for the info, then made our way to the exit.

"See that color," Dad said as the automatic door opened to the parking lot, blasting us with sticky August air. He was pointing towards the underside of the roof's overhang, which was painted a pale shade of aqua. "It's called 'haint blue.' The locals say it keeps evil spirits away. It fools them into thinking the blue is actually water, and they can't cross over bodies of water."

"Well, I guess *you'll* be safe here, Grandpa!" Abby laughed.

She was giving my father a goodbye hug when Bernadette called to us from the hallway. I couldn't understand what she'd said, so I asked her to repeat it.

"It's a Gullah blessing," Bernadette replied with an apprehensive smile. "It means, 'May God keep His eyes upon you.'"

Abby and I drove south after leaving the Blue Heron, crossing a series of bridges that spanned creeks, rivers, streams, inlets, salt marshes. In between the waterways were islets and islands bordered by yellow-green grasses, with white

15

egret sentries keeping watch. Poplars, cypresses, and live oaks spread their long branches over the road, weaving a thick canopy above us; Spanish moss fluttered down from the limbs like tattered gray curtains. It was mid-afternoon, however once we'd crossed Penny Creek, the foliage overhead was so dense we couldn't see the sun. The only affirmation of summer was the intense heat outside: my dashboard thermometer pegged the exterior temperature at a sizzling ninety-four degrees.

"I think the road to Angel Oak is around here somewhere," I noted as we zoomed along, the passage before us an emerald tunnel forged into the woods.

"So where is this Bandun Gate already?" Abby asked, employing a Dracula-*esque* accent while pronouncing the name of our ominous destination.

"It's gotta be close. We'll find it."

I glanced in the rearview mirror; there was no one behind us as far as I could see. No one in front, either, or coming towards us in the on-coming lane. Thinking back, I didn't remember seeing any other vehicles since leaving the highway ten minutes ago, and the last house we passed had to have been miles back. I took my foot off the gas and let the van coast forward, both of us scanning the landscape for a turn-off into the marshes.

"There it is!" I shouted, spotting an unpaved trail a hundred yards ahead. "I'm pretty sure it's down here."

"Is that even a real road, Mom? It looks like somebody's driveway."

We slowed almost to a stop. A rusted street sign was leaning over into the ditch; it looked as if it had been knocked down ages ago and no one ever bothered setting it right again. Or perhaps like someone had pushed it over on purpose, hoping to obscure the intersection. I inched closer and could see that the name of the road had been completely obliterated by buckshot, until all that remained was a rusty rectangular strip pocked with bullet holes.

"Well, there's a street sign here, or at least what's left of it," I offered. "Must mean this goes *somewhere*."

I turned onto the narrow passageway, the van creep, creep,

creeping forward. If another vehicle had come at us from the opposite direction, one of us would have to pull over to let the other pass, and even then, it would be tight. Luckily none did. We were alone on this overgrown byway, no one else coming or going. As we moved further along, Abby made a disconcerting observation: there wasn't a single telephone pole, streetlight, mailbox, power line or *any* sign of civilization down this long, desolate stretch.

After about a mile or so, the road took a sharp leftward lurch and spat us onto a rickety wooden bridge. Abby grimaced as we trundled over it, not sure the rotting framework would withstand the weight of our van. I was ready to ditch this search and head back to Charleston as soon as I could find a safe place to turn around, but when we came off the bridge, Abby and I were greeted by a ribbony gray splash threaded against the dark vegetation.

We were riding alongside it: Bandun Gate in all its creepy, captivating glory.

Chapter Two
The Vermicular File

Bandun Gate and its adjacent fence ran parallel to the dirt road's eastern side, beginning just past the crumbling bridge. The structure was set back into the brush about ten feet, allowing ample room for me to pull over and park. Nothing was growing along the front save for some patchy carpetweed and an occasional dandelion popping through the sandy soil. A lone oak sapling stood sentry just outside the archway's right column. I let the van roll to a stop then cut the engine.

"You weren't kidding. This is amazing!" Abby said, scrambling out.

As she flung open the passenger door, the South Carolina summer swept in and washed over us. The air was hot and damp, leaving me immediately uncomfortable, even in the shade. A swamp symphony greeted us: chittering insects, trilling songbirds, the creek's steady gurgling as it flowed under the bridge we'd just crossed. The scent of wet decay layered with salt wafts from the nearby ocean was overpowering. Abby swatted a mosquito as she stepped toward the fence.

"Too bad you didn't know about this place when you were writing your Hell book," she said, staring up at the gate's archway. "This would've been perfect for the cover!"

I smiled, but felt a twinge of unease remembering my recent nightmare, oddly relieved I hadn't told her about it after all. On the heels of that came another, much darker memory: a grim foray I'd made into the abyss a few months before Abby was born.

One summer afternoon in 1995, a family friend who'd spent thirty years in law enforcement showed up at my door. Hank heard I was writing a book about the netherworld and offered me a look at his own captured demons.

"You wanna know about Hell?" he said, holding up a big cardboard box that smelled like cigarette smoke and old cheese. "I'll show you Hell!"

For the next five hours, Hank walked me through the contents of his carton. He had police reports, crime scene photos, depositions, artist sketches, informants' testimony and forensic curiosities collected from around the country and dating back forty years. Their common denominator: every item figured into an investigation allegedly linked to devil worship, ranging from satanic graffiti on underpasses to homicidal maniacs claiming to be the Antichrist.

At first, I found Hank's collection intriguing. Much of it was fairly tame: gang members who used demonic names as aliases, aggressive panhandlers raising funds for 'shrines' to Lucifer, teenage vandals with a fondness for scrawling '666' onto church doors. Some items were even amusing, like the suburban couple who called themselves 'Apollyon's Apostles' and insisted the money they earned hosting weekly pay-to-play orgies was 'religious income' and therefore tax-exempt. These oddities were interesting, sure, but none quite fit my subject criteria. I was writing a book about Hell, not about Satan or his various devotees.

Other items in the box, however, offered a sinister glimpse into the realm of absolute, unmitigated evil. Those were downright nauseating.

Among Hank's papers were witness statements describing rapes, mutilations and murders designed to create 'Hell on earth.' The Feds ultimately dismissed most as hoaxes; however the accounts were still stomach-turning in their gruesome detail. Which was worse, I wondered, that these horrible crimes might actually have been committed, or that people could concoct such depraved fictions to amuse themselves? Many reports were so awful I couldn't read them all the way through.

And then there were the photographs. They were, by far, the absolute worst of his cache. I'm sure the fact that I was six months pregnant at the time made Hank's visuals all the more repugnant. *Reading* about violent, perverse acts was bad enough, *seeing* them was a whole new universe of revulsion.

"What — exactly — am I looking at here?" I'd asked him, thumbing through a paper-clipped bundle of black and white glossies.

Hank glanced at my bulging belly. "Sorry, kiddo. Forgot those shots were in there. They're stills from an eight-millimeter film made by some nut-job obsessed with Charlie Manson. 'Banquet of the Unbaptized,' he called it. Claimed it was real, an occult 'power ritual' or some such bullshit. Our guys say it's fake."

The first photo showed thirteen black-robed men crowding around a wooden altar, their faces partially obscured by white eye-masks. In the next shot a swaddled infant lay at the altar's center while one of the men held a large scorpion-shaped dagger over the baby. The rest of the pictures appeared to depict child sacrifice and ceremonial disembowelment, followed by enthusiastic acts of cannibalism.

"It's just doll parts slathered in chocolate syrup," Hank said. "Looks awful just the same. I get it. These sickos know how to push people's buttons."

He had numerous similar photographs in varying degrees of depravity. Hank provided background and specifics on each vile case. Animal torture, S & M orgies, eviscerations, blood-letting ceremonies. Lots of the pictures were even more sickening than the faux infanticide. None of them were fit for public consumption. I made a few notes and thanked Hank, telling him I might be able to use some of his data on background for my book (though at the time I doubted I would review any of it again, *ever*.)

"You can keep this stuff," he'd said, leaving me a stack of pictures and several case reports. "You never know."

I didn't want to mix Hank's stuff in with the rest of my research since none of it would likely be submitted to the publisher. I did, however, think it wise to hold onto his notes and photos 'just in case.' I dug through my desk and found an empty accordion-style folder decorated with squiggles — what artists call a 'vermicular' design — and that became the storage repository for Hank's contributions. I dubbed it the 'Vermicular File,' and over time it would grow and metastasize as I fed in more and more unsavory material that required 'special handling.'

By the time my Abby was born three months later, the folder had already expanded considerably. Alongside Hank's monstrosities were detailed instructions for summoning 'malicious demons,' a 'do-it-yourself' guide to human sacrifice, recipes for lethal 'hellfire potions,' lurid accounts of 'homage killings' done in the devil's name, and the firsthand testimony of a practicing exorcist. There were more abhorrent pictures, too, all of them unsuitable for publication.

"Yeah," I said to Abby, shaking off the ghosts. "This looks like the neighborhood park where Lucifer and Mephistopheles would bring their kids for birthday parties. Just the right temperature for them, too." A steady trickle of sweat had been sliding down my back since I'd left the van. "What do you think the snake potential is here?"

Abby had her phone out taking pictures; she stopped to survey the grounds. "Uh, you really wanna know?"

"I guess not. But I'm staying right behind you, so watch where you step."

We walked along the fence-line past the van and back toward the ramshackle bridge. When we got to the final post, we saw it was anchored in the shallow creek, a bicycle training-wheel fastened right above the water. Abby bent down to inspect the other items attached: a chipped coffee mug, three crescent wrenches of different sizes, a hand bell, an old padlock with its key sticking out. Everything painted that strange dreary shade of not-quite-gray.

"Beelzebub, did you remember to bring the ball and bat?" Abby said in a demon-growl, pointing to a catcher's mitt strapped to another smoky-colored post.

She snapped a photo, then leaned in closer, squinting.

"Hey, Mom, I don't think this thing's painted *gray*." She dragged a ruby fingernail across the coffee cup's pallid surface. Her scrape removed a thin line of dirt and mildew, revealing a more vibrant color underneath. She repeated the motion a few more times, expanding the newly-clean strip, then turned toward me, amused. "It's haint blue."

"Wow, that's not creepy at all," I replied, angling in for a better look.

She was right. I did my own scratch test on one of the wrench handles, and sure enough, under a long-accumulated layer of grime was the same hue my father had shown us at the Blue Heron. "Must be a popular color here."

Abby and I doubled back the way we came, stopping below the guardrail-turned-archway to observe its suspended curios. One of the baby shoes had fallen since I'd taken the photo that had so rattled Bernadette. It was lying sideways on the ground beside my front tire. Midway up the left-side pole was a plastic Halloween mask (Superhero? Clown? Ghost? Impossible to tell through the haint blue overcoat.) Its eyeholes stared off into the distance, gazing down the lonely country road. Somewhere overhead hidden among the treetops, a lone osprey began screeching.

The opening below the arch was wide enough for a small truck to pass through, but I doubted any vehicle had driven under it in a long, long time. The trail beyond the fence's border was thick with chickweed and foxtails and more sapling oak trees. A few yards further in, the woods had taken over completely. There was no house, no mailbox, no driveway we could see, nothing to indicate anyone lived at the end of this unkempt path. *So why such an elaborate gate?* I wondered.

"How far do you think the fence goes this way?" Abby asked, gesturing toward the side we hadn't yet explored.

I took a step backwards and gave it a look. Not too far ahead, the road curved sharply to the left and the fence followed, making it impossible to determine how deep into the brush either continued.

"Let's go check it out," I responded, and we began walking again.

As soon as the two of us rounded the curve we could see

that the fence ran on much longer this side of the gate. Like the stretch we'd already examined, there was almost no vegetation in front, providing a smooth path for us as we made our way along. More peculiar decorations here too, the strangest being a spiked dog collar that looked big enough to fit a moose. We kept tracing the fence, ignoring the heat and the bugs, curious where it might lead and what other surprises the strange structure had in store.

"Getting a bit soggy here," Abby said as we rounded another bend and she noticed charcoal sludge pooling around her sandals. I checked my own feet; murky mud was about to overspill my flip-flops and ooze between my naked toes. A half dozen mosquitoes were feasting on my legs. The swamp's musty odor had changed, too, taking on a stink of rotting fish. We were definitely coming into the tidal marshes.

"I think we better head back," I told Abby, feeling a sudden surge of snake-panic.

"Yeah, ok. Just let me grab a couple more pics."

She held up her phone in the direction we'd been going and hit the button. We could see where the odd fence eventually petered out, but it was too deep into the swamp for us to reach without getting really dirty. Mold had turned a tapering section of the last posts from haint blue gone wispy gray to blotchy-black.

"That must be the high tide line," I surmised.

No decorations adorned this final section of fencing, or perhaps whatever embellishments had been attached were since lost to the briny waters.

Despite the heat, the insects, and my paranoia over wriggling reptiles, I had really been enjoying this Bandun Gate adventure with Abby. The only other time I'd been to the site was with Dan, and he did not find it anywhere near as interesting as I did. We'd discovered it by accident while trying to find a shortcut to a local vodka distillery, and at the time, all he cared about was getting back to the highway.

Dan wasn't sure where he'd made the wrong turn after we'd left the main road, but one thing was certain: we were lost. At first it was fun, flitting through the countryside on a budding March morning, enjoying a part of the lowcountry neither of us had ever seen before. But after about forty-five minutes going in circles, both of us were frustrated and ready to be back on track. I'd been surveying the scenery, searching for some recognizable landmark or road sign when the fence caught my eye.

"What is *that*?" I gasped as we rolled off an old bridge and got our first glimpse of the structure.

Dan slowed down and gave it a once-over.

"No idea. Looks like somebody's 'found art' project," he said, putting his foot back on the gas.

"Wait! Pull over for a minute. I want to see it up close!"

Dan rolled his blue eyes but obliged. He slid up alongside the gate and let the engine run, an unspoken indicator that this stopover would be ever so brief. He checked his phone while I got out to take a few pictures.

"Still no cell service, no GPS. *Great*."

"Hey, Dan. You think anybody lives back in here? This road doesn't look like it gets much use."

"Who knows?" he shrugged, barely looking up from his phone.

The springtime air was warm not hot, and the morning smelled of damp earth and honeysuckle. I could hear bluebirds singing over the steady 'whoosh' of wind through the trees, the sound rising and falling like the tides. Dan leaned out the window and peered ahead, toward the bend where the dusty road made its leftward twist.

"This can't be the right way," he announced. "We need to turn around and go back the way we came."

I could tell he was getting antsy, so I snapped another photo or two then returned to the car.

"I'd hate be lost in these marshes after sundown," I said as he did a U-turn and started back across the dilapidated bridge. "God knows what it's like out here in the dark."

My walk back to the van with Abby would've been much more enjoyable if not for the intense heat. With the high

August humidity, every breath felt like inhaling shower steam. And the bugs were killer; I could feel them jabbing me, crawling along my skin, buzzing in and out of my nostrils. Abby ignored the annoyances and kept stopping every few steps to scrutinize some part of the structure. She was fascinated by the entire Bandun Gate experience: the gateway, the meandering fence, the absurd adornments, the woodsy-wetlands setting. If I'd been up for it, she would've set up camp and spent the night there. Maybe a couple of days.

"Hey, Mom! How creepy would it be if we were following the fence, but it just kept going on and on, and we never got to the van or to another road or anything?" Her green eyes were wide, dancing. "We just keep walking forever, like *Blair Witch* in the swamplands!"

"Hmmm, I think I still might choose *that* over seeing a snake while I'm in flip-flops."

Abby glanced at her phone. "There's no service out here. We're already halfway to a *Twilight Zone* episode."

Inspired by her comment, I shouted, "Scary movies! I'll say a line, you have to give the film's title."

"Let's do it."

"'I see dead people,'" I whispered.

"Easy. *Sixth Sense.* How 'bout 'I ate his liver with some fava beans and a nice chianti?'"

"*Silence of the Lambs.* Um, 'They're heeeeere!'"

"*Poltergeist.* And in keeping with the 'here' theme — 'Heeeeeere's Johnny!'"

"*The Shining.* How about, 'Walk this way,'" I spoke in a thick British accent, shuffling forward with an exaggerated limp.

"Aerosmith!" Abby laughed, strumming an air guitar. "No, I know — *Frankenstein*, or maybe *Young Frankenstein?* One of those!"

"Yeah, I'll accept that."

We came around the curve and could see the van parked up ahead. Alas, there would be no horror story involving the two of us lost in the shadow of Bandun Gate. Not the way she had joked, anyway.

"My turn?" I paused, trying to come up with a tough one. "Got it! 'This is no dream! This is really happening!'"

Abby stopped walking for a moment, concentrating on the quote. For a minute I thought I'd stumped her, but then she resumed her stride, picking up the pace a bit.

"Nice try, trying to trick me into saying *Nightmare on Elm Street* because of the 'dream' thing. But it's *Rosemary's Baby*."

"Can't fool you with Satan's spawn, I guess. Wish they would've *shown* the kid. I always felt ripped off, not getting to see the devil-baby. Anyway, your turn."

"'They're coming to get you, Barbara.'"

Abby was having fun with this, parroting the inflections and accents, even the facial expressions.

"*Night of the Living Dead*," I laughed, watching her do the 'zombie stagger.' She really was good at her craft. "Okay, 'be afraid. Be very afraid.'"

"*The Fly* remake with Jeff Goldblum, who still looks pretty good these days."

"Yeah, he's your Aunt Sharon's celebrity crush."

When we were almost at the arch, I paused to pull the car keys from my pocket.

Abby was still focused on the game, and in her best Robert De Niro-hillbilly accent she wailed, "'Come out, come out, wherever you are!'"

I was about to say *Cape Fear* when I looked over to her, panic suddenly seizing me. Abby had reached the opening a few steps ahead of me, and while blithely howling her line, had turned to walk through Bandun Gate and into the unknown wilds beyond. I lunged forward and gripped her shoulder just as she was under the archway, yanking her back with such force it spun her around so that she was facing me. If Abby hadn't grabbed the metal pole to steady herself, she would've toppled over.

"What?!?" Abby demanded, irked. "I was just gonna go in a little ways! Aren't you curious what's back there?"

"Are you SERIOUS???" I shot back. "Geez, Abby. Have you ever *seen* a horror movie? That's exactly how the adventurous dolt becomes a lumpy red puddle!"

26

Abby knew I was *not* kidding about staying on this side of the gate. I'd spent three years immersed in twisted tales of the supernatural while working on *Encyclopedia of Hell,* and believed to my core that it was crazy-dangerous to take unnecessary risks with the unknown. I didn't mess with Ouija boards, I didn't attend séances, I didn't have my tea leaves or tarot cards or aura 'read.' And I certainly did not walk through gates that look like they were designed and constructed by Clive Barker. Studying eerie oddities from the outside was one thing, sure, but breaching those barriers was quite another.

"Okay, okay. I get it!" Abby relented. "It's too hot out here, anyway."

I smiled, hoping I hadn't spoiled our afternoon. "Come on, get in the van. We'll stop for sodas on the way home. Better yet, I'll buy you dinner, wherever you want."

Abby nodded and smiled back. "Deal."

As I slid into the driver's seat, I noticed something strange. That ghostly Halloween mask, blue-gray and mildewed, was glaring down at me with vacant eyes. I would have sworn it had been gazing leftward before, out towards the road that ventured deep into the marshlands. But now it seemed to be staring straight at the van, watching as Abby and I made our departure. It must've shifted in the wind while the two of us were off exploring Bandun Gate, though from the time we arrived I couldn't recall there being even the slightest breeze.

Chapter Three
Writer of Wrongs

On the ride home, Abby and I continued discussing matters macabre. We debated the relative merits of horror classics *Nosferatu* and *Psycho* versus modern masterpieces *Halloween* and *Scream*. Abby told me about ancient ghost legends she'd heard while studying in Ireland over the previous summer, how she got chills at Saint Michan's Church where Bram Stoker found inspiration for his *Dracula*. I speculated on the possible origins of Bandun Gate.

"It's probably folk art. Y'know, one of those 'trash into treasure' transformations."

"Or could be a recycling thing," Abby countered. "Why dump useless crap into a landfill when you can hang it up to welcome houseguests?"

"But there was no house."

"Not one we *saw*, anyway. Could be anything out there in those woods."

The conversation moved on, neither of us imagining at the time that the true backstory of Bandun Gate would turn out to be something far more nefarious — and deadly.

We stopped for drive-thru at Melvin's, Abby's favorite Charleston barbecue joint, and by the time we got home I was ready for a quiet evening. However as we walked in from the garage, I spotted an unwanted souvenir of our wetlands excursion.

"Oh, God, Abby! There's a huge bug in your hair!"

"Ha, ha, very funny."

"No, seriously, Abby. There *is* a bug in your hair. Looks like a giant locust or something."

"Yuck! Get it out!" she said, pawing the back of her head.

"Hold still so I can grab it."

She stopped squirming, and I sifted her hair for the insect. If it was a locust, it was unlike any I'd ever seen before. Its head was way too big for the body, the wings resembled shards of broken glass and the whole thing was a sickly shade of olive green. Plus the bug was huge — three inches long, at least. I managed to untangle it from Abby's hair, but the pest darted across my hand and scurried into the hall closet before I could squash it.

I flung the door open and had just begun looking for the unwelcome invader when my cell phone rang. The screen showed a picture of Charles. Abby was running her hands along her scalp, making sure nothing else was hiding there.

"It's your little brother. I better get this."

"Hey, Madre," my youngest cooed in his breezy, light-hearted manner. "How're things in South Carolina?"

"Pretty good," I said, continuing my search. I stood on tiptoe, checking the closet's high shelf. Nothing. "Your sister's here already and Dad'll be back Monday. You still coming down with Roman?"

"Yeah, he's gotta work Friday, so we're heading down early Saturday morning." He paused a beat before continuing, which I knew from Charles-history meant he was about to make some request. "Hey, you remember my friend Sophie?"

"Sure," I answered, thinking but not saying, 'Sophie's hard to forget.'

"Can she stay with us a couple days? She has some volleyball tournament thing at Clemson University that ends Friday, and I told her I was going to be in Charleston, and she wants to meet up, hit the beach over the weekend. Is that okay?"

I hesitated for a second wanting to say 'no,' then caved. "Sure, why not?"

"Thanks! She'll be there late Friday. I get there Saturday afternoon, so you only have to entertain her *solo* for a few hours. And Abby can help keep her occupied."

"I'll make it work."

"Thanks, Madre. Can't wait to see you. Love ya."

"Love you too," I said and returned the phone to my pocket.

Abby had given up the bug hunt while I was talking to Charles and had taken our food out to the back porch. I spent another minute or so shuffling through the shoes on the closet floor without finding the insect, then joined my daughter outside. *At least locust don't sting*, I told myself.

"What'd Charles have to say?"

"Sophie's coming on Friday, staying the weekend."

"Your favorite person."

"She's not so bad," I lied. Sophie was the *worst*.

It was an absolute mystery to me how someone as likable and easy-going as Charles could possibly be friends with a shrew like Sophie. He was smart, charming, funny, and everyone loved being around him. The stereotypical 'baby of the family,' Charles had a knack for making witty remarks and endearing himself to others, equaled by his total lack of ambition and aversion to taking on adult responsibilities. He was almost twenty, just thirteen months younger than Abby, but while she was graduating college in May, Charles had been bouncing from major to major and was still years away from a degree. His soft blue eyes, quick wit, and killer smile, all inherited from his father, likewise a youngest sibling, were buffers against suffering life's consequences, and he used them masterfully.

Sophie, on the other hand, was cold, aloof, dismissive, and always on some self-aggrandizing mission. She rarely smiled and only seemed content when she was complaining about something. Her physical characteristics were equally stark. Sophie stood almost six feet tall and was all muscle. She wore her long dirty-blonde hair pulled back in a tight ponytail, and her voice was tinged with a perpetual 'I can't believe I even have to *say* this' inflection. Her favorite sources of entertainment were knocking people off-balance and initiating awkward interactions.

I had first met Sophie when Dan and I were still living in Northern Virginia. She'd come over to the house with Charles following their first semester midterms at the local community college. The two had been in the same public speaking course and they'd bonded over shared disappointment with the class syllabus. During their introductory chat, Charles and Sophie realized they had several mutual friends, including Sophie's on-again, off-again boyfriend Ethan and two of Charles' lacrosse teammates from high school. The pair had been *compadres* ever since.

Charles had brought her into the kitchen where I was preparing lunch and introduced us.

"Nice to meet you, Sophie. Can I make you a sandwich?"

Sophie'd studied the ingredients on my counter, an expression of disgust spilling across her face. "Is that *commercial wheat bread*? That's nothing but starch and chemicals! I can't believe anyone still eats that!"

I was taken aback, but Charles found the exchange amusing.

"So I guess that's a 'no' on the sandwich offer, Sophie?" he quipped, winking at me.

"I have other stuff," I'd offered, hoping to salvage the situation. "There's some lettuce, tomatoes, and cheese. I could make you a Chef salad."

Sophie didn't miss a beat. "Is that dairy cruelty-free?"

"Uh, I don't know." I thought maybe a little humor might ease the tension. "But I'm pretty sure I've got peanut butter that is!"

"I guess you think that's funny," she said, then walked away.

And that was pretty much the high point of our relationship. I'd seen Sophie a few times after that. Charles brought her by now and then, or I'd bump into her on campus when he needed a ride home. All our exchanges were similarly tense and uncomfortable. She found my taste in literature unrefined, my clothes outdated, my music clichéd. I know this because Sophie told me so in great detail under the guise of wanting to 'help me improve myself.' Charles always seemed entertained by her surly disposition, or maybe he felt sorry for her and thought she could use a friend. As I said, it's a mystery I could not begin to unravel.

31

Abby and I finished our barbecue and potato salad out on the porch, watching an egret scooping minnows from the pond behind our house. We mulled over strategies for dealing with Sophie, who would land on our doorstep in a mere forty-eight hours.

"Might be a good time for me to head up to Aunt Ruthie's for a few days," Abby said, half-jokingly. "If I leave now, I could be at there by ten."

Dan's sister, Ruth, lived in Myrtle Beach, about two hours north of Charleston. Whenever the kids came to visit, they always made a side-trip to her place.

"We got a couple days before the Sophie-invasion, no need to rush off in such a hurry."

"If I go up now, I could spend all next week here in Charleston with Dad and the boys."

I shrugged. "Whatever you want's fine. I'm pretty tired. I think I'll take a shower then hit the sheets. If you're here in the morning, maybe we could go to Isle of Palms, see the sunrise over the ocean."

"Sounds good. Love you, Mom."

"Love you too," I told my daughter. I kissed her forehead and left her there, alone beneath the darkening August sky.

As I brushed my teeth and changed into pajamas, I thought of my recent nightmare again. Something about it kept nagging at me, a veiled message I couldn't quite decipher. The dream hadn't even been that bad, really, compared to the ones I'd experienced when my Hell book research was in full swing. Those terrors ripped me to the core and could still bring me to tears all these years later.

Charles was born about a year after Abby, in October of '96. Big brother Roman, three years older, looked exactly like Dan but with my brown eyes; this new boy-child had his father's baby-blues and my chubby cheeks. Caring for two toddlers and a newborn was exhausting, especially since, at the time, I was also putting the final touches on *Encyclopedia of Hell.* One night during this phase, Dan found me slumped and shaking over Charles' crib.

"You okay, Miriam? It's 3 a.m."

"Bad dream."

"Wanna talk about it?"

I hesitated; there was no good answer to that question. Dan knew I'd been having nightmares; he'd often been awakened by me thrashing or crying or screaming things that left *him* unnerved. They had gotten progressively worse over time, yet I'd never given my husband anything more than vague accounts of the night terrors. Why put such troubling images in Dan's head, too? The Hell book had been *my* undertaking, there was no point making him suffer for it.

The nightmare that sent me running to Charles' cradle had been especially brutal. I was seated at a table across from a dark-robed hooded figure. He said something in a low, growling voice, sounded like "sustenance, Miriam," or maybe "*sustain us*, Miriam." I'm certain he used my name. There was a knife on the table; I grabbed it and shoved it into his chest. Blood poured from the wound, I felt its warmth spread across my hand, smelled the hot copper. Then I noticed the knife was the scorpion dagger from Hank's 'Banquet of the Unbaptized' photos, and I was wearing the same black robe as the men in the film. The wooden table, however, was the one in my own kitchen.

I lunged forward and pushed the hood back from my victim. Beneath it I found not some hideous ghoul, but the sweet face of my seven-month-old son Charles. His little body fell across the table, and he rolled over onto his back, the dagger lodged near his heart. Twelve more figures, all clad in long black frocks and white eye-masks, drifted toward the table. They held sharpened spoons. My boy looked up at me, smiling, with an expression that said, 'it's okay Mom, I still love you,' then he wrapped his tiny hand around my finger and squeezed. I stood frozen, knowing he was dying, and that there was nothing I could do to stop it. The dozen defilers began closing in...

A savage sound woke me then, wet, and fierce, and guttural. It was my own sobbing.

"I'm fine, hon," I'd lied to Dan in reply. "I'll be back to bed in a minute."

There were other dreams, more vivid and vile, before the Hell book was completed. More questions from Dan. More denials from me that anything was wrong. And more worry from both of us the nightmares were taking a toll, or worse, might never stop.

Yes, but they had *stopped*, I reminded myself as I turned out the bathroom light, or at least they'd become rare. *I'm just being an idiot resurrecting those phantoms.* Exhausted from my marshland adventure with Abby, I fell asleep almost immediately. Next thing I knew I was awakened not by a dream, but by a shrill blare from the family room just outside my door. *Abby must have drifted off in front of the TV,* I thought. *With all that screaming and shouting, sounds like a horror movie.* I looked over at the nightstand clock: 1:42 a.m. *Terrific.*

I got up and went into the family room, hoping Abby wasn't lying on the remote so I could turn off the set without waking her. But to my surprise the television wasn't on; the lights were off too, and the room was empty. The noises I'd been hearing hadn't stopped, exactly; they were steadily decreasing in volume and intensity. When the sound finally bottomed out, it became a soft chanting that emanated from one of the bedrooms upstairs.

Okay, Abby *had* dozed off watching some screechy show, but up in the guestroom rather than the family room. Whatever scene had jolted me must've been deafening for Abby, forcing her to turn the volume down. Since I was now wide awake, I decided to go check on her.

Midway up the steps I realized the noise wasn't an electronic signal, it was coming from Abby herself. She was murmuring something in a weird sing-song monotone, like a kid reciting a jump-rope verse. When I got to the upstairs hall, I could see her door was half-open, and Abby was sitting upright on the bed with her back to me. She had a candle burning; I recognized the familiar scent of Biloxi Rain, one of my favorites from a candle shop in our Virginia hometown. The flame's glow waltzed orange and yellow around her dark silhouette.

I paused outside the bedroom, listening to Abby's warble.

"Heed, now - the rope must be twisted, sister insisted.
In a fever she smothered what brother uncovered.
Ere the blood on the swather left Father unbothered
And the canticles chanting sent mad Auntie ranting.
Her concoction fed dozens of guzzling cousins.
The hexing portended such resplendent descendants.
I should like to have missed it, but sister insisted."

Abby repeated the rhyme three times in a peculiar voice that bore a distinct Southern drawl. She started a fourth round when I knocked lightly and stepped inside her room.

"Abby, what are you doing? You okay?"

Her body stiffened at the sound of my voice; she stopped singing but didn't respond. She held the glass candle-jar in her left hand and was cradling something --- her body blocked it from view --- protectively in her right. In the flickering light I saw the bathroom trashcan toppled beside her bed, its litter strewn across the floor. Used dental floss, receipts, a potato chip bag, gum wrappers peppered the carpet.

"Abby? Did you lose something? Threw it away by accident, looking for it in the garbage, maybe?"

Still no response, then her upper body pivoted from the waist. She didn't turn far enough to face me, but I could see her profile glowing golden in the wavering candlelight.

For a moment I thought Abby was messing with me, staging an elaborate reprise of something that had happened back when she was working at Zombie High. She'd come home one night without removing her ghoul make-up, and was tiptoeing up the stairs, trying not to wake anyone. Around the same time, I'd gotten up to use to the bathroom and decided to see if she was back yet. We almost ran into each other in the dark hallway, and the shock of coming upon a toothy, ashen-faced creature with blood dripping from its eyes nearly gave me a heart attack. I let out a shriek that woke the neighbors a block away. Abby screamed in response to my reaction, then we both realized what had happened and began cackling hysterically. Dan and the boys came running out of their rooms to see what was going on, but Abby and I were laughing so hard we couldn't talk. That incident immediately became a staple of family lore.

Maybe that's what she's doing now, I thought. *Abby heard me coming and is putting on a show.*

"I'm fine, just go away," she said in that same strange tone.

No, whatever was going on, Abby was not doing this for entertainment value.

Recalculating, I decided she had to be talking in her sleep. Abby must've been worn out from the day's events and the intense South Carolina heat, and this was how her body was reacting.

"It's time for bed now," I said in my best calm-but-firm mom voice. "Blow out the candle and go to sleep."

She sat motionless for a moment, and I took another step into her room. Slowly, Abby brought the glass jar to her face. The flame dwindled down until it was finally gone, like the sound from the non-existent TV show. A coil of white smoke ascended, lingered, and disappeared. Abby remained stiff and upright, then leaned down to set the candle on the floor before curling into a fetal position on the bed.

"Goodnight, Abs," I said. "Love you."

I'd waited a beat although I knew she wasn't likely to say anything back. Satisfied that Abby was settled, I headed downstairs.

As I returned to my room, the previous night's dream resurfaced, the one I'd meant to share with Abby but never did. In it, I was walking down a long hallway with mud-brown carpet and harsh fluorescent lights, reminiscent of a low-rent office building. I proceeded along; however it was no longer a hall but an overgrown thicket of thornbushes surrounding me like a prickly tunnel. I could hear a low buzzing sound and smell stagnant water. Soon the passage changed again, becoming a narrow rock-hewn channel barely wide enough for me to pass through. Its smooth walls were slick with condensation, and I could feel cold slime under my bare feet.

The corridor was incredibly dark, illuminated only by a dim yellow glow somewhere in the distance ahead.

Just before I awoke, a gaunt figure had floated toward me, a lanky shadow against the muted light.

"My apologies for the delay," a (woman's?) voice purred seductively. "Satan will see you now."

Chapter Four
Excellent Wretch

I had a rough time getting out of bed the morning after Abby's bizarre sleep-walking-talking incident. Most days I'm up and dressed before dawn, but at half past eight, I was still in pajamas. I hoped Abby hadn't been waiting for me to go to Isle of Palms for an ocean sunrise because that event was long gone.

A couple more yawns and stretches, then I changed out of my PJ's and went to the kitchen. Abby wasn't in the family room or on the porch, so she had either gone to the beach without me or was still asleep herself. I looked out the front window and didn't see her car, but that didn't really tell me much. When the kids visited, they usually parked around the corner where there's shade all day. I made breakfast quietly, just in case, and took my toast and juice out back to eat. I was finishing up when Abby appeared in the doorway, hair uncombed and traces of yesterdays' eyeliner smeared down her cheeks.

"Will you take me some place?" she asked without so much as a 'good morning.' She seemed groggy and was in the same jeans shorts and Social Distortion T-shirt she'd had on the day before. Even her voice was gravely and slurred.

"Did you sleep in those clothes?" With everything else going on the previous night, I hadn't even noticed what Abby was wearing during her chanting stint. "And geez, Abs, run a brush through your hair, wash your face!"

She just glared at me, miffed. Abby was usually upbeat in the morning, but whenever she was overly tired or angry, she would go into 'sullen mode.' The menacing looks and grumbled comments could last hours, even days, if she was particularly perturbed. I wanted to cut this episode short, so I tried chiding her about her midnight performance.

"Do you remember last night, that weird song you were singing?"

Abby gave me a blank stare.

"The candle?" I prompted. "Trash all over the floor. What was that all about, anyway?"

"I wanna go someplace. Say you'll take me."

"Okay, grumpy!" I said with an exaggerated frown. "Where do you wanna go?"

"It's out past Awendaw. I can show you how to get there."

"Fine. When did you have in mind?"

"Now."

"*Now*?" I took another shot at coaxing her out of her bad mood. "We'll miss Wayne if we go now!"

"Who's Wayne?" she asked, not even trying to hide her irritation.

"Wayne *Brady*! *Let's Make a Deal,* remember? Comes on at ten." I reached over to 'boop' her nose, but she pulled away.

"I wanna go. *Now*."

I sighed. This was not how I wanted the day to begin. I figured the best way to get her out of her funk was to get moving, so I shrugged and grabbed my keys. Getting Abby to put on her seatbelt was a chore; in the end I had to buckle her in myself like I did when she was a kid. Halfway down the driveway she abruptly lunged forward, pointing to the crepe Myrtle tree at the edge of our front yard.

"Wait!" she shouted. "Can you gimme some flowers?"

I looked over at the pink blooms. There were only a handful that hadn't withered completely in the August heat, and even those were starting to brown around the edges. I had no idea why Abby wanted them, but if it would help shake off the 'crabbies,' it was worth indulging her. I hopped out of the van, snapped off a half dozen clusters, and handed them over. Abby laid them in her lap then turned and stared out the window.

"*You're welcome*," I said sarcastically, settling back into the driver's seat.

Silence.

"Okay, so where exactly are we going?"

"It's a place I been before," Abby said, still mangling her pronunciations. "Go north on Savannah Highway and I'll show you where after that."

We were heading away from Charleston, so traffic was light on the trek to Abby's mystery destination. Instead of sprawling live oaks draped with Spanish moss, this journey took us past mile after mile of pine forest. Even the air was different, still warm and thick with humidity, but free of the musty smell that permeated the marshlands.

Inside the van, the atmosphere was also nothing like what we'd enjoyed on the way to Bandun Gate. Abby barely spoke the entire drive, limiting her utterances to 'turn here, take this next road, go that way.' There was no conversation, no happy banter, no talk of the weather or the beach or what to do for lunch. About ten minutes in I tried to get a 'music performers with foods in their names' challenge going, but she refused to participate.

"Spice Girls!" I said, trying to engage her. "Salt-N-Pepa! Meatloaf! I'm gonna win, Abby. Already up by three!"

Nothing. She just slouched in the passenger seat with her forehead pressed against the window.

"You awake, Abs?" I asked after we'd been driving for the better part of an hour.

Maybe she'd fallen asleep. After the night she had, it made sense she might've dozed off as we made our way north to wherever. I did a quick review of my options: 1) wake her up, since I had no idea where we were going, 2) pull over and let her sleep for a while, resume our travels when she was refreshed and hopefully in a better mood, 3) turn around and go home, try this little jaunt again later. Before I had a chance to decide, Abby sat upright and looked about intently. I thought she was ready to play 'Food-Band Trivia' after all, or at least to want to chit-chat.

Instead she declared, "take this turn — we're almost there."

I complied. We rambled down a dirt road that twisted through a mile or so of woods then past a small open meadow, eventually dead-ending where the forest line resumed.

"This's it!" she said, pointing to a burned-out shack at the edge of the clearing. "Stop! Lemme out!"

"Geez, Abby! How did you ever *find* this place? And when were you here before?"

Abby ignored me yet again and clambered to get out, spilling the Myrtle sprigs onto the floor as she struggled to unbuckle her seatbelt. I hit the 'release button,' freeing her. She stopped long enough to scoop up a handful, then sprinted towards the scorched ruins. There wasn't much there, really, just two crumbling brick walls and a stone chimney overtaken by Wisteria vines. *Strange.*

I stayed in the van, puzzling over Abby's connection to this place and my many unanswered questions. What did she mean she'd been here before? When? Who'd brought her? (Dan, maybe, because it sure wasn't me.) How was she able to find her way back without making a single mistake in the directions? And how, after being semi-conscious all morning, had Abby summoned the interest and energy to scurry off like a jackrabbit the instant we arrived? None of this made sense.

The phone rang as I was pondering the possibilities. *At least there's cell service out here.*

"Hey, calling to check in with my girls, see what you're up to," Dan's voice said from the other side of the country.

"Just waiting for you to get back, wishing you were here now."

"Me, too, Bunner. Me too."

'Bunner' is my husband's shorthand for 'honey-bunny.' He's called me that ever since we started dating back in the 80s.

When people ask us how we met, Dan loves telling everyone I'd been 'working the bar' when he found me. He'll say I wouldn't stop chatting him up, peppering him with questions about his background, his life, his plans for the future. And he'll add, smirking, that I'd asked him for his picture during that very first encounter. And while all of that is *technically* true, this is one of those cases where context really matters.

Our paths crossed in 1987, when I was a reporter for the

city newspaper, and Dan played bass in a local band. I was assigned to write a story about his group, which was performing at an area cocktail lounge. That meant conducting interviews and taking photographs. So yes, I was in fact 'working' at a 'bar,' probing Dan for info and requesting his picture the night we met, just not in the way he gleefully implies.

One thing he does have right: from the moment I arrived, I could not take my eyes off him.

People talk about 'love at first sight' like it's being struck by lightning, or getting hit with a tidal wave that washes everything else away. That's not how it was for me. When I met Dan, I felt as if this was someone I had known forever. *Forever.* Someone I could be my true, unguarded self around, with no fear of awkwardness or judgment or rejection. It was obvious he felt the same way. We clicked immediately, like old friends who'd run into each other after years apart and simply picked up where we'd left off.

I finished my interview questions that night: how did the band get together, when did you first perform, what are your musical influences? during a break between the first and second sets. Normally I would've left after that, (I wasn't much of a night owl even in my twenties) but at one a.m. there I was, smiling at the blue-eyed bass player as the band performed the evening's final song.

"We're going for breakfast after we pack up," Dan said as he came offstage. "Love to have you tag along."

We went to an all-night diner, and one by one the others left until only the two of us remained. Dan and I stayed for hours, talking. Through the course of the conversation we realized we knew lots of the same people but had never been around them at the same time, just missing each other our whole lives. I joked that we'd either overcome the forces trying to keep us apart, or finally gotten onboard with the forces trying to bring us together. Dan said whichever it was, we'd better go with it, or else risk unraveling the fabric of the universe.

Around dawn I left the table to go to the Ladies' room, and while I was gone, Dan told the waitress it was my birthday (not even close.) When I returned, she plunked a slice of chocolate cake in front of me as Dan led the entire restaurant in a rousing chorus of *Happy Birthday to You*.

"You don't look a day older than when we first met!" he declared amidst light applause from our fellow breakfast patrons.

Three weeks later we were planning our wedding.

Now Dan was off on the west coast, and I was roaming the backwoods of South Carolina's lowcountry, our daughter baffling me with her odd behavior.

"Abby's in one of her moods," I told my husband. "She's barely speaking to me, and when she does talk, she sounds like she's got a mouthful of marbles."

I decided against sharing what had happened the previous night, not sure I could describe the strange events without worrying him. My phone beeped then, indicating another incoming call. The screen showed Abby's number. I looked across the clearing and saw her crouching next to one of the tumbled walls; neither hand held a cell phone.

"Your girl just butt-dialed me," I said, hitting 'ignore.' "She is *really* out of it today. Hey, did you ever take her to an old crumbly house near McClellanville? Says she's been before, but it wasn't with me."

"Um, I don't think so. Could she mean when she was a kid? Your dad was always taking them on vacation adventures when they were little."

"Maybe that's it. We had lunch with him yesterday. Could've triggered her memory, I guess. Still, it's weird she remembered exactly how to get here. Especially in her current funk."

"Well, hope she's out of it soon. Tell her Dad says 'hello,' looking forward to seeing her."

We said our goodbyes, and I started towards the rubble. Abby, who had been standing by the debris just moments ago, was nowhere to be seen.

"Abigail? Hey where are you? You called my phone. Abby?"

No response.

I circled around the piled bricks and checked behind the chimney frame. She wasn't there either.

"Abby?" a bit louder this time, more demanding. "Abby! ABBY!"

Still nothing.

The formerly-mild morning air felt suddenly hot, stifling. I shouted her name again, zigzagging through the trees that separated the meadow from the deep forest. Half-annoyed, half-alarmed, I was rushing back toward the van when a gust of wind tore through the trees, diverting my attention. It was followed by a screeching sound, shrill and strident, like a flock of angry gulls. Gray-black clouds rushed in behind the gust, devouring the blue sky. A storm was coming up from the south.

A few yards into the woods something else was moving, too. It looked like my daughter.

"Abby! Didn't you hear me?!?" I shouted as I approached her. "I've been screaming my head off!"

"I'm right here," she spat, perturbed.

Abby was standing inside a small stone enclosure wedged in among the pines. Its walls ran maybe six feet long and two across, and were about a yard high. On the narrow end closest to me was an iron gate bound with a heavy chain and secured by an old-fashioned padlock. The post's top left hinge had rusted through, causing the gate to gape forward. At the far end of the walled space was a weathered concrete tombstone.

Abby had climbed through the gap and was standing at the foot of the grave, facing the marker. The wind was roiling her dark hair into a lion's mane, obscuring her face. A bouquet of the sprigs I'd snipped from our myrtle tree rested against the headstone.

"Wow, this is almost as creepy as Bandun Gate," I said. "Whose grave is this, Abby, do you know?"

I didn't wait for an answer but walked along outside the wall to get a closer look at the marker. There was barely room inside for Abby, and if I'd joined her, it would have been uncomfortably crowded.

There was no name on the gravestone, just the inscription '? – *1948*' stamped into the cement, along with the epitaph '*pax in morte.*' Peace in death.

"Weird there's no name, or even what year the person was born. Wonder what he or she's doing buried out here all alone. Drifter, maybe, or someone nobody knew anything about? And why is it all closed-in with walls?"

Abby said nothing.

I circled around to the opposite side and made another odd discovery. Just a yard or so away, barely three feet long and half as wide, was a small mound. It also had the look of a burial site, but without a headstone. A concrete angel had been placed beside the little hill, facing away from the walled grave. The statue had a cord tied around its neck, and whatever was dangling from it made a clinking sound as it whipped in the wind.

I crouched beside the figure and slid my finger down the coarse twine until it came to something firm and cool. It was a smooth gold band without stones. A wedding ring. I lifted it closer, squinting at the inscription inside. Its interior had been engraved 'K.A.L. + M.J.F. 06-27-08.' The wind picked up again, snatching the ring from my hand and sending it back against the angel, reprising the metallic clink, clink, clinking.

The first raindrops began to fall, heralded by a sharp thunderclap. Then I heard Abby, sounding impossibly far away, say, "Can we go now?"

I stood up and turned. She was no longer at the gravesite. Through the trees I could see her leaning against the stone chimney, the rain darkening her auburn hair. How on earth had she managed to travel that distance so quickly, and without making a sound?

We rode home in silence. Abby maintained her crumpled stance slouched against the window, then disappeared into the guestroom the minute we got to the house. *Just as well*, I thought. *Maybe all she needed was a good nap to be her sunny self again.*

While Abby was upstairs, I started prepping for Sophie's visit. I decided to put her in the 'office,' which was really just a nook off the front hallway big enough for a pull-out sofa and a little desk. Between Abby's brooding behavior and the imminent arrival of our belligerent lodger, my dreams of a fun-filled get-together with the kids were fading fast. Until that moment, I hadn't realized how much I'd been missing my trio's unique and lively dynamic.

Roman, Abby and Charles have always been extremely close. Born within three years of each other, they grew up as a pack, sharing their own coded language, pastimes and rituals. Middle-child Abby, the only girl, had her 'princess side,' but she would climb trees and catch caterpillars right alongside her brothers. Many a-time we'd see her out in the yard playing kickball wearing a tutu and tiara. The boys would reciprocate, joining their sister for tea parties or unicorn makeovers or ballet revues. The three of them did just about everything together.

Once, when Abby was five, I found her standing on the toilet seat straddling the bowl, her pink nightgown hiked up around her waist.

"What are you doing, Abs?"

"Peeing. The boys say you have to pee standing up. Sitting down is only for pooping."

It took a considerable effort for me to convince her otherwise. She did not want to break ranks with her brothers.

That same autumn, I came upon Charles (the only one who hadn't started school yet) standing by the front window, staring out at our driveway. He appeared so sad, I asked him what was wrong.

"Two people who aren't here," he said somberly, never looking up from his post.

Their bond endured through the typical scrapes and squabbles common with siblings, from school days to the teenage years, and now into adulthood. Sure, they might fight amongst themselves, but they always had each other's backs when it came to the rest of the world. When Dan and I moved to Charleston, Roman and Charles got a place together not far from where Abby was living while she finished her last year of college. We took comfort in knowing the kids remained such good friends and that while we were watching over my dad down south, they'd be together in Virginia. There was nothing they would not do for each other. *Nothing.*

By the time I had finished converting the office into a temporary guestroom it was half past three on Thursday, and Abby and I only had another day of Sophie-less bliss left before the peace would be shattered. I realized my daughter had been upstairs since noon, so I called her down to get something to eat. She sulked, protested, and pouted, insisting she wasn't hungry. I held firm.

"How about burgers? We can have a cookout," I said, hoping to spark her appetite and lift her mood. "Go on outside and I'll get everything ready."

Abby flopped down in a wicker chair off the porch while I shaped the meat into patties. I was midway through when my phone rang, but by the time I'd wiped the goo off my hands, the call had gone to voicemail. I looked at the notification — it said the missed call was from Abby. *Weird*, I thought, as I watched her sitting out back fidgeting with her hair. Just like earlier that morning, she wasn't holding her phone; *must be another butt-dial.* As I mulled what these phantom calls from my daughter might mean, a text came through. It read:

Got to Ruthie's ok last night. Tried to call earlier – call me back if you want.

Be back Sunday. Love you.

The message had originated from Abby's number.

I looked from my screen to the woman in the yard then back again. *The system is on some kind of delay,* I told myself. *HAS to be. Abby must've sent the text last night when she was planning to go to Myrtle Beach, but changed her mind and stayed home after it had already gone through. Her words floated in cyberspace, finally hitting my cell all these hours later.* So why did I suddenly feel so queasy?

A quick check of Abby's phone would clear things up, I thought. I poked my head outside.

"Hey, Abby. Can I see your cellphone?"

She turned, giving me that same peeved look I'd been getting all day. Only this time, it shifted to something else as she glared. Replacing her agitation was an expression of absolute contempt. For the first time in twenty-one years I didn't recognize my daughter.

"Your PHONE, Abby!" I demanded, trying to hide my alarm. "Let me see it!"

She ignored me and went back to toying with her hair.

I strode over and frisked her, my hands searching for the familiar shape. She sat silently seething as I patted her down. No phone. I ran upstairs to the guestroom, but it wasn't on the nightstand or dresser, either. Thinking she might've knocked it over during her sleep-chanting drama, I dropped to my knees and checked under the bed.

No cellphone, but something else was hidden there in the darkness: a pair of peculiar items I had never seen before.

I slid the first out slowly, careful not to cause any damage. It was a crudely made doll-form, about three inches long. The body was fashioned out of used tissues scavenged from Abby's trashcan, flattened, then twist-braided together and tied off with lengths of dirty dental floss. The doll's 'head' was a soiled cotton-ball (crimson-stained and smelling like nail polish remover) capped with seven strands of Abby's red-brown hair stuck on with a wad of chewed gum. About a third of the way down on either side of the figure fingernail clippings, bearing traces of Abby's signature dark-red enamel, had been attached with drips of blue-green wax. I recognized that scent, too. Biloxi Rain.

The second find was equally chilling. Beside the doll lay the husk of that enormous green locust I'd found in Abby's hair when we'd gotten home from Bandun Gate, only now the insect was bleach white. The carcass was lying atop another discarded tissue, this one with a symbol that looked like a circle with some squiggly lines inside drawn on with the tip of the burned match. I gently removed the dead insect and held the tissue up to the light. Several tiny holes were clustered in a smear of dried mucus — the bug had eaten Abby's phlegm.

I grabbed a washcloth from the hall bath, gently wrapped

the items inside, and went back downstairs. Abby was sitting on the lawn with her back to me. I slipped my discoveries into a kitchen drawer and took my cellphone from the counter. My mind was racing, unsure what to do next. After some thought, I ducked into my bedroom and texted Dan's sister:

Hi Ruth. Everything going ok in MB?

It felt like an eternity as I stared down at the screen waiting for a reply. One minute crawled by, then another. Nothing. When the third ticked away, I decided Ruth must either be busy or didn't have her phone handy. My next option was to call Abby's number, which I did *not* want to do, not if I didn't absolutely *have* to. I wasn't prepared for the possible outcomes. I pocketed my phone and stepped back into the family room, trying to come up with another plan to settle the storm brewing in my stomach.

Abby must have heard me. She got up and moved to the back porch, glowering at me through the glass door. I couldn't tell if she was curious or angry or maybe just hungry; her eyes were hollow, empty. *What is going on, Abigail?* I caught sight of the raw hamburger and improvised a plan. Fishing through the trash I found some eggshells and a half-rotted banana peel. I pressed them into the meat, then, forcing a smile, walked outside.

"Lunch is ready," I said, offering Abby the platter.

She hesitated. I struggled to appear calm while she scrutinized my face. After a moment, Abby took the plate and sat down on the grass. Smirking, she shoveled a fistful of the putrid mixture into her mouth. She continued until the muck was gone, swallowing it without chewing, like dropping quarters into a vending machine. When she'd finished, Abby licked her lips and gave me a sinister wink, never breaking eye contact. I had to look away.

Dropping my gaze, I noticed Abby wasn't casting a shadow.

This isn't happening, this isn't happening, THIS ISN'T HAPPENING! My heart was pounding hard enough to crack through my rib cage. I steadied my nerves and asked the thing that looked like my daughter. "What's your middle name, Abby?"

No response, but she stood up. The empty platter toppled to the ground with a soft thud.

"What's your middle name?" I repeated, losing the fight to stay calm. "When's your birthday? How old is your younger brother? Where'd you go to high school? What did I give you for Christmas last year?"

A peppy chime interrupted my interrogation, signaling an incoming text. I took out my phone and read Ruth's message:

Just watched Sweeney Todd with Abby. She's not feeling great - went to nap. Hoping to see the boys this weekend

Confusion, bewilderment, dread coursed through me as I tried to wrap my mind around the horrible truth: this creature beside me was *not* my daughter.

Whatever she was skittered over and slapped the cellphone out of my hand. I felt it hit the top of my foot while my eyes remained locked on the Abby-thing. Grinning hideously, she reached her right hand across her body and grasped her left elbow, then tore the arm off clean at the shoulder. There was no blood or ragged tissue; the limb simply popped out like a plastic doll part. The monster with Abby's face opened her mouth and began inserting the severed appendage. As she did, the detached arm re-emerged at the empty shoulder socket, fingertips first then wrist then elbow, until the entire limb was back in place. She licked her lips again, let out a rancid belch, and blew me a kiss with the newly-restored left arm.

Throughout the ghastly spectacle I stood transfixed. My brain was working feverishly to make sense of this impossible scene. I couldn't stop staring at Abby's Social Distortion T-shirt, her absolute favorite garment ever. It was jet black and emblazoned with the rock group's mascot 'Skelly,' a smiling skeleton holding a cigarette in one hand and a martini in the other. The Abby-beast must've sensed I found the familiar image comforting and decided to use it against me. Skelly became animated, took a drag off the cigarette and swig of his drink, then hurled both at me. The substances combined in a fireball as they burst forth from the shirt, creating a bright orange flash. I could smell the smoke hanging in the air between us.

Not-Abby crept closer, leaning in until her face was almost touching mine.

"Just STOP now, *Mama*," the monster snarled, dropping her half-hearted attempt to imitate Abby's voice. She spoke in the same southern accent I'd heard the night before singing that bizarre ballad. "You know I'm not your girl, so let's don't pretend. Why couldn't you just be nice and play along? Now, this isn't gonna end well for *either* of you!"

Chapter Five
Dispossessed

The world went gray around me. I had a thousand questions I wanted to ask the beast masquerading as my daughter. *What ARE you? Why do you look like my child? Is Abby in danger? What brought you here to us?* And, most important, *how do I send you back to whatever Hell you came from?* I knew in that moment there was no way I could've processed the answers, not with Abby in peril. Reality as I'd known it had dissolved like a chalk-picture in the rain, blurred into unrecognizable smears as I watched, helpless. I had no idea what new scenario was about to replace it.

Stay calm, my researcher-brain whispered, *approach this like any other investigation of the preternatural. You've done this before, and you know a methodical approach works best in assessing the facts.* But my maternal side kept pushing back hard, screaming, *RUN! Go to Abby, NOW, make sure she's okay, and do whatever it takes to protect her!*

I drew a long breath and let it out slowly, trying to reconcile the conflicting impulses. The sky was marred with patchy clouds leftover from the morning storm, and the afternoon heat had become overwhelming. I stood drenched in sweat; Abby's imposter remained cool, taking obvious delight in my distress. *Deep breaths. Inhale, exhale. Inhale, exhale.* I forced every other thought from my mind and focused on the only thing that mattered: making sure Abby was safe.

"Is my daughter all right?" I asked, surprised at the ragged sound of my own voice. "Is Abby in any danger from you?"

"You mean, *this* girl?"

The impersonator's smile widened. She put her hands on her hips and did a slow 'model on the runway' twirl, then took a step backwards and began to shrivel. In a matter of seconds,

Abby's five-foot-eight stature dwindled down to almost nothing. I thought she was going to melt away completely, but the shrinking stopped, and the form morphed into something else. I recognized the small figure immediately; it was Abby as a baby, her tiny body wearing the Social Distortion T-shirt like a dress. Then the monster reversed course and started growing again: Abby the wide-eyed toddler, the smiling schoolgirl, the athletic teenager, the college co-ed who had been at my side just yesterday. The progression of years continued forward still, manifesting a middle-aged version of Abby with streaky gray hair and wrinkles at the corners of her eyes.

"She'll never get this far," the fiend taunted. "Thought you'd like a peek at what might'a been."

"That's not Abby," I said, refusing to let myself consider her implication. "*You're* not Abby. Abby's at her aunt's now, safe. Who are *you*?"

The creature flashed a smug grin and resumed Abby's true-age appearance. "You can call me Rylah. And I'm the one who's gonna be wearin' your girl's skin, that's who I am, *Mama*."

Don't show alarm — that's what she wants.

"So, then, what? You're a ghost? Some kind of phantom?"

Her smile fell away, and she hissed. I'd hit a nerve.

"You're a *haint*," I continued, remembering Bernadette's warning about Bandun Gate. "A woman died not long ago at that place we went to, there'd been an accident or something. You, looking like Abby. It's just a trick. You're really that dead woman's ghost, aren't you?"

Rylah flew at me and slammed my shoulders, knocking me to the ground.

"Don't you *ever* talk to me like that!" she spat, standing over me, blocking out the sun. "Ever! *EVER!*"

Seeing the monster so agitated was surprisingly reassuring; the angrier she got, the less she resembled Abigail. And while this 'Rylah' was showing me her true self, she was coming unhinged at the same time, losing her hold over me. I needed to keep pressing before she could regain her composure.

"You're a *haint* and nothing more," I said with all the

resolve I could manage. "Yeah, you *look* like Abby but you're *not* her. Never will be. You're just putting on a show because your own body is rotting in its grave."

Rylah hovered above me, clenching and unclenching her fists. Fury had contorted the Abby-thing's face into an ugly mask. I had to look away from her beautiful, terrible green eyes.

"You're gonna know about dead and rottin' soon enough!" she growled, her pompous smirk returning. "Your girl's gonna get weaker and weaker until the least little touch'll do the trick!"

Rylah abruptly stopped and stepped away from me, her expression changing from contempt to concern. She'd caught herself revealing a secret.

I leaned into her angst, determined to probe that exposed weakness, and get her to give me more. *Anything* I could use against her. An image of the tissue-doll under Abby's bed popped into my mind. Rylah didn't know I had hidden it in the kitchen drawer, and maybe without it she wouldn't have any power over Abby.

"I've taken your toy away," I said, standing up to better read her reaction. "Your little wax and snotty-tissues craft project."

"That doll-baby? I don't need that anymore! That was just so I could mirror her. But I'll be *wearin'* your girl soon enough now!"

"What does that mean?" I shouted, grabbing her arm.

I have no idea what Rylah said next or if she replied at all, because touching that ghastly beast purged everything else from my consciousness. Her flesh was ice cold and gelatinous, sheathed in loose, leathery skin. Underneath I could feel frenzied squirming, like hundreds of maggots writhing in pudding. My fingers began to tingle and burn as they sank into the mottled rot, releasing a stench of rancid sewage and clotted blood. I yanked my hand away and vomited onto the grass.

"Poor Mama," Rylah chided as I spat out a mouthful of bile. "Feelin' sick, are you? Not near as sick as your girl is gonna be, I promise you that. Of course, she really isn't *yours* anymore. She's mine now."

This isn't happening, I said silently, as much a prayer as anything. *Please, God! It's just another nightmare. I'm going to wake up and Abby will be herself and we'll go to Isle of Palms and watch the sunrise at the beach and pick up seashells and get donuts on the way home and soon Roman will be here and Charles will be here and Dan will be here and everything will be fine and Abby will be fine and I will be fine and*

I could feel myself sliding into the dark well of my own fear, sinking into a murky place where I'd surely drown. Abby would have no one to help fight whatever horror was threatening her if I caved, and God knows what this abomination would do to Dan and the boys once they arrived in Charleston. *Try to focus on that.* And yet the numbing bliss of denial, even oblivion, was compelling. I felt its undertow taking me down, down, down.

A sound, soft and distant, accompanied me on my descent. At first it was too muddled to identify, then I recognized the deep, bold voice of Father Frank, a priest I'd interviewed decades ago for *Encyclopedia of Hell.* His words, stark and somber, drifted back to me across the chasm of years.

"When confronted with anything supernatural, our initial reaction is to reject it outright," Fr. Frank had told me back in my 'Hell days.' "It's the mind's coping mechanism, yes? 'This vision or demon or apparition isn't real, so I do not have to contend with it. I am safe in my little world with everything secure in its proper place.' But that is, of course, a grievous mistake. It's an error from which a person might never recover."

He would know. Father Frank was an exorcist who had assisted in hundreds of liberation rituals during his forty-plus years in the priesthood. A leading expert in demonology, he'd written extensively on the subject and given lectures all over the world. I came across his writings while researching my book and contacted him, hoping he'd give me a few minutes on the phone. Instead, he invited me to meet him in person the following week at Catholic University where he'd be giving a speech. Five days later I was sitting in the campus library with a tape recorder and six pages of hand-written questions, about to conduct the most fascinating interview of my career.

"We, all of us humans, yes? We fear the unknown," the priest had said. "It's only natural. A lesson we learned back in Eden, a collateral effect of pride. We want to be in control, and we tell ourselves that we have everything figured out, always. We, of course, do *not* have everything figured out. Some of us, in point of fact, have appallingly little figured out; that is an unfortunate truth regarding the human condition."

Then he'd smiled and asked me a peculiar question.

"What was the first thing you were truly afraid of when you were young, Miriam? Think back to when you were yet a little girl. What scared you? Not 'I have lost sight of my mother in the grocery store' scared, but deeply, chillingly, frightened to your very soul?"

It had surprised me how quickly those early memories of fear leapt to the surface. "Well, there was this green monster with an oversized head at the end of *Star Trek*'s credits; I had to look away whenever it came on or I'd have nightmares," I'd told him. "Oh, and when I was thirteen, my friend Tara gave me a copy of *'Salem's Lot* for my birthday. Stayed up all night reading it through. For the next few months I slept with a rosary around my neck, it freaked me out so bad!"

"And what about those did you find so fearsome? Frightening enough that the images stayed with you, followed you into your dreams? Did you believe they were real?"

I had paused, reflecting. "No, not exactly. But I thought they *might* be real, *could* be real. Even the possibility was pretty upsetting."

"Precisely!" the old priest had shouted, slamming his fist against the oak table. "You were not really scared of a monstrous face or a brood of New England vampires, yes? You were alarmed, *terrified*, to realize the world was not the cozy, protected place you always imagined it to be, that there are other possibilities in play. We like to think everything in life fits neatly into little boxes that we understand, that we can control, but that is not so. Your discoveries pulled back the curtain, brought you face to face with the most terrifying thing in human experience: the unknown."

He was right. As an adult, I'd come to recognize a 'separation of fears,' a sort of line of demarcation between practical worries like 'do I have cancer, what would happen if I lost my job, is there a snake in the lawn that might bite me,' and true horrors that defy logic or rational explanation. The things most people fear, and that people fear the most, are the 'maybes' shrouded in shadow, the unknown and the unknowable: vampires, ghosts, demons, intergalactic aliens, Hell itself. That is the stuff of visceral terror.

"That was when you first came upon the truth that fear is the mind's way of saying 'something is wrong, and I cannot make sense of it, cannot devise a workable resolution,'" Fr. Frank had continued. "There are two things that can make fear exponentially worse — sometimes to the point a situation becomes unrecoverable. One is to succumb, the other is to ignore it altogether. If we give in to fear it paralyzes us, yes? Strips away our ability to fight back, to escape. However, if we tell ourselves everything is all right and we will be fine, no need for further action, then we are unprepared for whatever might happen next. And take my word, something *always* happens next."

"So how do you deal with it?" I had asked him that long-ago day in D.C. "It must be terrifying, facing down demons, but you do it all the time."

"One practice has always sustained me when I feel particularly imperiled," he'd said, giving me a wink. "I allow the evil entity to think it has the upper hand, that it is prevailing against me, and I am cowering, powerless. That keeps it distracted, wallowing in its own deadly pride, and affords me time to formulate a counterattack."

Father Frank's words coaxed me back from the blackness, arming me for the task at hand. If I could force myself to stop worrying about Abby and focus attention on Rylah, maybe I could uncover her vulnerabilities and find a way to defeat her.

I just had to let her believe she was still in control, lull her into letting down her guard. Rylah clearly relished lording her power over me, so I decided to give her an opportunity to brag.

"So what exactly is your plan now, *haint*?"

"You best not call me that again!" she screeched.

"Okay, *Rylah* then. You said the least touch would do, right? So you need to make physical contact with Abby to do, whatever it is you're planning. That can't happen while she's a hundred miles away. So what now?"

I was struggling to put the pieces together, what few I had, hoping she'd give me more.

"Oh, you'll find out soon enough."

"Why can't you just *go* to Abby, search her out, find her, somehow? You're a ghost, can't you fly or 'appear' there or whatever? Or if you need a body to 'wear,' why not just take mine? I'm right here. You could do it right now!"

"I couldn't wear your skin even if I wanted to, which I do *not*!"

Rylah's rage was palpable, radiating off her in piercing waves. I could see in her eyes how much she wanted to hurt me, kill me even. Something was stopping her. I couldn't understand why she was holding back, then it dawned on me: maybe she didn't have a choice.

"You *can't* hurt me, can you?"

Rylah turned away, hiding her face from me. I continued, emboldened.

"I mean, sure, you can rough me up, put your cold, wormy hands on me, but you can't *really* harm me. Something's preventing you from doing what you want to me. Is it because I'm Abby's mother, that we're connected somehow, bonded by blood?"

"Oh, Lord, you're such a fool! That's got nothin' to do with it!" She stopped then, and I could tell she was performing a mental calculation: was the risk of revealing her secrets worth the thrill of watching me squirm? Rylah wanted me to know her formidable abilities, hoping that knowledge would crush my spirit. After a brief battle her ego won out; she brought her hand up to my face, stopping just short of contact.

"You ferried me 'cross the water, is all. Put yourself in my service, made yourself my aid. So I can't wear you, and I don't *want* to because you're old and ugly!"

The puzzle was beginning to come together, giving me a glimpse of the bigger picture. 'Across the water.' How many bridges had I taken on the way home from Bandun Gate? A dozen, maybe more? And what had my father said regarding the 'haint blue' paint? Something about southern ghosts being afraid to cross over water and that's how to keep them away, by disguising doors and ceilings as waterways.

Of course! That's why this monster hadn't followed Abby to Myrtle Beach. She *couldn't*. The pond behind our house straddled the entire backyard, fed by a creek running along the property's eastern border. The western boundary was marked with a line of maple saplings, and a few feet beyond them the ground sloped downward into a long stretch of soggy swampland. Out front, a drainage channel paralleled the street, and ever since we'd moved in, we had never seen it completely dry. After a heavy rain Dan and I would jokingly refer to it as our 'moat,' almost too deep to drive through. That culvert intersected the little creek on one side of the house, then emptied into the wetlands on the other. The result: our entire lot was bounded by water.

And even if Rylah *could* find a way off our property, she wouldn't get very far. There were all sorts of streams and creeks and ditches she'd have to cross just to get back to the main road. And what then? The lowcountry is one big labyrinth of waterways that continues for more than a hundred miles. She'd be confronted by one dead end after another. No, Rylah was stranded at our place, unable to get anywhere on her own. This meant Abby was safe, at least temporarily. The realization exposed something else, too: Rylah required a chauffeur to leave, and as far as transportation went, she was at *my* mercy.

"You have to be *invited* by me, don't you? To take you anywhere," I said, another big piece falling into place. "This morning, when we went to that burned-out house to visit a friend of yours, or family maybe, buried out in the woods. You made me say the words. You didn't just hop in the van and say, 'let's go!' I had to agree first, otherwise you're stuck here with old, ugly me and my water-encircled homestead."

The vile thing could sense the power shifting away from her, and she was *not* happy to have it go. I could feel Rylah's fury flare up like a belching furnace. Like any cornered animal, she became ferocious.

"That's right, I'm stuck here, but your girl is stuck, too! Stuck being sick, stuck hurtin', stuck helpless with nothin' you or anybody can do to help 'er. And that's just the *start*, Mama! Don't you have boys gonna be here soon? A man, a couple sons? Heard you talkin' about that last night. Here, lemme show you somethin'."

Rylah sauntered over to one of the little maple trees at the yard's edge. There was a fat gray squirrel sitting beside its trunk and a pair of wrens scratching at the grass beneath. She waved at me, flashing a lovely smile that made my heart ache for the real Abby, then turned towards the animals. A low grumbling sound rose from Rylah's throat, causing all three to look towards her. The squirrel fell dead instantly, blood pouring from its ears. Both birds flitted about wildly, uttering panicky screeching sounds. They began to fight, pecking each other's eyes out while continuing their dreadful shrieking. One of the wrens took flight, slamming against the kitchen window so hard it left a crimson splatter on the glass. Stunned, the bird stumbled backward then launched itself against the window again, this time breaking its neck. The other wren staggered, blinded, towards the pond, then plunged into the muddy water and disappeared forever.

"What did you do to them?" I whispered, horrified.

She turned toward me; Abby's sweet smile replaced by Rylah's wicked grin.

"I showed 'em who I am," she said, crossing back and placing an icy hand against my cheek. "You got a fear a'snakes, isn't that right?"

This time, instead of squirming maggots, Rylah's touch became a serpent sliding along the side of my face. It slithered through my hair, then curled around my ear, flicking a spiky tongue against my neck. I could hear hissing as I stood frozen, waiting for its fangs to rip into my skin.

Rylah pulled her hand away, having made her point.

"I can't wait 'til your family arrives so I can show 'em all the things I can do, things you can't *imagine*," she cooed. "Gonna take my time, have some fun with 'em, before they're all used up. I hope they'll be nice and play along, truly I do. You can watch. You *will* watch. It's gonna be quite a show."

The tide was turning again, going against me. Yes, Abby was safe for the time-being, but no one else who came to the house would be. Rylah couldn't harm me (not physically, anyway,) but there was nothing to stop her from attacking Roman and Charles and Dan while I stood by, helpless. *No one* was safe while she was around. Another wave of nausea began to rise, distracting me from my mission. I fought it back. There had to be something I could do to escape this nightmare. *Had* to be.

Rylah walked, no, glided up to me, kissed the spot on my cheek where her repulsive hand had just been (a jolt of pain exploded where her lips made contact), then slowly melted into a pool beside the back door. A black puddle with Abby's face at its center, like a reflection in an oil spill. The liquid slid to the door then under it, re-forming into my daughter's image once inside. Rylah skittered backwards up the family room wall and clung to the ceiling, her red-brown hair cascading downward, cloaking Abby's counterfeited face.

I remained in the yard, thinking about the advice Fr. Frank had given me before Abby was born: *let the evil entity think it has the upper hand, then devise a counterattack.* Okay, maybe Rylah could be bested, but would I be able to get it done before she destroyed someone I loved? The clock was working against me, against my family. I dreaded to think what horrors she might unleash while I struggled to destroy her.

Just start with the basics: to take down an enemy, you concentrate on its flaws. I began composing a mental inventory of everything I had learned about Rylah, determined to find a chink in the armor that would lead to her downfall:

61

1) She was a spirit, almost certainly human rather than demonic

2) She had copied Abby's form, but Abby was still alive (although in some unspecified danger)

3) Rylah's copied body was not truly human: it was capable of unnatural things but also limited in what it could do (can't cross water)

4) For Rylah to 'wear' (take over?) Abby's body, she needed to make physical contact, she could not do it remotely

5) 'Wearing' Abby almost certainly meant killing her

6) Rylah mentioned not being willing to 'give up' Abby's body – which meant breaking whatever connection they had was possible

7) By assisting Rylah (bringing her over the waterways), I was now serving as her familiar, so she couldn't kill me

8) She was wary of revealing anything about herself or her past, meaning she knew there were things that if discovered could be used against her

9) Rylah could not leave our property without my help, and she had to be invited by me to go anywhere (so she couldn't just hide in the van or sneak away)

10) Not only could Rylah harm or kill others, but she also loved inflicting agony and watching people suffer

11) She seemed a creature of her time, with no awareness or understanding of modern technology (like the cellphone)

Modern technology! Inspiration hit and I went inside, purposely avoiding even glancing at the dark, gurgling mass in the corner of the ceiling. I went straight into my bedroom, closed the door, and took out my laptop. If I could determine who Rylah was, where she'd come from, how she died, what unresolved grievances and grudges she might have, maybe I could find a way to force her to cross over, or at least relinquish her hold on Abby.

I opened a search engine and typed in "South Carolina + woman + fatality + accident + Bandun Gate." A news article immediately popped up: 'Hiking Venture Takes Deadly Turn.'

Beside the blurb, the photo of an African American woman smiled back from my screen. I clicked on the link and began reading.

March 23, 2011. Kadisha Fontaine, 31, died of anaphylactic shock while hiking along the Wadmalaw River marshes. The Philadelphia native and graduate of Temple University appeared to have suffered an extreme allergic reaction after consuming food containing nuts or nut products. Paramedics attempted to revive her, but despite their efforts she was pronounced dead at the scene.

With the victim at the time was husband Michael Fontaine, 30, an architect with a firm in downtown Charleston. Fontaine said his wife had been despondent following the deaths of her mother and sister, who were killed in a recent car accident, and must have inadvertently eaten the nut-tainted pastry. Early indications are the death will be ruled accidental. Police, however, are continuing their investigation.

I skimmed over the next few paragraphs until a familiar name caught my eye.

Yesterday's fatality is the latest in a series of misadventures associated with the place locals call Bandun Gate that date back to the 1600s. Fontaine's death is the first documented fatality in the area since the drowning of an elderly transient almost a century ago. Bones, teeth, and other human remains have been recovered from nearby marshlands over the years, however almost none have ever been positively identified. Likewise there is no documentation or forensic evidence to support allegations of disappearances at the site spanning almost 400 years, though rumors and local legends about Bandun Gate abound.

I read the article again, confused by elements that didn't seem to add up. The woman who had died at Bandun Gate was a Philly girl with a college degree; Rylah's vocal patterns and vocabulary were more like those of a Southerner who'd never made it past grade school. And the death described occurred only five years ago in 2011, surely the deceased would've owned a cellphone, or at least been aware of what they are and how they work. I took a closer look at the photo. Kadisha Fontaine had gentle eyes and a sweet smile. I couldn't reconcile the woman in the picture with the sadistic hellion currently inhabiting my family room. Something was definitely off.

There had to be more to her story that would explain the contradictions. I started thinking that perhaps Kadisha Fontaine's death wasn't an accident after all, that she could've been murdered and now her spirit was lashing out in anger. Maybe her misdirected wrath was causing a horrible psycho-spiritual mutation, and somehow Abby had gotten swallowed up in it.

I opened another tab and searched "Michael Fontaine + architect + Charleston." Sure enough, a millisecond later I had his photo, business address, and contact info. The computer clock showed it was 4:15 in the afternoon; he was most likely still at work, so I dialed the office number. *This is going to be a weird conversation* I thought as the call rang through.

Before I could figure what I was going to say, a man's voice answered.

"Mike Fontaine."

"Uh, hello, Mr. Fontaine," I stammered, unsure how to proceed. "Um, I'm sorry to bother you but, well, I don't even know where to begin, really. Let me start by saying I'm so sorry about your wife's tragic death."

"Who is this?"

"My name is Miriam Van Scott. I didn't know your wife, but I think we might be..." I struggled for the right word, "... *connected*, somehow."

Silence. I continued.

"I was with my daughter Abby yesterday (*God, had it only been a single day since my world had fallen apart?*), and we visited a place out in the marshes called Bandun Gate. I think it's the same place where your wife died, and something happened that I can't explain..."

Click. Mike Fontaine had hung up.

I dialed him back immediately. He picked up and before I could speak, said, "Listen, I have nothing to say to you. Please don't call again."

Another 'click' as the line disconnected.

I waited a few minutes before a third try, taking time to compose my thoughts. This time, as soon as he answered, I blurted out, "if you hang up again, I'm going to come to your office in Charleston and wait there until you *do* talk to me."

No response, but he stayed on the line. I continued in a gentler tone.

"Again, I'm sure this must be incredibly upsetting, and I really am sorry for that, but I think you might be able to help me."

"Help you with what?"

I took a deep breath. "Saving my daughter." I thought he might bail once more, but when he didn't, I kept going. "Her name is Abby. She's twenty, going to be twenty-one next month. We went to Bandun Gate yesterday and when we got home she seemed fine. Was herself, I mean. Sometime during the night Abby started acting weird, and today... Okay I know how crazy this sounds, but the woman who's in my house now isn't Abby. She looks like Abby, but she's *not*. Looks *exactly* like her, but she's *different*. The way she talks, the things she can do. Calls herself 'Rylah,' says she's 'wearing' my daughter. It's like she's in an Abby costume, but everything about her is just *wrong*."

A long pause, then Mike Fontaine asked, "What is it you think I can do for her?"

My heart leapt. He hadn't decided this was some prank or that I was insane, or asked me what in the world I was talking about. He was willing to keep listening, perhaps even help if he could.

"I think maybe your wife, her ghost, her spirit, whatever, has attached itself to Abby. I think she might be angry, and is lashing out for some reason."

"Just stop, please," he replied, his voice cracking.

But I couldn't stop. Mike Fontaine was my only lead.

"I think your wife, Kadisha, is haunting us somehow."

"Don't say that."

"I am so, *so* sorry to have to tell you all this, Mr. Fontaine. I simply don't know where else to turn. But this started after we went to Bandun Gate, where your wife died, and it seems like your wife…"

"Stop saying that!" he interrupted, raising his voice. "Stop saying she's Kadisha! That miserable bitch you're talking about is *not* my wife!!!"

Chapter Six
Mangled Angels

"You *do* know something about what's happening!" I blurted out, my eyes filling with tears. There was hope.

"I can't have this conversation while I'm at work," the man whispered into the phone.

"Of course, I understand. Can you meet me somewhere, tonight? Any place you like, I can be there."

There was a pause and I thought he might hang up on me again, but Mike Fontaine spoke. "You know that hot dog place on seventeen in Mount Pleasant?"

"Jack's! We love that place, go there all the time." Jack's was hard to miss, with its canary yellow exterior and kitschy silver 'rocket' perched out front. It had been on our 'frequent eatery' list for years.

"Meet me there at 7:30, on the patio, around the side. They close at eight, so it should be pretty quiet."

"I'll be there. And thank you, Mr. Fontaine. I didn't know where else to turn."

"I have to go." He softened his tone. "And you can call me Mike."

After hanging up I checked the time; it was just after 5 p.m. In two hours I'd be sitting down with a stranger who might've murdered his wife and would see me as a threat. Maybe he would decide to get rid of me, too. Who knows? Or he might turn out to be a good man who'd have the answers I needed. At this point, it didn't really matter, this was a risk I had to take.

Besides, anything was better than being in the house with Rylah, wondering what fresh torments she was planning to unleash on me.

Before putting away my laptop I did one more search, this one on "haints + lowcountry + southern ghosts." Some of the results I already knew — they're malevolent spirits who prey on the living, they can't cross water, they're bloodthirsty and vicious. And of course that they're intertwined with Gullah folklore. After all, who would know more about residual evil than people who'd been ripped from their homeland and forced into slavery?

The articles provided some new insights as well. One said the phantoms move by night, and unless they take on a physical form will burn up in sunlight just like vampires. (Not sure about that — Rylah hadn't gotten the least bit smouldery when we were out back. Maybe Abby's copied body was enough to shield her?) Another insisted they only target people who are weak or compromised, and have tricks for making humans vulnerable to them. Most entries mentioned something I already knew, that haints love inflicting pain, and feed off the dark energy. They'll prolong agony as long as possible, often chasing their victims to death from exhaustion, or slowly siphoning their life force away. That was Rylah to a 'T.'

Then I hit upon something I could use immediately in my preternatural battle. Lowcountry ghosts are obsessive when it comes to repetitive activities such as counting straws in a broom or crystals in the sugar bowl. Duping them into performing these tasks would keep them distracted for hours. They can't resist printed materials either, and will stop whatever they're doing to read every last word.

Perfect! I ran into the family room and grabbed a copy of *Encyclopedia of Hell* off the bookshelf. (The publisher had sent me a case of hardbacks years ago and I still had ten left.) I got out the scissors and tape, then hustled over to the back wall. The Hell book gave a sharp *crack!* as I forced it open, breaking its brittle spine. I sliced through the binding and pulled pages out by the handful, careful not to tear them. When I had a sizable pile, I taped them up side by side on the glass doors that led outside, and as far up the adjacent wall as I could reach. Familiar names and phrases flashed past as I worked: Hiyoya, the Papuan underworld, the Buddhist 'hot

Hell' Jigoku, Mot, ancient Canaanite lord of the damned. An illustration of Dr. Faustus glared at me, glum and unrepentant.

Sometime while I was papering the place with my torn-out pages, Rylah had ebbed down from the ceiling for a closer look.

"Here you go," I said, waving a hand at the haphazard collage. "Thought you might be homesick. This should help."

She was standing a yard away, both hands pressed against a jagged-edged paper detailing Orpheus's doomed trek to Hades, devouring it with her eyes. I backed slowly out of the room and down the hall until I reached the garage door, dropping more loose pages as I went. Rylah never looked up or spoke a word; she was too busy obsessing over the display. I got in the van and went down the driveway. There was a soft *splash* as my tires dipped into the culvert, sending watery ripples in either direction. I smiled and drove off, leaving Rylah marooned on her own private 'island.'

Jack's Cosmic Dogs was a twenty-minute drive from the house. Mike wouldn't be there for another hour, and I was desperate to keep my mind off Abby. I knew if I let myself obsess over her current situation, I wouldn't be able to function. Or worse, I'd race off to Myrtle Beach to try to find her, impetuously abandoning the only hope I had of vanquishing Rylah.

My first inclination was to head to the shore for a quick refresh before my ominous rendezvous. Nothing helps me put things in perspective like gazing out at the vast, lulling sea. I left the main road and headed for the Isle of Palms causeway, the August sun a yellow balloon in my rearview mirror. About halfway there, an old steeple poking up through the trees caught my eye; it seemed to be summoning me. I'm a cradle Catholic, but learned a long time ago that faith of any kind is powerful, and I needed whatever divine assistance I could get.

The aging structure turned out to be a Baptist church, one of several denominations in the Charleston area. Its white bricks were storm-worn, and the northern wall was laced with tufted vines. I parked in the empty lot, no one around on a Thursday evening, and stepped into the sultry summer air. An A-frame sign listing the times for Sunday services greeted me, assuring passers-by *'Jesus Never Takes a Vacation from Loving You!'* I circled the building until I came to a shady spot, sat down, and leaned against the wall. It was surprisingly cool, even the humidity seemed to have tapered off a bit.

Sitting in the shadow of this picturesque little church, in the sheltering embrace of the Holy City, I was tempted once again to dismiss everything that had been happening as nonsense. Product of an overactive imagination. Musings. Delusions. Crazy from the heat. My rational, *'just the facts, ma'am,'* researcher's voice insisted *there's no such thing as ghosts, you know that! Snap out of this and get real!* If someone else had told me this same story, that they were being threatened by an evil spirit intent on stealing and inhabiting their daughter's body, I would've smiled politely and thought *what a nutcase.* Now, here I was questioning my own senses, wondering if I was the lunatic and this entire crisis existed only in my head.

The longer I stayed, listening to the *whoosh, whoosh* of passing traffic, smelling the ocean air, staring at the steeple's ivory silhouette against the sapphire sky, the crazier I felt. After a few minutes I took out my phone and dialed Abby's number. *She's really gonna laugh when I tell her what I'd talked myself into believing! I'll never hear the end of it!* No answer, which probably meant she was off somewhere with her Aunt Ruth, splashing in the waves or shopping for funny T-shirts or gobbling shrimp at an all-you-can-eat seafood buffet. I tried again anyway. The call went straight to voicemail.

A twinge of panic crept up my neck, whispering, *what did you think was going to happen?* I called a third time, then a fourth. I was listening to the intermittent hum of unanswered rings on my fifth attempt when it dawned on me I was not only coming unglued myself, but seeing so many 'missed calls' from 'Mom' was likely going to alarm Abby when she finally checked her phone. My daughter's perky, pre-recorded voice came on the line, telling me, "Sorry I missed you! Leave a message and I'll get back as soon as I can."

God, I loved hearing that voice. Abby. Really and truly, Abigail.

I inhaled slowly, struggling to sound nonchalant.

"Just calling to see how you're doing," I managed. "Ruthie said you weren't feeling well earlier. Hope you're better now." After a quick gut check to make sure I could say it without bursting into tears added, "Love you, Abs. Talk to you soon."

I lingered a bit after hanging up, enjoying the delicious shade and peaceful churchyard, shutting out everything else. What *had* I been thinking? As I was getting up to return to the van, my phone chimed with a text from Abby.

Sorry Mom cant talk head buzzing bad wont stop going to Ruthies dr maybe will let you no love you 2

I read the words over and over again, not realizing I was crying until a stray tear splashed onto the screen, magnifying the word 'bad' in a glistening fisheye effect.

A doctor won't help, I thought as I wiped my face. *No medical professional will be able to diagnose what's wrong. Even if they could, there's nothing they could do to fix it.*

Just like Roman, a phantom voice taunted. *Remember? Only this time, it's SO MUCH worse.*

Eleven years earlier, a late-winter flu hit our household hard. Dan and I had both gotten ill right away with chills, body aches and projectile vomiting. No sooner were we on the mend, Abby and Charles began a week-long cycle of symptoms, recovery, relapse. But the one who fared worst was Roman. He became so sick so fast, we almost lost him.

He was twelve at the time, and what at first seemed a simple bout with the virus took a sudden, deadly turn. One evening Roman complained about excruciating headaches; I told him he was being dramatic and a good night's sleep was all he needed. The next morning he couldn't walk without staggering. By the time we got to the doctor's office Roman's speech was slurred to the point of being unintelligible. His regular physician couldn't determine what was wrong, so Roman was whisked by ambulance to the local emergency room, then by helicopter to Children's National Hospital in

Washington, D.C.

Even after a battery of tests, the doctors could not offer a conclusive diagnosis. Their best guess was Roman might have acute disseminated encephalomyelitis, or maybe a meningitis variant. A lesion had developed on his brainstem and was expanding, slowly destroying various functions as it grew. He'd already lost the ability to walk and to speak, and within hours he couldn't stay awake for more than a few minutes at a time. No one was certain what might be affected next.

"Right now, we're attempting 'diagnosis by process of elimination'," his pediatric neurologist Dr. Mackey had told us. "So far, we've ruled out brain cancer, a tumor, stroke, aneurism, epilepsy. Frankly, this has everyone stumped. We're not sure *what* we're dealing with, but we're not giving up."

No diagnosis meant no treatment plan. And while the evaluations proceeded, Roman's health continued to deteriorate.

For the next two days, the team tried all sorts of procedures without success. His condition worsened by the hour. Three days after being admitted, Roman went into a coma and had to be put on a feeding tube. His doctors were running out of options, and my son was running out of time.

"Is Roman going to die?" Abby had asked me when things were at their worst.

"I don't know," I had to tell her, not wanting to lie. "But everyone is praying for him, and the doctors are working really hard to help him get better."

The truth was, Roman was slipping away and no one could stop the slide. Hours after I had to tell my little girl she might never see her brother again, Roman was rushed to intensive care. He could no longer breathe on his own and required a ventilator.

That had been the worst day of my life, seeing my boy unconscious, so thin and fragile, surrounded by beeping machinery and with a tangle of wires attached to him. I had never felt anything remotely comparable to the savage desperation that clawed at me while I sat at Roman's bedside, as helpless and forlorn as he appeared.

"You need to prepare yourself emotionally for all outcomes," Dr. Mackey had told us, handing me the card of the hospital's 'grief and loss counselor.' "If he does pull through, he's likely to have permanent brain damage. We don't know yet how severe."

After Roman was intubated, one of the nurses brought me to a room across from the Intensive Care Unit. It was cavernous, jammed with cots, sofas and reclining chairs, about half of them occupied by people trying to sleep. Along the far wall was a counter piled with fruit, mini cereal boxes, and peanut butter crackers. There was a glass-front refrigerator stocked with milk and juice.

"This is for I.C.U patients' parents," she'd said in a hushed tone, trying not to wake anyone. "You can sleep here, help yourself to something to eat or drink whenever you want. There's no cell service, but there's a bunch of phones just outside in the hallway you can use. Dial nine for an outside line."

The 'parent dorm' experience was beyond surreal. I sat in one of the empty chairs, trying to take it all in. Many of the moms and dads sharing the space were asleep, others seemed lost in thought. The ones who were awake and alert smiled or gave me a little 'welcome to the club' nod. It took everything I had not to burst into tears.

A man who'd been stretched out on a sofa in back came over and introduced himself. His name was Cole and he lived in North Carolina. He had seven-year-old twins, a boy and a girl. His daughter Sally's appendix had burst, (the local doctor thought she had food poisoning and sent her home the day before it happened, saying she just needed 'to get some rest,') sending infection throughout her body. She was fighting sepsis and catastrophic organ failure. Cole told me Sally had been in I.C.U. for nine days and might remain there for weeks, maybe longer, but it was better than the alternative.

I drifted off to sleep thinking of Cole and how much he must miss his wife and son back home. How long, I wondered, would Dan and I be spending time here while Roman's crisis played out? At least we could drive back and forth between the hospital and our house an hour away, alternately tending Roman, and parenting Abigail and Charles, until our child was healthy again. That was more than most of these parents had.

I did not let myself consider the other possibility. Not *at all.*

When I finally dozed off that night my sleep had been restless, punctuated by fragmented dreams: laughing with Dan and the kids in happier times, riding through the Virginia countryside in my father's old hatchback with my brother and sister when we were young, pouring water on a fire that could not be extinguished. One dream was so vivid it seemed real. Father Frank, who I hadn't seen in years, was gently shaking my shoulder.

Could he really be here in this odd place of hope and despair, come to shepherd me through this darkest valley?

"Thirty-three down, ten letters, 'no explanation,'" he'd said as I stared, confused. "You should know this one, Miriam!"

"Father Frank? What are you doing here? And what are you talking about?"

"The crossword!" he said, tossing a folded newspaper onto my lap. "Cross. Word."

I picked up the object he'd dropped and held it closer, but it wasn't a printed puzzle. I'd found instead the corner of a thin white blanket stamped 'Children's National Hospital.' Someone jostled my shoulder again. When I'd looked up, I recognized the nurse who'd escorted me to the room earlier that evening.

"You're Roman's mother, right?" she'd asked. "Come with me, quick!"

"What's wrong?" I had mumbled, scrambling to my feet.

"Dr. Mackey sent me to get you," she'd said as I followed her across the hall. "She wants to see you about your son. Said to get you quick. That's all I know."

The world went silent then, my thoughts spinning.

Oh, God Please God please God please God PLEASE GOD PLEASE PLEASE PLEASE

I'd run to Roman's bedside, my stomach doing somersaults, fearing the worst. To my shock, he was sitting up, wide awake and rather annoyed.

"I think we've turned the corner," Dr. Mackey announced, smiling. "I was going over his chart when he suddenly woke up and started asking for you."

I'd looked at the doctor then back at my son, jamming my fingernails into my palms hard enough to feel the sting, worried this might be another dream.

"Roman. I can't believe it! How do you feel?"

His voice had sounded scratchy and was nearly inaudible from days of non-use, but he'd managed to grumble, "I want OUT of here!" then asked for a donut, and promptly fell back asleep.

"I can't explain how he improved so quickly," Dr. Mackey had said with a shrug. "But he's obviously light years ahead of where he was this morning. His vitals are good, we're sending him back to a regular room. If he continues like this, he'll be able to go home in a couple days."

Roman's astounding recovery left his medical team baffled. Two days after being unhooked from his respirator and feeding tube, he was walking and talking normally. He showed no signs of long-term damage, physical or cognitive. Later that week when Roman was discharged, I'd asked Dr. Mackey if they'd learned anything more about his illness.

"The truth is we'll probably never know exactly what caused the crisis, or how he recovered so fast. It's like something had a tight grip on him then simply — let go. I'm just glad he's leaving here healthy. We don't always have this positive an outcome."

She didn't need to spell that out for me. No one did. I was painfully aware of how easily things could have gone the other way.

Now here I was a decade later with another child in grave danger. And me, again, powerless, anxious, desperate. *Familiar territory.*

I pulled into Jack's parking lot at quarter past seven. All the outdoor tables were empty, so I went inside and looked around. A few people were still munching their food or waiting on an order, but Mike wasn't among them. Normally I'd get an

Atomic Dog (chili, onions and spicy mustard) and a side of fries, but nothing about this visit was normal. I doubted I could choke down anything at all.

I bought a chocolate shake and took it out to the patio's back-corner table. Still no sign of Mike. Vintage metal signs for Pez and Nehi glinted in the late day sun, a 1950s era canister-vacuum fashioned into a robot leaned against one of Jack's exterior walls. He'd been part of the décor since the kids were little. Years ago they'd named him 'Cyborg Steve.' The metal man was a bit rustier now, but still a bittersweet reminder of happier times. I thought about how much Abby and the boys would love to be here with me, taking pictures with Steve and dipping fries into my shake.

Mike arrived not long after I sat down and parked in the side lot. I recognized him from his internet photo and walked over, extending my hand.

"You must be Mike Fontaine. I'm Miriam Van Scott. Thank you so much for agreeing to meet with me."

He looked surprised as he returned the handshake.

"Sorry, I didn't think you'd be …"

"White?" I smiled.

Mike chuckled. "I guess when you said your daughter had some connection to Kadisha, I was picturing someone who looked more like her."

My laugh was clumsy, Mike's disarming.

"Do you want something to eat?" I asked as we made our way to the table where I'd left the milkshake. "Or a soda, ice cream?"

"No," he said, taking the chair opposite me. "Let's just get this done. You start. Tell me what happened with your daughter."

I recounted everything for Mike: our trip to Bandun Gate, how Abby had been her usual, feisty self after we got home, the incident with the strange bug. Then I described her nighttime episode, her bizarre chanting, the difference in her voice and her demeanor, finding the insect husk and the tissue paper doll. All of that leading to Rylah revealing herself and showing off her hideous abilities, boasting how she was going to kill my daughter and inhabit Abby's body.

"Oh, and while I still thought she was my daughter, Rylah had me take her to this burned-out shack north of here, past Awendaw. It wasn't much more than a pile of rocks and a chimney, but she was *really* intent on going there."

When I'd finished relaying that last detail, Mike took a heavily-creased paper out of his wallet, unfolded it, and handed it to me. It was a photocopied newspaper story from 1948. 'Woman Dies in House Fire.' Below the headline was a photograph of the house I'd visited that morning, smoldering and less deteriorated, but definitely the same place. Further down the page was another picture, this one showing a young blonde woman with pale skin and piercing eyes. She was identified as Virgilia Jane Hodges, the fire's lone fatality.

"Oh my God! This is the place we went!" I laid the paper flat and pointed to a spot in the photo. "There's a grave back behind the trees, over here. Not a *graveyard*, just one grave all by itself with a rock wall around it. No name on the headstone. She put flowers on it, like she was paying her respects."

I glanced up at Mike, who was staring down at the article. His face had turned to stone.

"What does this mean?" I asked him, tapping the photocopy. "Is Rylah connected to this house? Did she set the fire, kill this woman? And what does it have to do with your wife?"

"Read it," he said, pushing the paper towards me. "Then I'll tell you what I know."

I picked up the weathered copy and scanned the story. According to the article, Virgilia Hodges was alone when a fire began sometime after sundown, originating in the kitchen. By the time someone saw the smoke (her closest neighbor lived almost three miles away) and got help, the entire structure was in flames. It took a while to get the blaze under control, and when the fire-fighters finally got inside, they found the victim's body slumped against the bedroom wall. She was clutching a large metal box to her chest, a crowbar beside her on the floor.

At first it appeared to be a tragic mishap: something left too long on the stove, or an oil lamp that had fallen over. At that time, most houses in rural South Carolina did not have electricity. An investigator from Charleston made several troubling discoveries. Both the front and back doors had been barricaded, and all the house's windows were nailed shut — from the outside. The expert was quoted in the article as saying that the victim still might have been able to escape if she'd let go of the box and focused on prying open a door or window.

The piece offered some background info on Hodges, too. She had moved to the area two years before the incident, and no one could say with certainty where she'd lived before that. Conflicting accounts had her coming up from Georgia or down from the North Carolina coast, or possibly from some shrouded alcove of the Holy City itself. Everyone agreed on one thing: as soon as Hodges moved into the little shanty, bad things began happening with alarming frequency.

The county sheriff had been summoned numerous times over complaints she was hurting area children, however no charges were ever filed. Victims were either too young to give credible testimony, or their injuries could be explained away as accidents. In many cases, parents had abruptly withdrawn their accusations without explanation. It seemed people were afraid to go against Hodges, worried what she might do in retaliation. There had been one man who refused to back down and had threatened to contact state authorities if the locals wouldn't arrest her. Within days of issuing the ultimatum, he, his wife and their two young sons vanished without a trace, leaving all their possessions behind. And once again, there was no hard evidence linking Hodges to their disappearances.

The article concluded by stating an anonymous benefactor was handling Hodges' burial arrangements, which would be private.

"Newspaper uses her given name, Virgilia," Mike said when I'd finished reading. "But folks who knew her say she went by 'Rylah'."

I took a closer look at the picture of Virgilia Jane Hodges. She appeared to be in her mid-twenties, tall and slender, wavy blonde hair bound in a loose bow. Her intense stare must've made whoever shot the photograph incredibly uncomfortable. I'd never seen the woman before but recognized that expression immediately — it was the same look of festering contempt I'd been seeing all day plastered on my daughter's counterfeited face.

"So Rylah was evil," I said as I studied the photo. "*Really* evil. And it eventually caught up with her."

Mike nodded. "The paper gives a hint what she was like, left out a whole lot of things. *Disturbing* things. I tracked down some of her old neighbors the last couple of years, a few old-timers are still around. They were just kids when Rylah was living in that house, but they all remembered her."

"I'm guessing not in a good way."

Mike shook his head.

"No, not in a good way at all. A man named Bill told me about an incident with his sister, Marlene. She was six at the time, playing in the woods not far from Rylah's place, running around, you know how kids do. Marlene tripped in a little hole that had been covered with leaves and twigs, hiding it, covered up *deliberately*. She caught her foot in it, slipped, broke her ankle.

"Well guess who just happened to be there to see it all. Marlene told her parents she couldn't get up, just sat there crying and crying with Rylah watching her. Watching and *smiling*. Then, when Rylah finally did come over, she yanked and twisted Marlene's leg, making her scream, making the girl beg her to stop. Marlene *swears* Rylah was laughing the whole time, tortured that child for who knows how long, had picked her up to take her Lord knows where when Bill and his buddies came looking for her.

"Rylah told the boys the girl was mistaken, said the accident had just happened and she was trying to keep Marlene calm, figured out how badly she was hurt. She was taking her to the doctor, although Bill swears she was heading the opposite direction from town, heading back into the woods. *No harm intended*, Rylah said, *just trying to help*. Bill said things like that happened with Rylah all the time."

Mike took a deep breath and leaned back against the patio railing.

"There were other things too — stories about raunchy sex stuff, filthy things she'd do to men, let them do to her. Orgies, rituals, conjurings. Neighbors said she was a witch, wanted her *gone*. Finally, Rylah pushed them too far."

"Well, obviously the fire was no accident. Did you find out what really happened?"

"I talked to a lady from the Watkins family. They owned a patch of land back in the day, up by Mechaw Creek. She was eleven back in the winter of '47, had a three-year-old cousin named Sammy who went missing two weeks before Christmas. He and his folks lived four, five miles from Rylah's place, and right off, there was talk she had something to do with it. So everybody's out looking for the little guy, frantic, you know, not sure if he wandered off by himself or maybe somebody took him. Maybe *she* took him. Not sure which was worse. Went to her house, Rylah smiles like she doesn't have a care in the world, invites them to look around but they didn't find anything.

"Couple days go by and still no Sammy. Looked everywhere. Then a week after he's gone — likely dead, everybody's thinking but didn't want to say with Christmas so close — an old man is out hunting and hears a child screaming. 'Blood-curdling' is the way she says he described the screams. So he follows the sound deep into the woods and sure enough, there's Sammy sitting on tree stump, clothes all dirty, one of his hands all bloody like an animal got him. Man thought he heard something else, too. *Saw* something moving in the trees. Had his gun ready and thought about going after it, but decided he best get help for Sammy instead.

"He picks up the boy, wraps his scarf around the bloody hand, rushes him home to his folks. Looks now like maybe Sammy just wandered off and stayed lost in the woods until the hunter found him. They take Sammy to the doctor to get him checked out and that's when everything changed.

"First thing doc notices is the boy doesn't have any signs of frostbite or hypothermia, even though temperatures were down around freezing most nights he was missing. Kid didn't have a coat or sweater or anything. Sammy wasn't malnourished either, after going so long without food. There's no wild berries or bugs or anything he could've eaten out there, not in wintertime. Then the doctor examined Sammy's hand. The little finger — pinky finger — on his left hand, was gone, and so was the top knuckle of the finger next to it. And not torn off like an animal bite, but *sliced* off clean with a blade.

"Doc said the pinky wound had been cauterized and had started healing over. Was a couple days old already. But the cut on Sammy's ring finger was fresh, *real* fresh. Still bleeding, like that's what the boy was screaming about when the hunter heard him. There were other cuts on him, too, and burns, made in a pattern on his back. Somebody had been *keeping* Sammy, hurting him on purpose. Would've continued, what was being done to him, if the man hadn't found him that morning. Lucky for both of 'em he had a gun when he came upon whatever was going on."

I sat listening to Mike's tale, already knowing the answer to the question I was about to ask.

"It was Rylah, wasn't it? She'd taken Sammy and was... maiming him?"

"That's what everybody suspected, but nobody could *prove*. Sheriff came by, asked her a bunch of questions, had a look around her place, couldn't find anything. He saw the metal box, the one the newspaper mentioned. It was the size of a big shoebox, like boots would come in, maybe a little deeper. Had a lock on it, he asked her to open it, but she said she'd lost the key. Just kept the box for sentimental reasons, had been in the family forever. Swore she had nothing to do with Sammy or his injuries, so there was nothing the sheriff could do.

"A month later, Sammy and his mom are visiting a neighbor when Rylah shows up at the same farmhouse, looking to buy honey. Sammy takes one look at her and loses his mind, screaming, crying, trying to get as far away from her as possible. While Sammy's having his meltdown, Rylah walks up to him playing 'peek-a-boo.' All smiles. Then she leans down and tells him, 'be nice and play along,' in a real spooky voice. Sammy pukes then takes off running.

"'Poor Mama,' Rylah says to his mother, with that big grin still on her face. 'Boys can be so hard to control. Sometimes they just get away from you,' then sashays out the door.

"Sammy's mom asks the sheriff to check into Rylah again, so he goes back and re-interviews everybody. The man who found Sammy didn't have anything new, but the doctor who'd treated Sammy sure did. He hands over the boy's medical report and sheriff sees something that turns his blood cold. Doc had drawn a sketch of Sammy's cuts and burns, and sheriff's seen the design before. It's the same one on that metal box of Rylah's, at least part of it. Looked like a fancy candelabra with a circle drawn around it, something like that. The one on the box had lots more detail, but sure looks like whoever hurt Sammy was copying the same pattern onto the boy's back, just didn't finish. Didn't get the chance to.

"Sheriff sends it up the chain, but it's still not enough to bring Rylah in. Could just be a coincidence, or somebody trying to make it look like she did it, or maybe those marks could look like anything you wanted them to, you know? Whatever reason, Rylah was off the hook again. And it didn't worry her, everybody knowing. She *liked* that they knew what she'd done, what she was going to get away with *again*.

"That was the last straw. Three days later, the fire," Mike gestured toward the article. "Everybody got tired of worrying what she might do next, who she'd hurt, felt they had no other choice. Took matters into their own hands."

"What was in the box?" I asked. "The authorities must've recovered it from the debris."

"Another mystery among mysteries. Rumor is, whoever made her final arrangements got hold of it. But even that's only a guess. Some say it was put it in Rylah's coffin with her, or buried beneath the rubble of the old house, or melted down and destroyed. Could be somebody still has it, along with whatever god-forsaken shit was inside."

I picked up the article and read it again, peering at the picture of the dead-but-not-gone Rylah. Mike reached over and touched the paper's edge.

"I'm going to need that back when you're done. I keep it with me, take it out when I get to thinking about Didi, question my recollections. I use it to remind myself what I was dealing with, why I did what I did."

"I still don't get what this has to do with your wife, or Bandun Gate. That's *miles* away from this house. Or with me and Abby."

I looked across the table. Any suspicions I'd once had about Mike being a murderer evaporated. He hadn't hurt his wife. I could see it in his face. Whatever tragic fate had befallen Kadisha Fontaine, her husband had nothing to do with it. Even after five years, his grief was still raw.

"What was she like, your wife?" I asked. "Tell me about her."

The first tears slid down Mike's cheek. He brushed them away and cleared his throat.

"Kadisha — everybody called her Didi — was smart, beautiful, kind. And funny! Lord, did she have a great sense of humor. Always kidding around, laughing."

I handed back the article. Mike folded it carefully and returned it to his wallet.

"Look, maybe this was a mistake," he muttered. "I think I should go…"

"No, wait, please. *Please.* I don't have anywhere else to turn. Please tell me. What happened with Didi?"

Mike let out a long sigh, took a napkin from the table dispenser, and dabbed his eyes. He nodded and gave me a sad smile.

"She'd want me to help you. Help your girl. That's who Didi was. Always."

I smiled back as the day's dying sun turned the sky indigo to plum, and listened as Mike poured out his incredible tale.

Chapter Seven
Consumed

"Didi and I loved taking long walks. 'Explores,' she called them. It was our favorite thing to do together. She grew up in the city, Philadelphia. Not much nature there, so she loved living in Charleston. All the trees, birds, flowers, beaches, wetlands. Every chance we got, we'd pack some sandwiches and just start walking until we found a spot then stop and picnic. We'd talk about whatever was on our minds, just enjoy spending time together.

"That's how it started, that morning. Didi was having a real hard time. Her mom and sister Darla had been killed by a drunk driver not three weeks before, barely a mile from Darla's house. Didi had lost her dad to cancer when she was in high school, and she and her mom and Darla were already close even before then, *really* close. After he died, they were a force onto themselves. One for all, all for one, you know? Almost kept Didi from moving to South Carolina. Didn't want to be so far away from them. But Darla and her mom told her they'd come see her all the time, which they did, and she'd go back to Philly whenever she could, keep things close. She'd been offered a good job down here and they wanted her to be happy.

"And I think she was, I truly do.

"Anyway, after we came back from the funeral, Didi was really hurting. *Bad.* Never seen her so sad, just quiet all the time. I thought getting her back into a routine would help pull her out of it, so I suggested we go do an 'explore.' Go someplace we'd never been, see something new. So we drove up seventeen, parked off an old dirt road, and started walking. It was spring, nice weather, lots of birds singing, flowers blooming. Started off a beautiful day.

"Didi was quiet, but she'd smile and say something upbeat now and then. I could tell she was trying. We kept on, after a while started looking for a place to have our picnic. We saw a little house that looked like it had burned down years ago, just on the edge of the woods. Seemed like a nice spot for lunch.

"'How 'bout here?' I asked her, she smiled, nodded, so I took off my backpack and spread out the blanket, got our sandwiches out, got everything set up. Meanwhile Didi was wandering around, checking out what was left of the house, watching the birds fly by. When I had everything ready, I looked up, couldn't see Didi anywhere, started calling her name.

"'I'm over here, Mike,' she said, and I could tell she was crying. Heard it in her voice. I looked over and saw her through the trees, hunched over something. Thought maybe she'd tripped, hurt herself, couldn't stand up. I ran over and found her inside this little stone frame, walls about waist-high. Walls around a grave. Didi was leaning on the headstone, sobbing. Her whole body was shaking back and forth she was crying so hard. A chill ran through me, felt like my heart turned to ice. Didn't know why then, but something in the back of my mind was shouting, 'no, no, no!'

"'Whoever's buried here is all alone,' Didi says, hardly able to talk. 'It's not right being out here all alone, and without a name, even.' Something like that. I knew she was thinking of her mom and Darla. The two of them back in Philly in their final resting spot, her down here, so far away. There was a gap where a gate met one of the walls. I started climbing through to hold her, give her some comfort. But there wasn't a lot of room in there and while I was trying to figure out where I could stand without crowding her, she stood up and sort of waved me off.

"'I'm all right,' Didi says. 'Just give me a minute.' She looked over and smiled at me. Beautiful smile. Silver line down each of her cheeks from the tears, made her look even prettier. It was really Didi, I *know* it was. I said 'okay' and went back to wait for her at the edge of the woods.

"I never should have done that, left her there. I should have listened to that voice trying to warn me.

"Didi knelt down again, put her hand back on the headstone. I could see her body hunched over. Stayed there another minute or two, not long, then she got up and that was the first thing that made me think — made me *know* — something was wrong. She didn't *stand* up exactly. Looked more like something pulled her up from behind by her shoulders until she was all the way standing. It was — unnatural. Reminded me of a puppet being pulled up from the ground by its strings. Then she sort of pivoted and stepped through the gap and came toward me. Her face was just blank, and her eyes were empty, but there was something else, too. The whole time she was walking over I kept staring at her cheeks — they were dry. *Bone* dry. Not like the tears had been wiped away, but like they had never been there at all.

"'Take me away from here,' she said, real calm. Scared me, because it sounded like Didi's voice, but it *didn't* sound like her, too. Like she was imitating Didi and almost got it right, but not quite. Again, I told myself she's just shaken up by seeing the grave, what with Darla and her mother just buried and us not long back from the funeral. Of course, we didn't want to have a picnic near an abandoned grave. So I packed up and we left.

"She didn't say a word the whole way home. Just watched me drive, studying everything I did — not watching the road, but watching *me*. We got back and she wandered through the house like she'd never been before. Didn't know where anything was. Poured over everything like she was in a museum or something. Just strange.

"'You okay, Didi?' I asked. She didn't even look at me. Like she didn't know her own name anymore, either.

"Our dog Otto runs over to her — big ol' German Shepherd Lab mix Didi got before we met — and she jumps back like he was an alligator about to take a bite. She didn't want anything to do with him, and that was *not* like Didi at all. She loved that dog. *Loved* him.

"The rest of the day she's the same kind of strange. Can't find a thing without me showing her where it is. She had a bunch of old birthday cards and letters from her mom and Darla laid out on the kitchen table, just swept them into a box and tossed them in the closet like they were rubbish. And the whole time she's quiet, not sad-quiet like she'd been since losing her family, but quiet like she was concentrating, focusing. Maybe *planning* something.

"I told myself it's just the heartache Didi was struggling with. She's going through the stages of grief. Must be taking a huge toll on her, making her act strange, feel out of place in her own home, her own life. But that wouldn't explain what happened next.

"The night after we found that old house, Didi heated up leftover spaghetti for dinner. Not in the microwave, but in a pot on the stove. Couldn't figure out the coffee maker, either. I had to show her how to work that, too. Put the water in, press a button, but she couldn't quite get it. Okay, whatever. She gave me my noodles, then sat down and started eating hers. Didn't say the meal blessing like always, just dug in. I picked up my fork, looked up to say, 'smells delicious,' and she's staring at me. Eyes wide, this strange grin on her face. Freaked me out, *bad.*

"I stared down at my spaghetti, gave it a good close look. There was broken glass mixed in. And not a *piece* of broken glass, but shards of it mixed all through the noodles and sauce. I picked out a big chunk and held it up, couldn't believe what I was seeing. Looked over at Didi. Her grin was gone. She looked mad, you know? Disappointed.

"'How'd that get there?' she says, not sounding surprised. She got up in a hurry, took my plate, dumped it in the trash. I see she's eaten half her plate, no glass in her food. Not one single piece.

"That was just the beginning. I go to wash my hands and there's sewing needles pressed in the bottom of the soap. Poured some coffee and it smells like bleach. Didi always hovering nearby, watching. Hardly ever says a word to me, pulls away when I touch her. Doesn't use her laptop or cellphone anymore, like she's forgotten they exist. Doesn't answer to her name most of the time. She'd taken a leave from her job — she did accounting for a real estate firm downtown — when her mom and sister died, now says she doesn't want to go back to the office, ever. After a couple days of this, I was convinced it wasn't just grief over Darla and her mother. Something was really, *really* wrong. But I had no idea what.

"So I call Didi's best friend Jill and ask her to come by, help me figure out what's going on. Jill comes that afternoon and Didi acts like she's never seen Jill before in her life. Finally after some awkward conversation, Didi tells us go sit on the back deck and she'll be right out.

"'She's just upset, losing them both so suddenly must be incredibly traumatic,' Jill says to me while we're alone, trying to explain Didi's behavior. 'She needs grief counseling, maybe anti-depressants.' While she's talking, Didi comes outside, smiling, with a big mug of coffee for Jill. Now, even *I* knew Jill never drank the stuff — got her caffeine from sweet tea — but here's Didi bringing her coffee. I'm thinking about the glass in my spaghetti, thinking I should say something to stop her from drinking it. Before I can get a word out, Didi spills the whole steaming-hot cup onto Jill's arm. She jumps up screaming and Didi just stands there, watching her friend's arm turn beet red. I rushed Jill inside to get ice, wrapped it in a towel around the arm, which is scalded pretty bad.

"Jill says she best go home and soak it in cold water, and I agree, then here comes Didi holding Jill's purse out to her.

"'Sorry you have to leave so soon,' she says, smiling her weird little smile.

"She follows Jill out to her car, but before getting in, Jill stops to tell Didi she's sure the arm will be fine, she'll come back soon to visit, catch up. Didi seems to be rushing her along, 'just get going already,' you know? Then Jill tries to open up her purse to get her keys, but she's having trouble what with her arm all scalded and wrapped in a towel. Drops her bag on the ground — and a copperhead crawls out.

"Jill screamed. I jumped too, and got out of the way as the thing crawled off. Didi didn't move a muscle, didn't say a word, didn't seem surprised. All I can think of is what would've happened to Jill if the snake hadn't gotten out until she was in her car, driving herself home.

"Finally Didi goes, 'gee, I guess Mr. Copperhead slid in there when we were out in the backyard.' Talks like it was a bunny rabbit, no big deal. Doesn't even ask Jill if she's all right.

"Something about the look on Didi's face made me remember what'd been nagging at me when she was crying over that grave. It was a story I'd heard years back, when I was a boy. I couldn't quite remember it before, but it was coming back to me now.

"After Jill left, I told Didi I had to go into the office, wouldn't be back for some time, don't wait dinner on me. I drove to Beaufort to see a friend from grade school, boy named Malikai. Well, to see his gramma, really, who lived in the Gullah community near there. She's a root worker — that's a healer who can do white magic, lift curses, things like that. Kind of like a shaman. Everybody calls her Sungila, which means 'helper.' I needed help.

"When I was little, I'd sleep over at Malikai's, and she'd tell us stories about spirits and spells and omens. One time she warned us never to cry in the graveyard, because if you did, restless spirits would come after you. They'd steal your body, wear your skin. Haints, she called them. Sungila said she knew a boy who was taken over by a haint, did all kinds of awful things before he was 'returned to the other side.'

"So I went to Sungila's place and told her what had happened, how I found Didi crying over that grave, how she was different after that, just like you say your girl is different now. Told her about the glass and the coffee and the snake, told her everything I could remember about how Didi wasn't herself anymore. When I'd finished, she put her arms around me and said, 'I'm so sorry, your wife's spirit has crossed the river Jordan and the haint has taken her skin.'

"'How do I get Didi back?' I asked, but she just kept shaking her head.

"'Didi has crossed the Jordan,' Sungila says. 'She's with the ancestors now.'

"After I pulled myself together, I said, 'then how do I get

rid of the haint?' and Sungila told me about Bandun Gate.

"She said that the strip of land had been cursed going back hundreds of years, before slave times, even. People were living there before the white men came, natives called the Kiawah, but they didn't last long after. A bunch of white colonists calling themselves Goose Creek Men would kidnap Kiawah and ship them to Barbados as slaves. Used those marshlands as part of their hunting grounds. It was illegal, what they did, but they didn't care. There was money to be made. Same natives who'd helped the newcomers survive in the Carolinas. Now they're being enslaved or dying of white men's diseases. Special place in Hell for them. Has to be, you know?

"After the Kiawah came the Africans. Forced to work in the marshes, full of snakes, gators, bugs carrying all sorts of ills. That area was all rice plantations and indigo, anybody doing that labor died young. Even the children were forced to work. Kids — babies, really — made to keep drinking from the swamp so they could taste when the tide was bringing in salt water, give the signal to close the irrigation gates so the rice paddies didn't' get contaminated. Who knows what else was in that water they had to keep taking in, day after day after day? Making indigo was no better — harvesting the plants, working the vats. Just miserable, brutal work.

"The war put an end to slavery, but the abominations along that stretch of swampland carried on. People drowning or disappearing. Accidents. When the tide comes in the water rises fast, and it's easy to get caught up. Others maybe not so accidental, you know? Nobody knows how many bodies are buried back in there, or stuck in the black mud under those marshes.

"The whole tract is surrounded by creeks and marshes, still full of snakes, 'gators, what have you. Place wasn't much use to white folk, so Gullah from Stono River, Wadmalaw, Edisto, all put their money together, bought it cheap. They built the fence and gate along the section that wasn't on the water, one where the road runs. Families decorated it with objects that had special meaning to them. They held a blessing ceremony to keep any evil spirits inside, stop them from escaping to *our* side of the gate. Over the years, folks painted it Haint Blue, added more decorations, kept it up.

"Sungila said I should take the haint to Bandun Gate, force her through it however I could. Once she was out of Didi's body, the haint would be trapped there. Wicked spirits can't cross water, can't get passed the blessed objects. We talked about some possible ways to do what had to be done, then she gave me some Life Everlasting tea. I thanked her, told her how good it was to see her again after all these years, said goodbye.

"The whole drive home, I kept telling myself, 'this is crazy! My wife isn't possessed by some evil spirit, she's just mourning her mother and her sister. She'll be herself again soon.' I'm feeling more than a little foolish, truth be told. By the time I got back to my house I'm laughing at myself for letting my imagination get the best of me. Haints? Magical gates that hold back evil spirits? Please! I'm an educated man, earned two Masters degrees. What was I thinking?!? I'd decided to tell Didi about my foolishness, about the haint stories, Sungila, Bandun Gate. We'd laugh about it together.

"Then I walked in the door, and I wasn't laughing anymore.

"The first thing that hit me was the smell. It was godawful. I looked down at the floor, and there was a line of puke and shit all the way from the living room through the dining room around the corner into the kitchen. Next to it were a couple footprints. *Didi's* footprints. Then I heard the sound, worse than the smell, even. I followed the puke-shit trail, and I came into the kitchen, and there was Otto, laying on the floor and making this heart-breaking whimper, his whole body shaking. Didi was standing over to him, watching Otto suffer, that grin on her face. And she was holding a bottle of cleaning spray.

"I could tell from the marks on the floor, she'd started making him sick in the front room, and he was trying to get to his bed in the kitchen. Place he felt safe. Dragged himself through his sick, Didi walking along beside him, tracking through the muck. He almost got there, but collapsed just short of the bed. She would have let him die there, *watched* him die in horrible pain, if I hadn't come home just then.

91

"I grabbed up Otto and rushed him to the vet. He was in bad shape, but she was able to save him. I gave her a story about how Otto'd gotten under the sink and into some chemicals, asked could he stay there overnight so I could make sure everything was put away safe before bringing him home. She said, 'sure.'

"I drove back home, angry, sad, lost, not sure what. Didi hadn't cleaned up the mess, when I came up to her, she didn't even ask if her dog was still alive.

"'Otto's going to be fine,' I announced, but she just looked at me like she had no idea what I was talking about.

"'Your DOG!' I shouted.

"She started giggling. Swear to God, *giggling* like a schoolgirl! Points at the bottle on the counter and tells me, 'I sprayed my hand with that stuff, told the beast 'be nice and play along,' and it kept lickin' and lickin'. Then it shat itself, and I sprayed its face, and it licked *that* off, too!' She can't stop laughing.

"That was it. I knew this sick witch wasn't Didi. *Knew* it. No way in Hell. All doubt gone. Didi loved that dog. It would've *killed* her to see Otto suffering like that. No way would she have hurt him on purpose, ever.

"Then, my phone rings. It's Jill.

"'Sorry to bother you at work,' she says. She'd come back by the house while I was gone to show Didi her arm wasn't so bad; reassure her she didn't blame Didi for the snake — just one of those weird occurrences Jill says. Didi told her I'd gone into the office, and I wasn't in any shape to correct Jill and tell her what'd been happening at our place.

"'I wanted to give you some good news about Didi,' she tells me. 'I know she's been so distressed the last couple days, but she's definitely coming out of it.'

"'Why do you say that?' I ask her.

"'Well, I convinced her to sign up for volunteer work at the church. Didi says she's not ready to go back to the office just yet, but she wants to get out of the house and do some good.'

"'What kind of volunteer work?' I say.

"'Pastor Thompson is starting a program to help parents of

children with autism or developmental delays or other health issues that make it hard for them to find childcare,' Jill tells me, all excited. 'Didi's going to be babysitting kids with special needs, isn't that wonderful?!?'

"I say, 'yeah, that's wonderful,' thanked her for calling, hung up. I knew what I had to do.

"This next part, it's not easy to talk about, even though I know I did the right thing. *Know* it. We're strangers, you and me, but if there's something I can do to help your daughter, I owe it to Didi to try. That's what she'd want, no doubt in my mind. That's who Didi was.

"You know your girl. You see how different she is from the thing that's in your house now, so you can understand where I was then. The place I was in. What *had* to be done.

"I was dealing with *evil*. Absolute evil. The kind most people never face in their life. And this haint, this Rylah, was a very particular kind of evil. Not like a serial killer — someone who'd murder you outright then move on to the next victim. In some ways, what she was, was worse. *Way* worse. She's the kind of monster that likes to drag out the suffering. Cause pain, then watch it play out, keep it going long as she could. Twist the knife and listen to the screams, you know?

"A snakebite will kill you outright. But a hornet stings you, hurts like hell, but it's not fatal. You get past the pain, then it comes back, stings you again, and again, and again. Same hornet can sting dozens of times, maybe hundreds. Just keep dishing out the pain.

"Pretty soon you're afraid to go outside, no matter how much you love tending your rose bushes or your tomato plants. You don't toss a football in the park with your buds anymore, don't go for walks in the woods with your wife. A friend asks you over for a barbecue and you say, 'no, no thanks. Can't make it. Sorry.'

"Now all you do is find excuses to stay inside, hiding from any more pain. There's times you can't think about anything else. You might as well be dead. Who you used to be is gone. You're scared all the time, angry, worried about getting stung again. It's always on your mind. Pretty soon it taints everything in your life. *Sours* everything. Sucks away the color and the sweetness and the joy.

"*Lingering* evil, that's what she was. Parasitic evil eating others alive.

"And now she was going to be alone with kids who can't talk. Can't tell anyone what's happened to them. How they broke their leg or cut their hands or swallowed something that burned their insides up. Can't tell how they've been hurt in places where it doesn't show. Hated to think how many kids she could hurt before someone finally figured out these weren't accidents. Might take a child dying to put an end to her reign of terror. Might take several dying. That's something I knew I couldn't live with, especially not while she was pretending to be Didi. Couldn't stand the idea of people thinking my Didi was a monster.

"So there's a mini-mart by the house where they sell this pastry. It's like pound cake with icing and crunchy stuff drizzled all over the top. They got slices of it in plastic by the register. Not sure its real name. My gramma always called that sort of thing 'honey cake.' I *love* the stuff. Eat it all the time.

"When Didi and I'd just started dating, I got her a slice. I brought it over all smiles thinking she's going love it as much as I do, love me for getting it for her. Instead she takes one look and says, 'are you trying to kill me???' Turns out she's got a bad allergy to nuts. *Real* bad. The honey cake, she tells me, has got almonds, peanut oil, pecan chunks — all sorts of stuff that'll close up her throat, stop her breathing. She didn't even wanna *touch* it, her allergy's so bad.

"So now it's the afternoon everything happened with Otto and finding out about her babysitting plans. I tell her we should go for a drive, celebrate her new adventure, maybe do another explore. She didn't want to at first, but I said it would be good to get out of the house, away from the stench of the dog mess she's let sit there all afternoon. We'd get a treat while we're out. Finally she says 'okay,' so we stop at the mini-mart with the honey cakes.

"'What about these? Looks tasty, let's say we get a couple' I say to her when she sees 'em. She grins and picks up two slices, we pay for them and get back in the car.

"I didn't go to Bandun Gate right away, didn't want her to get suspicious. We drove around a while, went by Angel Oak, weaved through the area. Then we ended up there around 7 o'clock.

"'Here's a good place for our little picnic,' I tell her. Got out the blanket, spread it out right in front of the archway. Set the bag with the honey cakes in the middle. She comes over, sits down. I could tell she didn't like being so close to the fence, it made her uneasy, but she sits with her back to it and that seems to work for her.

"'How about digging into those sweets?' I say. She takes one out of the bag, unwraps it, takes a bite.

"I can tell she loves it; ate it up, no hesitation.

"As she's eating, I slowly empty my pockets out onto the blanket. Car keys, wallet, gum, handful of change, and her epi-pen. It was a test, you know? I had to be *sure*.

"'You can have my honey cake if you want,' I tell her, seeing hers is gone. She grabs it outta the bag without a word, tears off the plastic, starts wolfing it down. That was part of the test, too. But it was also so *she* was the one who'd done it. I had nothing to do with her getting into the honey cakes. I'd never touched either one.

"She gets about half that second one down before she starts choking, gasping for breath.

"'What's wrong?' I ask, but she just keeps clutching at her throat, trying to breathe.

"Ripped my heart out seeing my Didi's face contorted like that, eyes bulging, terrified. I start having doubts, scared what I'm letting happen to her. I had to be one hundred percent convinced it wasn't really my girl, so I pick up the epi-pen, offer it to her.

"'Do you want this?' I ask, but she wasn't even looking at me. She'd stood up and was waving her arms around, stumbling.

"'Didi, DO YOU WANT THIS?' I scream, loud, holding the pen right in her face. 'IT'S FOR YOUR ALLERGY! THIS

WILL STOP THE REACTION!'

"But I just got that lost, blank look and that's all. She had no idea what I was talking about.

"I knew then, *really* knew. Guess in a way I'd known since that first day. She wasn't my Didi. She didn't know the honey cake would hurt her, didn't know what the epi-pen even was. Didi was always so careful about everything she ate, but this thing was clueless.

"I put my hands on her shoulders and backed her towards the opening under the archway. "'Calm down and walk around a bit,' I tell her. 'You just need some air.'

"When we were right under the arch, I shoved her as hard as I could backwards through the gate, making sure I stayed on the outside. She fell and rolled further in, scowling at me. Lord, the hate in her eyes! She wanted to hurt me, *bad*.

"She starts wheezing even harder, trying to get up but can't. Falls flat on her back, sputtering, losing steam. I see her left leg is sticking straight out with her toes just under the arch, so I grab my umbrella from the car and jab at her ankle until she pulls away from me. Now all of her is on the other side. I couldn't take any chances.

"At the very last second, she pushes herself up on her elbows, glares at me with fury like I've never seen. Can't even describe it. Made me feel better — she didn't look *anything* like Didi anymore. Not one bit. Still, it was terrifying. I thought she was going to get up and come over and do Lord knows what to me. Maybe drag me under Bandun Gate so I'd be trapped there with her. Her and whatever else was on that godforsaken side. She'd figured out what I'd done, but it was too late. She didn't get up. The body convulsed one last time then flopped back down. Whatever hateful spirit was in her had departed.

"I waited a while more just to be sure. It was nearly sunset when we'd gotten to Bandun Gate. I sat there until it was almost full dark. By then I figured she was definitely gone.

"Picked up the umbrella, hooked the handle into Didi's shoe, and pulled until her foot was on my side of the arch. I was *not* going inside Bandun Gate. Not a chance. Didn't want

96

the police or paramedics to, either. I grabbed the foot and slowly dragged her body out, then picked her up, wrapped her in the picnic blanket, carried her over to the side of the road.

"I jabbed the epi-pen into her thigh, pushed the plunger. I knew it was too late, but wanted everything to look right when the ambulance came. Sat there another couple minutes, not touching the body or even looking at it. Just spent the time thinking about Didi, *my* Didi, who I had already been missing since that day at the old house.

"My phone didn't work out there, so I walked back to the main road, headed towards Johns Island. Not too long before a car came by, I waved him over. Told him 'my wife needs help' and where she was. He said go back and stay with her, he'd drive until he got cell service or came to someplace with a phone, get us some help.

"I walked back to Bandun Gate, scared, thinking maybe the body wouldn't be there. What would I do then? But it was there. The ambulance came, and the police. The paramedics took the body away, police bagged up everything else. They questioned me, what exactly happened, how did she die, what was my part in the whole thing.

"I told them about Didi's allergy, how she must not've known there were nuts in the honey cake. Said the epi-pen was in the glove box, but by the time I realized she was having a reaction, unlocked the car, found the pen, got back and injected her, it was too late.

"I was a wreck the whole time they were talking to me. That part I didn't have to fake. I could tell they still weren't convinced I was telling the truth. But a few days later the lab tests came back; it was only Didi's fingerprints on the honey cake wrappers, her bite marks and saliva on what was left of the half-eaten one. Their expert said if anybody had tried to force it in her mouth, the cake would have crumbled, and whatever was left would have traces of that person's DNA on it. There wasn't anyone's but hers.

"She had marks on her shoulders from when I shoved her under the arch. I told the police I was trying to get her to cough up whatever was causing her reaction, shook her pretty hard. Not sure if they pulled the security video from the mini-mart where we bought the honey cakes, but if they did it would show *she* was the one who picked up two slices and took them to the register, not me.

"And of course, everyone knew about Didi's mom and Darla dying in that accident not even a month before this happened. People figured she could've been distracted from the grief, maybe was taking some medication that made her foggy, got careless and ate the wrong thing by mistake. I'm sure some of her friends thought maybe she did it on purpose, she was grieving so bad for her family.

"So that was the end of it. Police declared it an accidental death, case closed. I took Didi's body back to Pennsylvania, had it buried with her parents and Darla.

"But her spirit's still here, still close by.

"After I got back from Philly, I started second-guessing myself, thinking maybe I had been crazy to believe all the haint talk after all. Maybe I'd convinced myself some ridiculous ghost story was true, lost my Didi as a result. So I started looking into the history of that old house and the grave behind it. Learned about Rylah, the stuff she'd done. The more I found out, the more I knew I did the right thing.

"I lost Didi that day when she was crying over that grave. That's when her spirit passed on. And I know she's happy. Wherever she is, it's a good place.

"When she was alive, we loved spotting birds on our 'explores.' Our favorite was seeing a painted bunting. Ever seen one? It's a gorgeous bird, cousin to the cardinal only lots more colorful. The male has that red breast but a bright blue head, yellow and green down its back. So pretty it doesn't look real. Females are this tropical-island green, sort of lemony-lime all over. Whenever we'd spot one, I'd tell Didi I wished they'd come to the birdfeeder in our backyard, but we never saw one there. Not once.

"Three months after she died, the day that would've been our third anniversary, I look outside and there's so many on our lawn I can't count them. All mated pairs. They stayed even when I went out the backdoor and walked right up to them.

Thought maybe I was imagining it, you know? I'd been dreading that day, spending it without Didi. But Arthur next door looks over, says, 'hey Mike, what birdseed you using?!? I've never seen so many buntings together like that!'

"'Didi sent them,' I told him. And I just stood there, watching them flying to the birdfeeder and back, playing on the lawn, until they finally flew away.

"She was telling me she was okay, but not just that. Didi was letting me know I did right by her. She didn't blame me for what happened, any of it. The buntings were her way of saying, 'I still love you, Mike. I always will. See you on the other side.'

"I owed it to Didi to get rid of that witch who stole her away from me, that ghost, to take her to Bandun Gate. I put her there to *keep* her there, thinking she wouldn't get out again. Not ever.

"I'm truly sorry about what's happening to your daughter, to Abby, but like I told you on the phone, it isn't Didi that has her now, it's Rylah."

Chapter Eight
An Eye for an I

Mike finished speaking, exhausted. I was so mesmerized by his story I hadn't taken a single sip of my chocolate shake; its maraschino cherry stared up from the clotted whipped cream like an angry red eye.

"That's Otto buried there, isn't it?" I asked. "In the woods by the grave. You put the angel statue there for him."

He looked up at me, surprised, then nodded.

"Lost the old boy this past spring," Mike said, clearing his throat. "We helped each other get through losing Didi, some pretty miserable days. Otto always loved being with her. And Lord, she loved that dog. I thought their spirits should be together. She'd have wanted that."

We sat quietly for a while, lost in our individual thoughts. I was picking through the bones of what he'd told me, trying to make sense of it, searching for something I could use to help Abby. I'm sure Mike was thinking about the wife he'd known before their disastrous trip to Rylah's gravesite.

I broke the silence. There were some big discrepancies between his situation and mine, and I was hoping he might be able to clear them up.

"Okay, so if this *is* the same spirit who's attached herself to Abby, *how* was she able to do it? Abby wasn't crying when we were at Bandun Gate; she was having fun. And *when* did Rylah take over? Abby was herself when we got home, we ate dinner together, talked about our plans — she was fine. Or how come Rylah can't harm me, or *won't*, but she was trying to hurt you from the very first day? And what about the body — Rylah *looks* like Abby, but that body isn't real — she can do impossible, *unnatural* things. When she took Didi, her body *had* to have been real or the nut allergy wouldn't have affected her."

I hesitated for a moment, reluctant to rub salt into Mike's freshly-reopened wound, then added, "And Abby isn't *gone*. I mean, something bad is definitely happening with her, but she's still here. Still alive."

"No idea," he said, shaking his head. "Wish I had some answers for you Miriam, for getting your daughter back. Wish I knew how to cage that devil for good."

"Oh trust me, you've done more than enough," I said, sincerely thankful for Mike's help. "I'd still be sitting at home thinking I was going crazy, that it was hopeless, if you hadn't agreed to tell me all this."

"What are you going to do now?"

"I don't know. I honestly don't know. If I get rid of Rylah, if that's even possible, what would that mean for Abby? She's got these terrible headaches now, and I'm sure Rylah's causing them somehow. Maybe I need Rylah to undo them, make Abby well again."

We talked a bit more, discussing possible scenarios and solutions. I asked if Sungila might be able to help me. He said she'd suffered a stroke that left her in pretty bad shape. Then I remembered Bernadette Aubelle, and Mike agreed it was worth approaching her for a conversation. By the time we'd finished talking, Jack's was closed. The only cars left in the customer lot were ours.

Mike walked me to my van. "One last piece of advice, if I may."

"Of course."

"Whatever you decide to do, you commit a hundred percent and *do* it. No hesitation." Mike scanned the lot, making sure no one else was around. "No matter how awful it feels, how you never thought you'd do something so terrible. Don't start doubting yourself or getting emotional or second guessing. She'll use that reluctance, that guilt, against you. Don't be afraid of her. Fear is weakness, especially against evil like hers."

I nodded, knowing he was right but not sure I'd be able to live up to that standard when the time came.

"Thank you, Mike. I mean it. *Thank you*."

"I'll be praying for you. Hope things work out, I truly do. But I hope you'll understand if, well..."

"Us getting together, talking about this, is a 'one and done?'"

"Sorry, I can't — I can't keep getting back into it, you know? The whole mess. Want to let the past be. I need to remember Didi the way she was."

"I get it. This meeting never happened. You'll never hear from me again, I promise."

I replayed the highlights of Mike's story on the way back to the house. Malevolent spirits. Cursed wetlands. A sacred barrier penning in the damned. Not as 'out there,' really, as it sounded. All over the world are places considered inherently evil or teeming with destructive preternatural energy: Japan's Suicide Forest, Xunantunich in Belize, Afghanistan's Shar-e-Golgola, the 'City of Screams.' During my years as a research writer, I'd learned about mountains that echoed with violent shrieking, placid lakes in which children inexplicably drowned, houses where horrible deaths occurred repeatedly over decades or even centuries. It wasn't such a stretch to think that the verdant marshes beyond Bandun Gate might be harboring similar dark and uncanny forces.

The lights were all out when I arrived home, but that didn't mean anything. A creature who can detach her own arm then force it down her throat and back through its socket could surely read in the dark. I sat in the garage considering my next move. Bernadette would've gone home hours ago and the only number I had for her was her work phone, so I'd have to wait until morning to reach out to her. The urge to go to Myrtle Beach and get Abby flit through my mind once again, but then what? Where would we go, how would Abby's affliction be lifted, what would happen to Dan and the boys when they got to the house? None of us would be safe until Rylah was out of our lives for good.

I'm not sure how long I'd been sitting there mulling over the grim dilemma when Roman's text popped up.

What's going on with Abby?

My heart stopped. I dialed Roman's number frantically, fearing Abigail's health had taken a turn for the worse and she'd contacted him about it. But he sounded calm, even chipper, when he answered the phone.

"Hi, Mom. What's up?"

"You texted about Abby," I said, trying to sound upbeat. "She's at Ruthie's. Did you know that? Went up last night. Today I guess she's not feeling so good."

"Yeah, I know. Ruthie called me, said Abby has a bad headache or something. I got tomorrow off. You want me to come down early, go by there on the way to Charleston, and check on her?"

"That would be great! What's tomorrow, Friday?"

"Yup. All day."

The wheels were spinning, churning out a plan. "How about you and Charles go to Myrtle Beach? Ruthie wanted you to come by anyway so that works out. See how Abby's doing and give me a report."

"Sounds good. We'll head out tomorrow morning. Should be at Ruthie's around three or four. I'll call you when we get there."

"Perfect. Just promise me one thing, Roman." I paused again, struggling to strike the right tone. "You kids, all three of you, *stay* at Aunt Ruthie's until you talk to me, okay? Don't come down to our place unless you call me first."

"Why? What's wrong?"

I could picture Roman raising an inquisitive eyebrow and stroking his thick brown beard as he evaluated my request. He'd been intensely analytical since his toddler days, always eager to solve puzzles and investigate phenomenon. A born engineer, the counterpart to my philosopher-son Charles who dealt in emotions, inclinations. If I were to inform both boys their sister had been imperiled by a ghost, Charles would pepper me with frantic questions: 'how did it happen, is Abby in pain, what does she know about her situation, how is she taking it,' and want to hear every last detail. Roman, on the other hand, would simply say, 'how do we fix it?' During this

103

pause in our conversation, it dawned on me that if I *were* to share the current predicament with anyone, it would be Roman. I would tell him before I'd tell Dan, even. Our eldest was definitely the pragmatist of the family.

"I didn't say anything was wrong," I replied, skirting the truth. "I just want to make sure everything's ready when you three get here — house clean, pantry stocked, fresh sheets on the beds, clean towels, you know."

"Yeah, makes sense. I'll call you tomorrow from Ruthie's. Give you an update."

"Thanks, Roman. Love you. Tell Charles and Abby I love them, too."

Another pause. Maybe I'd pushed too far with that last comment.

"Are you sure you're okay, Mom?"

I could hear the suspicion in Roman's voice, but there was no way I was going to even attempt an explanation of what was going on with Rylah. My son would think I'd lost it, or maybe was playing some elaborate not-funny practical joke. Either way, it would upset him. And if I could somehow convince him a malevolent force was threatening his sister (and that was a *big* 'if') what could he possibly do?

"Just missing you kids and your dad," I said. "I can't wait until all of us are together again, everybody happy and healthy."

That was the most honest statement I'd ever made in my life.

No more putting it off. It was time to face the fiend occupying my home. *Stay resolute, show no fear.* I went in, fumbling for the hall light switch. Rylah was skulking in the darkness just inside the door and we almost collided.

"You been to church," she snapped.

"How do you know that?" I asked, maneuvering around her, careful not to make contact.

"You stink of cat piss."

"Not a churchgoer, Rylah? That's a big surprise." *Focus on my anger, let it fuel my fight.*

104

I flicked on the lights. The place was a mess. Papers were scattered throughout the hallway and into the family room. It resembled a larger-scale version of the trash spilled in Abby's room the previous night. Rylah had apparently finished off the *Encyclopedia of Hell* pages and was still craving diversion, so she'd ransacked the kids' yearbooks and family photo albums on the bookshelf. Captured images of loved ones smiled up at me from the carpet. Rylah held several crumpled photographs in each hand.

"What *is* this?!?" I shouted, snatching them away from her.

"You were snoopin' 'round, tryin' to learn more 'bout me. Figured I'd do the same regardin' *you*."

"Did you find out anything interesting? Because I sure did!"

I wanted Rylah to be worried — *frantic* — wondering if I'd discovered some fatal flaw. She was much easier to manipulate when she was rattled, much more likely to unwittingly betray herself. And Mike was right about fear leading to weakness. I was ready for *her* to feel panicked for a change.

Instead of taking the bait, Rylah plucked the torn shell of *Encyclopedia of Hell* from the memorabilia pile on the floor and held it up, smirking.

"It's no wonder they hate you."

"My family doesn't hate me, Rylah. You're projecting."

"You revealed their secrets," she scolded, caressing the book cover. "Invoked their names without shred a'reverence. Made light of their powers, their *majesty*. And the ones you didn't bother mentionin' at all — why, they are simply *furious*!"

"I have no idea what you're talking about, and I honestly don't care."

I had almost made it to the bedroom when Rylah slid in front of me, blocking the door.

"You think you got the upper hand, knowin' I can't hurt you. Haughty fool! It's not *me* you should be fearin'. It's the others."

I still didn't understand Rylah's meaning, but a dreadful possibility was beginning to dawn in the back of my mind.

"The 'others'?" What others? Other *what*?"

"The *others*!" Rylah scoffed. "Surely you don't think I was there all by my lonesome!"

"You mean other ghosts? At Bandun Gate?"

It hadn't occurred to me that Rylah might not have been the only spirit prowling those cursed marshlands, taking notice of my daughter and me.

"Oh, there are many of my kind stranded in that wretched place. But most are from before."

Alarm bells started going off in my head, warning me not to continue this line of questioning. *Just ignore her and walk away. I can't handle anything else tonight.*

"Before what? Before you were put there?" I asked, in spite of myself.

Rylah pranced a circle around the family room, kicking up my treasured photos like a child splashing through a mud puddle, then repeated the little 'model twirl' she had performed when she'd first revealed herself.

"Before the *world,* Mama! From the world before the world!"

She bounced the ravaged *Encyclopedia of Hell* cover in front of my face, making the flames on its dust jacket dance.

"You got all sorts of words for 'em in your book, don't you remember?" Rylah taunted. "Demons! Devils! Asuras! Ghouls! Fallen angels! Incubi! Djinns! Why, some you called out by *name*!"

Rylah stopped frolicking, ran to the back of the family room and began reciting the litany of the damned.

"Apollyon! Bile! Belial! Iblis! Gwynn! Lucifer! Mephistopheles! Mot!" She darted along the back wall as she rattled them off, pointing to each in turn. Whenever Rylah spoke a name, the ink would spark and sizzle on its page, spitting puffs of black smoke into the air.

"Rati-Mbati-Ndua! Satan! Vizarsh! Yama! Why, didn't you think they'd hear you — *answer* you — when you called them? Maybe have somethin' of their own to say?"

I was baffled by Rylah's insinuation. What was she talking about? Cataloging malignant spirits was part of my research,

106

yes, but I had never *summoned* demons.

Then the bitter truth hit me. Of course I had. Twenty years ago, writing about Hell, I had indeed called those wretched beasts forth from their dark corners so I could take a closer look. How else could I have studied them, learned their intricacies, become familiar enough to describe them in detail? I'd spent countless hours with these foul creatures, scratching and tickling and enticing them to show their faces, bare their claws, spill their secrets. I wouldn't have been able to research them if they had stayed hidden in the shadows, so I drew them out. *Deliberately.* I had made myself their biographer, given them what every infernal creature desires most: attention.

Sure, that had been two decades ago, but what's a few thousand days in the scope of eternity? In relative terms, I'd spent more time choosing the color of my last toothbrush. The netherworld isn't bound by any schedule. For the damned, twenty years had passed in the blink of an eye, and now here we all were — Rylah in my house, Abby in limbo, me back in Hell.

"Is that why you came after Abby, because of my book?" I murmured, still reeling from this revelation.

"Why, yes, I s'pose it is," Rylah said, mockingly. "I might've missed you even bein' there if *they* hadn't seen you and started up the most ungodly wailin' and hollerin'. Never heard anythin' like it in all my days! I wanted to see what all the fuss was about, and that's when I saw your girl amblin' toward the boundary. Got a little nudge in your direction from an old acquaintance hopin' to settle a score."

The notion that Abigail was targeted because of something I'd done, however unintentional, was a knife in my heart.

"That's not fair," I muttered, trying to process Rylah's allegation. "How could my writing a book, when Abby was still a *baby,* make her weak, vulnerable to you?" I became angry as I pieced it together, my voice climbing. "She didn't do *anything* to deserve this! Why not just go after me since I'm the guilty one? *THIS ISN'T FAIR*!!!"

Rylah grinned through Abby's face, compounding my rage. "Oh, no, *Mama*, my mirrorin' her has nothin' to do with any weakness in your girl." The haint tried to put her hand on my shoulder but I pulled away. Amused, Rylah dropped her voice to a whisper and leaned forward before continuing.

"I'm mirrorin' her because she *invited* me to this side. Your girl gave me her hand. She looked right at me, then she summoned me away from that horrible place."

"Like Hell she did! Abby did nothing of the kind! I was *there*! I would know if she'd done anything remotely like that!"

I pictured the scene in my mind: the two of us walking the fence line, pausing here and there to admire a particular object, enjoying the adventure despite the afternoon heat. I could visualize Abby's hair peppered with orange highlights where sun had filtered through the leafy canopy, could smell the salty air tinged with earthen decay, could hear the solitary osprey screeching above. We had a competition of 'name that horror movie from its tagline' going. Just as we reached the van Abby *almost* went through Bandun Gate, but I had stopped her. She'd grabbed a post to steady herself, so yes, her hand — part of it, at least — *had* passed to the other side. But only for a second. It happened while she was taking her turn at our game with a line from *Cape Fear*, gazing into the marshes, at the very moment she said, she said…

"'Come out, come out, wherever you are,'" I echoed, horrorstruck.

Oh God, it was true. Abigail *had* made contact and invited Rylah to come forth, albeit inadvertently, while breaching the barrier of the ghost's lair.

Guilt swallowed me whole. *I* was the one who had taken Abby to Bandun Gate, who ignored Bernadette's warning, who suggested the game, who failed to act quickly enough to prevent her from breaking the unseen infernal seal. I was the one who laid the groundwork for this entire ordeal by choosing to write that damn Hell book before Abby was even born.

Rylah winked and blew me a kiss. I wanted to dig my fingernails into her face and claw it into mush, anything to stop her from defiling my daughter's image with that putrid smirk. Before I could make a move, she dashed to the scattered mementos on the floor and snatched up a photograph and one of the school yearbooks. She brought both over to me, beaming.

Rylah held up the picture first. It was a shot of twelve-year-old Roman in his hospital gown, taken at Children's National the day before he was discharged following his brush with death. Roman's face was ghostly pale, a grim contrast against his chocolate-brown eyes and crimson cheeks. In the background, the white marble dome of the U.S. Capitol towered over the surrounding rooftops. I had forgotten how frail Roman looked during that terrible time. Hard to believe that same little boy was now a burly college graduate who stood taller than his father.

As I reminisced, Rylah abruptly flung the picture aside; it fluttered to the floor like an autumn leaf. She snapped the yearbook open to the page featuring Charles' seventh grade class photo. In the margin, his friend Brandon had drawn a cartoon of Charles with big red droplets falling from his nose. Underneath the sketch he'd written, '*glad you didn't die in the bathroom — have a fun summer.*'

Rylah snickered. "Poor Mama. Seems you've *never* been good at keepin' your children outta harm's way."

Charles had always been prone to nosebleeds, going back to his toddler days. They were especially severe during his middle school years while we were living in Arizona. On several occasions he'd gotten one in the middle of the night, and by morning his pillowcase looked like a murder prop from *CSI*. The incidents appeared far worse than they actually were, and despite the grisly mess, Charles was never at any real health risk. At least, not usually.

The episode Brandon referenced took place right before the end of the school year. One morning during Social Studies, Charles experienced an exceptionally heavy discharge and decided to have a little fun with the situation. That afternoon his teacher sent me a rather irate email.

Dan & Miriam,

I wanted to let you know about Charles' behavior today. He got a bad bloody nose during my class. I asked if he was okay or needed the nurse. He told me no, he just needed to visit the bathroom. He came back, but failed to tell me that he had dripped blood all through the hallway, and left the bathroom a mess, including the sink being full of blood. Students were really sickened seeing the blood! A couple were feeling faint due to being squeamish. It was also a serious biohazard.

During the next class, boys were asking one-by-one to go to the restroom, and when Ms. Nathan asked what was going on, they admitted it was to see the awful mess. Apparently, the custodian hadn't attended to it yet. Charles grinned from ear to ear when I brought up the mess and apparently was very proud of it. I don't know if Charles was telling people to go see the restroom, or if that was done by a student who helped Charles, but this whole thing caused much more disruption than necessary. Charles was certainly relishing all the attention.

Please talk to Charles about making mature and civilized decisions. Thank you for your support at home.

Mrs. Tucker

The message was obviously intended to alarm me, however I found the teacher's communiqué absolutely hilarious. I read it aloud to Dan and the kids, after which the phrase 'make mature and civilized decisions' became a staple of the family lexicon. We joked about it for days.

What I did *not* do was take the opportunity to discuss the seriousness of his condition with Charles, opting instead to focus on the story's humorous aspects.

A month later, he suffered another severe nosebleed. Charles was in his bedroom when it started, and he decided to go downstairs to the laundry for a towel. Just before reaching the third step, he became lightheaded from blood loss, and tumbled the rest of the way down, breaking his right arm in two places. Charles needed surgery to set the bone and spent the rest of summer vacation in a cast.

Ha ha, Madre. Really funny.

Rylah was right; I had failed my children. All of them. It was bad enough with health issues, but now the danger I'd put them in was unfathomable. Abby was already in the clutches of this fiend, and if I didn't figure out something soon, the boys, Dan, my father, virtually anyone who came through our door could be Rylah's next victim. I fell to my knees, unable to hold back scalding tears.

The pictures strewn around me amplified my heartache. What I wouldn't have given to melt into one of these frozen memories! My mom and dad celebrating Christmas with their young grandchildren, Roman and his girlfriend Daniela dressed for Halloween as the Joker and Harley Quinn, Dan handing preschooler-Abby a popsicle, Charles and Ethan and Sophie at the Irish Festival in D.C...

"Oh my God — Sophie!" I gasped, grabbing the picture as I remembered she was due to arrive in less than a day. I didn't have her number, and would have to get ahold of Charles to relay a message not to come. What excuse could I give for canceling her visit? Maybe I could sell him on the idea there was some mystery illness going around and I didn't want Sophie catching it. That seemed plausible. Charles knew Abby was feeling sick...

"Deliver her to me," Rylah whispered as I fumbled through my mental machinations. "The one you were talkin' about the other night — that's her, right? Give this one to me and I'll release your girl."

"W-what?" I said, stunned. "You — you mean, you'd take Sophie in place of Abigail?"

"I need to wear the skin of a nubile female. It's no matter to me whose it is."

Rylah's words hung in the air between us.

I should have flat out refused immediately. *'I can't do that! Won't do it! I'm not the kind of person who trades one life for another! I'm not a monster like you!'* That was the only decent response to such an odious proposition.

What I did instead was to sit silent, staring into the face aping my daughter's, and allow Rylah to continue her repugnant pitch.

"We don't have to be enemies, Mama," she purred. "I can help you. We can help *each other*. You bring me this other girl, and I'll surrender your daughter."

"And Abby will, she'll be okay? She'll be herself again, no permanent damage?"

"Of course not!" Rylah let out a hearty laugh. "She'll be fine, same as before. Why, she won't even remember anythin' was vexin' her."

No, this can't be right. This doesn't add up. Rylah isn't telling me everything.

"Wait, wait. If you can take over another person, another girl, then why are you so intent on getting Abby? Why didn't you just have me drive you into town? You could 'wear' whoever you wanted and let Abby go!"

"It doesn't work like that!" Rylah barked, the syrupy '*we're buddies now!*' tone gone. "I can't journey flesh to flesh with anyone other than your girl."

She gave an exasperated sigh and rolled her eyes before laying the process out for me. "Your girl's the one who summoned me, the one I mirrored using the doll-baby. *Her* nails, *her* spit, *her* hair, *her* essence. We're linked now, bonded. So I need to either wear her or surrender her back where we made first contact. I can't enter any other vessel while we're still tethered."

"What about that bug thing, the insect in Abby's hair when we got home? I found it under her bed, all white and hollowed out. That was you, wasn't it? How does that fit in to all this?"

"That was just a sheath. I needed a physical form to get away from that place, but it was only a temporary vessel. To wear your girl, I had to accompany her home, then wait."

"Wait for what?"

"My opportunity."

I was connecting the grotesque dots in my mind. Abby 'called' Rylah at Bandun Gate, but my daughter was too strong for the fiend to kill outright like she had Kadisha Fontaine. So Rylah transferred her spirit to the locust and hitched a ride back to the house with us, planning to 'take' Abby during the night, weaken her somehow, through fear or pain — the insect crawling down Abby's throat maybe, or burrowing into her ear as she slept. Except Abby left for Myrtle Beach before Rylah could complete her ghoulish mission, so she had to go to Plan B.

Insect-Rylah had eaten the mucus from Abby's used tissue, which must have given her enough 'essence' to begin the transformation. Then it/she fashioned the little 'voodoo doll' with bits of Abigail from the trashcan, gaining strength as she went. The candle jar would've provided the final boost; trapped under its lid was Abby's 'breath' from the last time she'd blown out the flame. It still wasn't enough for Rylah to displace Abby completely, but it was sufficient to 'mirror' her and to give Rylah a counterfeit body to hold her over until she could snatch the real thing.

"Abby said her head was 'buzzing,'" I muttered, "in her text message to me. It's so bad she's thinking of going to the doctor. Buzzing — like a locust. You're making that happen, and that's not going to stop, is it? You're doing it to her and will keep doing it as long as the two of you are connected."

Rylah shifted back to playing 'pals' again. "Look, it's all very simple. All you have to do is take me where I first yoked your girl. We'll bring this other female — Sophie — along with us. I'll surrender your girl, take Sophie, and you will never see me again after that, I swear. No harm done. So what do you say, Mama? Be nice, and play along!"

My mind was racing, weighing her proposal and its bitter implications. Sure, I'd have my daughter back, but at what cost? Sophie's blood would be on my hands. I didn't know if I could live with that. Yet if I said no, would I be able to spend the rest of my life knowing I'd had a chance to save Abby but didn't take it? Would I ever be able to look my husband or my sons in the eyes again if I let her go? Could I face *myself?*

"I don't know," I sputtered. "What, exactly, would happen to Sophie?"

"Does it matter?" Rylah snapped. "You'd have what you want! You don't even like this girl, I heard you grousin'! I can't believe you're even hesitatin' on this! Don't you love your girl? Don't you *want* her back?"

Of course I did, but not this way. I felt like Eve being tempted in the Garden of Eden. *Hope this apple isn't too sour, because I'll be gnawing on it for all eternity.*

"There's somethin' else I can give you as well," Rylah added slyly. "I speak the language of the dead. I can teach it to you."

She held up my *Encyclopedia of Hell* cover again.

"Do you *really* wanna find out about the netherworld?" Her emerald Abby-eyes blazed. "What you got right, what you got wrong, what you missed completely. The dark beauty of it all?"

She gave me a playful smile that reminded me of everything I loved about my daughter. Everything I would miss if she were gone from my life forever.

"There's all different sorts of spirits," Rylah teased, "just like there's all different kinds of folks. And there are things, *so many things*, you *can't* know without enterin' their world. No amount of diggin' in books or talkin' to scholars could *ever* show you what's hidden on the other side. *My* side. But I could tell you. You like writin' books. I can give you enough stories to fill a hundred libraries. Deliver me the girl to wear, and I'll tell you tales you cannot *imagine*."

It frightened me how much I wanted to hear Rylah's nefarious secrets, to delve into that trove of aberrant knowledge. But was I ready to accept her dire terms?

"You're asking me to kill someone."

Rylah's blithe smile fell away, replaced by the angry scowl.

"You're not slayin' her, just deliverin' her to the gate!" she roared. "Besides, what choice do you have? You got family comin'. Friends. You can't keep folks away from here forever! One of your neighbors'll come by, or the postman bringin' a package to the door, and *I'll* be here to greet 'em. How you think that'll turn out? Sooner or later, *somebody* is gonna get hurt, and it's not goin' to be me who gets the blame. Who'll protect your girl — or *anyone* you care about — then?"

A caustic sea of frustration, rage, sorrow swirled in my gut. Rylah was right, there were no good options. Even if I could warn off Dan and the boys, it was just a matter of time before some unsuspecting visitor wandered onto our property and into the teeth of Rylah's wrath. How would I explain that away? *Oh, I didn't commit this terrible crime, officer, the real culprit is a marauding haint 'mirroring' my daughter.* Even *thinking* about saying that aloud was crazy. The *best* I could hope for was to be declared insane and institutionalized, leaving Rylah free to resume her rampage unimpeded.

And what about Abby? Surely whatever curse was making her ill would continue. Or worse, Rylah might find a way to overtake Abby and complete the blood ritual, sending my daughter into oblivion then 'wearing' Abby's body over her own malignant soul.

"You think it over, Mama," Rylah advised. "But don't dally. Things can happen so quickly now, can't they? Remind us how we're not really in charge of our fate and can't keep harm from befallin' our loved ones."

The ghoul stretched out her Abby-hand and skated her fingertips along the taped-up pages on the back wall. The entries I had written twenty years ago disappeared at her touch, replaced by the names of my husband and children repeating over and over again. The pictures changed, too. Each now showed someone I loved suffering the tortures of the damned: Dan drowning in a lake of fire, Roman being eaten by an enormous serpent, Abby and Charles impaled on hooks while horned beasts slashed them with swords. A putrefying stench filled the room, not the wet woodsy scent of the marshes, but an odor like rancid meat left in a dumpster in July. The stink of rotting flesh.

How can this be happening? It had only been a single day since Rylah upended my life, and now I was losing my family, my sanity, my soul. *One. Single. Day.*

Desperate and deflated, my Catholic school training kicked in and I began to pray.

"Our Father, who art in heaven, hallowed be thy name. Thy kingdom come, thy will be done on earth as it is in Heaven…"

Rylah erupted in laughter. She didn't have Abigail's laugh: girly, giggly, punctuated by snorts when Abby was especially amused. The imposter's was a thick, throaty rattle, tinged with a mocking undertone. *Good.*

"Pray all you want, *Mama*," she jeered, "for all the good it'll do you. You think you're the first to call on the heavens for deliverance? I've heard pleas from men who were shoutin' with pleasure right up until they started wailin' in pain! From women who swore to do *anythin'* if only they'd be spared! Oh, and the babies! You've never heard anythin' like the squeals of a hurt child. Why, they are absolutely *delicious!* Most of 'em call for their mamas, if they can talk, that is. Young or old, boy or girl, don't matter — they all want to be delivered from their fate. They *won't* be. Neither will your girl."

Rylah circled around me as she spoke, gloating. She *loved* twisting the knife. "The heavens never opened up and sent down angels for any of 'em — what's the chance YOURS is the prayer that's gonna get answered? Why, you sound like an old dog howlin' at the moon! Ah-woo! Ah-woo! Annoyin'. Pathetic. But in the end, nothin' more than just so much bothersome noise."

I saw an opening to knock her off balance and grabbed it. "You mean like little Sammy Watkins? Seems his prayers were answered. He got away from you."

The grin slipped, but only for an instant, then Rylah shifted to a pouty scowl. "Yes, that ornery boy evaded me. *Most* of him, that is. I *did* keep a lovely souvenir of our time together. Is that what you want for your girl — to lose a piece of her to me? A finger, or an ear, or maybe part of her pretty face? She's already gonna be damaged goods if I don't surrender her soon. She'll *never* be right again."

"No," I retreated. "There has to be a way out of this."

"There *is* a way! Deliver this other girl to me, or lose yours *forever*! Be nice and play along! You have *no idea* what you're dealin' with, Mama. Not the slightest inklin'. You think you know about evil from pennin' your silly book. I promise, you have *never* seen the likes of me!"

As she finished, I realized that I *had* in fact seen the likes of Rylah before. Worse, even. She had read through the *Encyclopedia of Hell*, but not everything I'd learned about diabolic creatures was in it. I still had an extensive archive of villainy Rylah knew nothing about tucked away in the next room: interviews, photographs, notes, advice — a veritable treasure trove of data on insidious beings. And perhaps, within my Vermicular File, I would find the key to taking down a vicious haint and sending her back to Hell, *permanently*.

Chapter Nine
Malum in Se

The time had come to raid a crypt I'd sealed almost twenty years ago. After *Encyclopedia of Hell* was published in 1998, I packed up all my research — including the Vermicular File — in a big cardboard box. I never dreamed I'd actually need any of it again, and certainly not like this. The only reason I'd kept the stuff at all was out of nostalgia, a souvenir of my 'fledgling author' days. I figured the materials would languish undisturbed, unremembered even, in perpetual storage.

But now here I was, rushing to the bedroom closet, desperate to get my hands on that wretched portfolio. I grabbed up the 'Hell box' — it was heavier than I remembered — and lugged it over to the bed. The packing tape had become brittle over the years, and one good *yank!* was all it took to pop it open. When I pulled up the flaps, a swirl of dust leapt into the air, like a forgotten ghost reasserting its dominion, then a wafting scent of old paper, tinged with a hint of something sweet. Cinnamon, maybe, or cloves. *Strange.*

The container was a time capsule, protecting artifacts of an era long since gone. On top was a collection of letters and other mailed communiques: permission forms from *Chaos Comics* to reprint artwork, an edict from Columbia Pictures denying usage of stills from *Bram Stoker's Dracula*, a personal note form director Linda Hassani, along with photos she'd taken on the set of *Dark Angel: The Ascent*. A few envelopes had been returned marked 'undeliverable', my handwriting still crisp below the post office's *'sorry can't help you here'* message. I scooped all of them out onto the bed, uncovering a stack of weathered comic books underneath. Faded monsters from *Weird Tales, Haunt of Fear, Pinhead*, leered up from across the decades.

Beneath the comics was a bunch of legal pads filled with scribbled notes, then assorted illustrations of demons and hellscapes, followed by magazine articles which contained highlighted passages about the underworld and its creatures. A plastic 'Grim Reaper' toy from *Bill & Ted's Bogus Journey* (part of a 'netherworld novelties' photo shoot) toppled out as I rummaged through the box, along with a 'fireball-scented' beanbag devil. *Ah, the source of the cinnamon-smell.* Further down were various relics of obsolete technology: floppy disks, a micro-cassette recorder and tapes, an address book full of hand-written numbers for landlines and fax machines.

There, at the very bottom of my *Encyclopedia's* ossuary, was the Vermicular File, its looping squiggle pattern impossible to miss. I lifted it out and swept everything else back into the box, then checked on Rylah. She'd returned to scanning the pages on the family room wall and didn't so much as glance in my direction when I peeked out. I closed the door, sat on the bed, and opened the folder.

So far, the grizzled bones I'd pulled from this tomb had all been rather tame: comic books, old mail, 'infernal' knick-knacks. That phase was over. The Vermicular File would have me slicing into Hell's rotted bowels, exhuming rancid atrocities. Simply *holding* it again made my stomach turn, remembering what was inside. Its secrets had not only fueled innumerable nightmares, they'd also revolutionized my long-held beliefs regarding the very concept of Hell. As a child I was taught that corrupt souls faced pitchfork-wielding demons and unquenchable fire in the afterlife. That image became more nuanced through my college years, expanding to include a hierarchy of punishments that fit the sin. After filling the Vermicular File, I realized damnation was actually an echo of insanity: the unsaved caught in a perpetual loop of toiling to forge order out of chaos while reliving malignant memories and trying to convince themselves everything is splendid.

I opened the folder and saw that the first document in the Vermicular File was an interview summary from a man named Levi. *Figures.* I could picture the slimy miscreant lying in wait for two decades (or however long it would have been) to take another stab at me. Levi stood out even in a battalion of villains, the arrogant sadist. The only thing he relished more than indulging his depravity was watching people squirm as he bragged about his exploits. He fed on revulsion. I know he enjoyed *mine*. But what I remember most about Levi is he was the one that showed me how precariously thin the boundary separating humanity from the realm of the damned really is.

I met Levi through Dr. Arden Matthews, a college professor with advanced degrees in comparative religion. We'd been discussing a recent survey that showed a sharp decline in belief in Hell among young adults. I'd asked if he was seeing that same disbelief among his students, and if so, what factors might be contributing to their skepticism. Dr. Matthews had speculated that the generation who'd grown up learning the horrors of the Holocaust and facing a constant threat from nuclear annihilation likely couldn't imagine anything worse. Most who did still believe, he'd added, tended to be deeply religious churchgoers. And then there were outliers like Levi.

"You should meet with him," Dr. Matthews had suggested. "Levi claims to be a sort of *uber*-warlock. He not only *believes* in Hell, he says he's been there many times, insists he can enter the underworld and visit whenever he pleases. His accounts are so vivid — he's either psychotic or a genius. Could be both, I suppose. Of course, there is another possibility: that he actually *has* made the trip."

"So, what, you really think this guy's some sort of afterlife 'frequent flyer'? How would that even be possible?"

"Tell you what, I'll set up a meeting. You can hear for yourself what he has to say. I'm certain he'd be happy to speak with you. He loves to hold forth on his escapades. I'll make sure it's somewhere public — Levi can be a handful. Spend an hour or two with him and see what you think."

I had agreed, intrigued. If nothing else, I thought Levi could put me onto some obscure texts or info sources I otherwise would never have stumbled upon. Later that day, Dr. Matthews had called to tell me Levi was eager to talk.

"I hope it isn't a mistake putting you two together," the

professor had said. "His excitement over being part of your research gave me pause. Levi is fascinating, no question. I'm sure you've not interviewed anyone like him. But there's a *blackness* as well. He'll share things you won't be able to erase from your mind — no matter how badly you might want to."

By that time I'd already encountered so much information about the dismal side of the afterlife, I didn't think anything a college kid had to say would rattle me.

I could not have been more wrong.

Levi was waiting at the counter when I'd arrived at the café. He greeted me cheerfully, introducing himself as a 'demon proxy *extraordinaire*.' I'd reached out for a handshake, but he swooped in and planted a wet kiss on my cheek. Levi was in his early twenties, with wavy black hair and hazel eyes, effortlessly handsome, unshakably confident. He reminded me of a young Elvis. I was a rumpled thirty-two-year-old toddler mom *sans* makeup. We made an odd-looking pair. Levi was acutely aware of that fact and reveled in it.

"Mind if we snag a table in the back, sunshine?" he'd said with a wink as he breezed past the hostess. "We're gonna want a little privacy, if you know what I mean. Something *intimate*."

Immediately I'd started regretting this decision. I had brought two pages of questions for Levi, but with this pompous behavior, I wasn't sure I'd get any usable answers. He'd acted as if he was only there to put on a show. I figured I'd let him talk a while out of respect for Dr. Matthews, grab a quick lunch, then be on my way.

Levi hadn't waited for me to ask him anything, he launched unprompted into his story. How he'd grown up in a small midwestern town, discovered demonology at sixteen after reading Jim Morrison's biography, became obsessed with the works of Arthur Rimbaud and Aldous Huxley. Levi said he had briefly practiced Satanism, but found its rituals and practices dull. He then began searching out a deeper, more 'interactive' relationship with the forces of evil.

"It was all just so — *theatrical*," Levi had explained that afternoon in 1996. "All candles and robes and inverted crosses. Everyone babbling gibberish in Latin. It felt like a bad music video. Not my scene, man, not my scene. I had to find a way through, and I did."

"*Through*? Through what?"

Another flash of that seductive grin, then Levi burst into a chorus of the Doors' *Break On Through to the Other Side*, drumming the beat with his knife and fork. An elderly woman at the next table glared at us disapprovingly. I don't know what reaction Levi had expected from me, but when I calmly got up to leave, he ended his serenade.

"Through the gateway," he'd laughed, motioning me to sit. "Past the veil, across the void, into the abyss — whatever terminology floats your boat."

Dr. Matthews had been right about Levi; the kid was beyond conceited, yet at the same time fascinating. I'd sat back down and listened while he then described numerous 'visits to Hell.'

On his first excursion, Levi claimed to have assisted a legion of devils, (green rather than red, Levi had insisted, and with multiple horns rather than a single pair) by chasing down human souls trying to escape. Once they had corralled the spirits, Levi and his new associates tortured them by various means. Some were thrown into a whirlpool of razor blades, others were forced to drink acid, a few were fed to a crocodile/vulture hybrid beast.

The leaders of the failed jailbreak were forced to re-enact the most shameful moments of their time on earth. Levi said he'd been in hysterics as the damned pantomimed bouts of bulimia, abusing disabled parents, molesting children that had been left in their care. One man had beaten his son's pet rabbit to death in a fit of rage, then fed it to the boy for dinner. That feat in particular had a powerful impact on Levi.

Convinced of his loyalty, Levi said the demon Eligos gave him seven succubi skilled in the 'secret pleasures of the flesh.' He had recounted the names of each one, the color of their hair, the firmness of their breasts, the sexual acts they'd performed on him.

"Those devil-gals taught me some things!" he had boasted. "Got me so hot I thought I was gonna melt down into a steamy puddle of awesome! But so what? I can get all the poontang I want *here* on earth. That's not what keeps me going back."

"Really? So what's a bigger attraction than a harem of your very own kinky she-devils?"

Levi dropped the sexy smile and gave me an icy look that had made me shudder. This was the *real* Levi, his 'charming man-boy' mask fallen away. And the real Levi was terrifying.

"Don't kid yourself, Church Lady. It absolutely *is* better to reign in Hell."

"What do you mean?"

"You know that feeling you get when you swat a mosquito, stomp a roach — how *good* it feels to snatch the life outta it, the power you feel seeing its crushed carcass? Well multiply that by a hundred. By a *thousand.* That's what it's like in Hell — hearing the damned scream for mercy. Begging, pleading, offering to do *anything* if only I make it stop. That look in their eyes when they know I'm in control and there's *nothing* they can do. It is *orgasmic.*"

Levi resumed smiling then, reverting to his casual cool.

"I'm working on my future; don't you get it?" he'd continued. "Making friends and banking chits. Building a castle in my 'forever home.' Won't be so bad spending eternity on *my* end of the whip down there. Getting a taste of it every time I go below. Hot damn! It sure beats anything on this side."

At that point, I had decided we were done and thanked Levi for his time. Sure, he'd given me some interesting imagery, but nothing I could use in my book. All of it was simply rehashed images from Dante and Milton, funneled through the prism of Levi's twisted imagination.

"Wait," he'd said as I rose to leave. "I haven't gotten to the best part yet — *how* I do it. Got the idea that first time under, when I was helping punish the damned. Anyone could do it, really. You could, if you wanted to. It's not hard at all."

"You mean, visit Hell?" I'd asked, never imagining what would come next.

"Yup. There's no secret passage or anything. No magic spell. You just have to create a vortex of pain and *voila*, you're there!"

Creepy, I'd thought, *but again, not that original*. Poets and playwrights have been devising such scenarios since Orpheus descended to Hades in search of his departed bride.

"What, like a ritual sacrifice? Slaughter a goat? Smear yourself with chicken blood? Maybe get a tattoo of Mephistopheles on your backside?"

I'd thought my flippant tone might anger him, instead he laughed and shook his head.

"Nothing that complicated. Just get a dog or cat. It's gotta be someone's pet, though. Something that's *loved*."

My smile evaporated. If this was his idea of a joke, it wasn't funny.

"You kill people's pets to visit Hell?" I'd said, still trying to read him.

"Oh, no, you don't *kill* them. Then it's over. That's no good. You want to keep the thing alive through everything — then you take it home, to its owner. That's part of the suffering. The *real* suffering. You need that to make it work."

I should *not* have asked this next question.

"What do you mean 'through everything'?"

Levi had hunched forward and rested his chin on folded hands, relishing the moment.

"Watch the neighborhood for a while — not your own, of course. Somewhere where you won't get recognized. Where they don't know your car. Look around for somebody with a cat or a puppy they *really* love." Levi's voice took on a mocking cadence as he continued. 'Who's a good boy?' 'Here, kitty, kitty! Come to Papa'!"

I had remained frozen, not sure if he was serious.

"Strays don't work," he'd said, leaning back. "There's no payoff at the end 'cause there's nobody to bring them back to, nobody to cry over what's been done. Or the *real* 'gotcha' — to have to decide what's gotta be done *next*. Do they let Fido suffer, limping, blinded, scarred, or do they opt to put him down? Either way, that's a wound that'll last forever. Curdles the memories. Every time they think about the li'l critter it'll hurt all over again. It's a lifetime of pain."

I had no reply. He spoke again, staring at me without emotion.

"Now, back to the opening act. The torment. You want to make it last as long as possible. Start with needles, then fire. Any lighter will work. Knives next, but you have to know where to cut or it'll kill them right off. The more they yelp and whine, the better. You *want* that. You also want a lot of blood, but again, not *too* much. Then when you've done *everything* possible short of offing them, you gotta maim them. Something permanent. Take an ear or an eye…"

"Just stop!" I'd snapped, louder than I planned. A man a few tables away threw a gravely *huff!* my way, indicating I better keep it down. "This isn't funny, it's sick. I don't want to hear any more."

Levi smiled again, pleased with himself. "Okay then, I'll show you."

He'd reached inside his jacket and took out a tattered white tube sock that had been stuffed and sewn shut. It had lines drawn on it like the markings butchers use to carve various cuts of meat. There were red circles inked in various places.

"All you need to learn is the torso," Levi explained. "It doesn't matter how bad you hurt the limbs because that won't be fatal. You want to make the most of those."

He'd set the sock-body down and reached into his coat again, this time retrieving what looked like a black cosmetic bag. Levi unzipped it, exposing an array of knives, scalpels, hooks and needles. Then he took a silver cigarette lighter from his pocket. He pulled out one of the skewers and slowly inserted it into a red marked area on the sock-thing.

"Here's your sweet spot. Maximum pain, not fatal. Just make one of these practice dummies, it's pretty basic. Once you've practiced some, you can scale it to any size animal then try …"

I don't know how that sentence ended. I had rushed out without looking back.

From the café, I went straight to Dr. Matthews' office,

demanding something be done to stop Levi. The professor said he'd already spoken with the police, but unless he had solid evidence Levi had committed a crime, there was nothing they could do. Even his 'torture kit' didn't contain anything illegal. He'd asked me if Levi had shown me a slaughtered animal, even pictures of one, or just talked about the procedure. I had to admit I hadn't actually seen proof of wrongdoing. For all either of us knew, Levi never did any of the things he claimed. His assertions could be nothing more than rantings from a Satan-obsessed lunatic.

Ultimately, there was nothing I could do but add the interview to the Vermicular File, and pray Levi was not the monster he'd claimed to be.

I never saw Levi again, but now I'd met his kindred spirit in Rylah. Inflicting pain wasn't enough for her, either; she wanted to savor the suffering. If the two of them were to meet, I wonder, would they become fast friends, compadres in cruelty? Or would each see the other as a rival who had to be destroyed, and employ whatever sick methods necessary to come out the winner? How ironic that despite their perverted similarities, Rylah was doing all she could to avoid Hell, while Levi couldn't wait to take his place in the dark inferno.

There were so many things in the Vermicular File that were equally soul-crushing. I found a folio on a cult called Legion of the Deathless Angel. Revisiting this account was particularly painful because I'd known the father of one of its members (or should I say 'victims.') The Legion had a lot in common with other groups. Strip away the particulars and weren't all cults, really, nothing but misogynist sex and macho power trips, preying on vulnerable women and using mind games to maintain control? I flipped through the notes. Seeing my handwriting on those yellow sheets sent a jolt of guilt, vintage 1990's, through me. Gary, the girl's distraught dad, had told me the sad story himself as I'd jotted down key points. At the time I'd uttered all sorts of sympathetic clichés, but in the end, I broke his heart all over again.

Gary lived in our neighborhood at the time, and his daughter Teresa had attended the same high school Dan had graduated from a decade earlier. Word reached Gary that I was writing a book about Hell, and he phoned me saying his daughter had been caught up in 'Satan's work,' would I hear him out?

"I'm not sure what I can do," I'd told him.

"The cult leader, Lark, he calls himself, is the devil. The *devil*. No exaggeration. Put him in your book, tell the world what he and these sick bastards are doing."

Gary spoke in waves of sorrow and fury. I didn't have the heart to tell him no. The following day he brought me a letter he'd received from Teresa's friend Kristen (that copy was in the Vermicular File, too, its pages held together with a rusty paperclip) describing their experience in the Legion. The two had joined together, but Kristen soon regretted her decision and managed to escape. She'd written up her experience in hopes that one day Lark would be brought to justice.

The Legion of the Deathless Angel was basically a mishmash of concepts pilfered from other ideologies. Lark began with bastardization of Taoism, mixed in some Gnostic precepts, then wrapped it in the philosophy of William Blake. Its overarching premise was that humans could achieve immortality by indulging the flesh. Traditional 'Heaven,' Lark claimed, was oppressive, its many rules and exclusions stifled rather than elevated the soul. Hell, by contrast, offered endless, exciting possibilities. The first step to enlightenment was throwing off antiquated moral codes in order to live wantonly, shamelessly, unapologetically. That, of course, is where the young ladies came in.

Even Lark's name was plagiarized from Blake's *Visions of the Daughters of Albion* (which, appropriately, is a poem about rape and victim-shaming.) The self-proclaimed 'Deathless Angel' claimed he was a 'celestial being God had allowed to visit earth and walk among humans.' He was supposed to return to Heaven after ten days but refused, pitying mankind for their 'ignorance' and choosing to enlighten the poor creatures instead. Lark said his eyes had been opened, that 'moral' people acted only out of vain pride so they could claim superiority over others but were, at heart, shallow and miserable. He took it upon himself to 'free' humanity from the 'prison of self-righteousness' and remained on earth, purportedly having spent the last few centuries fulfilling his mission.

Kristen's letter painted a very different picture of Lark and his exploits. She described how she and Teresa were recruited at their high school just weeks before graduation. Both girls had recently turned eighteen, came from troubled homes, and had no plans for what they'd do after receiving their diplomas. They were at a school softball game when a thirty-something woman calling herself Andromeda befriended them. The three chatted. Andromeda told the girls she'd also been having family problems at their age and had no vision for her future. Lark had helped her to 'find herself' and allowed her to 'reach her true potential,' she'd said, and he could do the same for them. Both were eager to meet him.

Within days of being introduced to Lark, Kristen and Teresa had been renamed Cassandra and Aurora, (immortal names from the stars) and had sworn undying allegiance to the Legion.

'The Deathless Angel lived in a motel in Alexandria, and we went every night,' Kristen's letter read. *'Other girls were there, plus Andromeda. She was in charge when Lark wasn't around. We talked about our lives, and school, and parents, whatever was on our minds. Lark said religions only cared about money and control, but his Legion cared about people like us. Teresa and I quit school in April and moved in. Lark bought us nice clothes, perfume, shoes, and took us to fancy restaurants. Most days Andromeda drove us to Ocean City or Rehoboth. We sold T shirts, hats, suntan lotion, and sunglasses on the beach til it got dark. Andromeda said when it got cold, we would go to Florida and sell stuff there. At night we went to parties, different places, mostly at big houses near the beach, or in D.C. Lark let us drink, smoke pot, hook up, whatever we wanted. Nobody forced us to do anything, except he made us take birth control pills. He didn't want to deal with any*

pregnancies. It was a party lifestyle too good to be true, but we were dumb enough to fall for it.'

The letter went on to reveal how things changed abruptly a month after the girls joined the Legion. One afternoon, Lark showed up in a ratty RV and instead of heading to the shore, he drove Teresa, Kristen and the other girls to a field near the West Virginia line. Outdoor party lights were strung up, and music blared from a boombox beside a bar made of wooden crates. They were the only ones at first, and Lark made them erect 'party tents' in the meadow. Andromeda set up a few air mattresses in each. As it was getting dark, two large buses pulled up.

"Our guest have arrived!" Lark announced. When the passengers got out, Kristen realized she and the 'Legion girls' were the only females there. She described the men as 'old guys' who were well-dressed but 'scary.'

Lark called the girls into one of the tents and gave each a hit of ecstasy. He told them it was time for their 'initiation rite,' a chance to prove their loyalty to him while 'opening themselves up to pleasure without limits.' Lark referred to the men as 'benefactors' and instructed the women 'do whatever you're told, and make our guests happy.' Kristen and the other girls were scared what might happen if they refused, so they complied. Kristen said she had sex with at least seven different men that night, maybe more; it was hard to keep track because sometimes there was more than one at a time.

From then on, it was the same thing every night. Lark took the girls to various locations — remote fields or abandoned buildings or sometimes they'd just park the RV in an empty lot — and offered them up as entertainment to 'donors.' Kristen said the sex wasn't the worst part, the violence was. Lark wouldn't let anything extreme happen to his Legion, (hospital visits or visible scars might lead to questions) but everything else was fair game. By day, the Deathless Angel would feed the girls drugs and alcohol between lengthy brainwashing sessions about how their pain was actually pleasure, if only they'd open their minds to it. By night, they were violated repeatedly.

129

'*I didn't sign up for that,*' Kristen had written. '*I wanted out. I was tired of getting hit, bitten, burned, hair ripped out. I wasn't going to keep screwing old men the rest of my life. I told Andromeda I was done, and she told Lark. He said he was sorry. He didn't know it was so bad on us. Lark told me to get in his car and that he'd take me home. I tried to get Teresa to leave with me, but she had fallen for his bullshit hook, line, and sinker. I said just ride along, make sure I get home safe, she can decide when we get there if she wants to go back or not. She came with. Only Lark didn't take me home. He drove us out in the woods to a shitty old camper. It was rusty and broken-down, and all the windows were blacked over. We're here, he says. Heaven.*

'*Inside there was no furniture, just a dirty mattress and a bucket for a toilet. The place stunk so bad I puked a little. There were chains bolted to the floor. Lark was smiling. He said trust me I would never hurt you, and chained us up by our ankles. He said I love you both, we just need to start over. Things will be different this time. First, we had to learn some lessons. Lesson one. This is what Heaven is really like, so decide if it's for you. Then he locked us in and drove away.*'

This event occurred in late June. 'Heaven' was unbearably hot during the day, pitch black at night, and constantly reeked of human waste. From the start, Teresa blamed Kristen for her misery, insisting it wasn't fair she was being punished alongside her apostate friend. She wanted to go back to Lark, and was willing to surrender herself to him, body and soul.

Lark returned late the following day. He brought with him a cage containing a little gray mouse they named Rocco. He told them their next lesson was to figure out how to handle helpless creatures. 'This little guy is going to teach you about trust,' he said. 'When you've learned the lesson, you can come back home' — which, of course, meant back to his travelling rape-mobile.

Kristen said 'Heaven' was so awful, she started thinking maybe she should just give in. Then Lark launched into another sermon praising himself as the Deathless Angel, saying that Hell wasn't so bad, that it had drugs, and booze, and endless parties, that paradise was the prison. The more he preached, the more Kristen hated him. She decided she'd rather die than go back to being his slave.

Before leaving, Lark got a bag of burgers and fries from his car. The girls hadn't eaten in almost two days and scarfed them down. Kristen realized he had drugged the food after she came-to hours later on the filthy mattress, naked and sore. Teresa was vomiting into the toilet-bucket and refused to talk about what had happened. 'You brought it on yourself,' was all she'd say.

Kristen's letter described how their situation continued to go downhill.

'Lark left us there another two days, no food or water, the place stinking from the shit bucket. Teresa stayed real quiet all the time except when she played with Rocco. Taking care of him kept us going, or we woulda gone crazy. We both told him, don't worry little guy, we'll get outta here soon, take you somewhere nice. Finally I hear someone unlocking the door, but it's not Lark, it's Andromeda. She had more water for us, but no food. I told her we're starving. She gave me a big metal spoon and gave Teresa a lighter. She said, you wanna eat? Kill Rocco with the spoon, then use it like a pan to cook him with the lighter. There's your food. Do it, and Lark will know you learned your lesson. He'll welcome you both back, no hard feelings. Then she left.

'No way we were going to kill Rocco. NO WAY.'

According to Kristen's account, Andromeda came back the following night, angry to find the mouse still alive. She told Teresa and Kristen that she'd give them one more chance, threatening that if they hadn't eaten the mouse by the time she returned, she'd take the lighter away, and when they finally got hungry enough, they'd have to eat their pet raw. Lark was going to be furious if it came to that, Andromeda scolded. Kristen said that by then Teresa was half crazy from hunger and dehydration and being locked up. All she wanted was to be back with Lark. He was their savior and they had been wrong to betray him.

Kristen realized Teresa was having a breakdown, so she

took matters into her own hands. When Andromeda returned the following day, Kristen grabbed Rocco, the spoon and lighter, then huddled in the corner with her back to the two women. 'I didn't think you'd be the one to crack,' Lark's enforcer laughed. 'I guess brats like you aren't as tough as you think.'

Andromeda gave Kristen a minute to complete the sordid task, mocking her the entire time. Teresa just stood by, silent. When Andromeda bent down to see if the mouse had been killed, Kristen whirled around, grabbed Andromeda by the hair, and pressed the spoon — which Kristen had been heating with the lighter — against Andromeda's left eye. Andromeda screamed, and Kristen shoved the molten utensil into the woman's open mouth, ramming it as far down her throat as she could. Then Kristen knocked Andromeda to the floor and dumped the toilet pail in her face. Andromeda yelped and gagged, trying to dislodge the hot metal as Kristen took her keys and unlocked the girls' shackles.

'Come on, now's our chance. Let's go!' Kristen reported shouting as Andromeda writhed in pain. *'Teresa called Rocco I thought she was bringing him along like we promised. She had a weird smile it scared me. She sat down next to his cage then picked Rocco up by the tail and put him in her mouth, still smiling that creepy smile. I ran, didn't look back. I locked them in the camper, got in Andromeda's car, and drove. There wasn't a real road, it was way out in the woods. I wasn't thinking, just wanted to get away. I went til I found a road, then another, then a house. The lady didn't believe me about what happened. Her husband gave me some hot soup and called the cops. They came, and I told them about everything, and they took me home. That's how I escaped the Legion.'*

It took Kristen two days working with the police to find the trailer again. She hadn't been sure which direction she'd gone or how far she had driven before finding the couple who helped her. By the time she returned with the authorities, Teresa and Andromeda were gone. So was the mattress, the bucket, the chains, and all evidence of Rocco. The camper had a new smell, too: bleach. Andromeda's car didn't yield any clues either; it had been stolen from a mall parking lot a few months earlier. Investigators weren't convinced Kristen's story was true. They thought perhaps she'd stolen the car herself, them made up the harrowing tale of captivity and escape to avoid criminal charges.

Lark and the rest of his Legion had vanished as well. The police went back to the motel where the girls had stayed, only to find that the rooms had been rented under a fake name and paid for in cash. None of the workers had gotten the license plate of Lark's car or RV. Employees remembered a man of his description coming and going, but couldn't, or wouldn't, provide any further details on his activities. All investigation of the Legion of the Deathless Angel ended.

Kristen moved back in with her parents and eventually shared her story with Gary. She felt guilty about everything: getting Teresa involved, not escaping sooner, leaving her friend behind.

Gary hired a private detective to go to Florida and look for Teresa, but after weeks of searching he hadn't unearthed any leads. The anguished father hoped I could generate publicity by including the Deathless Angel story in my book, believing maybe someone would come forward with information on his daughter's whereabouts. For months following our meeting, Gary would phone me and leave long messages on my answering machine, increasingly desperate, punctuated with sobs. Unfortunately Kristen's story, though riveting, didn't fit my book's parameters, so his info went into the Vermicular File. After a while I stopped responding to Gary, and he quit reaching out to me, in what I know must have been another heart-breaking dead-end.

The last I heard, (a decade and a half ago, maybe more) Teresa was still in the wind. After *Encyclopedia of Hell* came out, I was busy publicizing the book, then pivoted to tending my own children, forgetting all about Gary's. I felt horrible losing track of him over the years, never following up to see if he'd found his daughter. Now I knew what it was like to have a girl in jeopardy and to feel lost, hopeless, wishing there was someone — *anyone* — who might help get her back. Maybe this was my karma.

I shook off the self-recriminations and continued sifting through the Vermicular File, desperate to find *something* to use against Rylah. There were notes from an Indonesian *dukun* detailing his exorcism experiences, how he'd talk with demons after removing them from human hosts; all they really wanted was an audience to hear their stories. There were a few gory crime scene photos, too, and recipes for cooking human flesh, some pornographic drawings involving saints and Satan. All of these items I had considered too taboo for public view twenty years back; now, thanks to the internet, material a hundred times more repulsive is available twenty-four seven on an easy-access electronic buffet.

Of course, some things in my Vermicular File could *not* be found online. I'd picked up a homemade *grimoire* at a Virginia estate sale, the leather-bound book crammed with hexes and spells and instructions for fashioning powerful talismans. It contained hand-copied passages from *The Lesser Key of Solomon*, too, describing how to summon demons for various purposes: wealth, power, sexual prowess, revenge.

Accompanying the guide was a page of sigils identifying each demon. One stood out. Andras, Great Marquis of Hell, sewer or discord, thirty legions of demons at his command, a vindictive spirit who will smite a reckless conjurer. Beside the text was an illustration of the demon. He was depicted as an angel with a raven's head riding a wolf and wielding a huge sword. Below the drawing was Andras' sigil. It resembled an ornate candelabrum inside a large circle.

I lingered on the design, wondering if this was the same symbol carved into Rylah's mystery container and little Sammy Watkin's back. It certainly appeared to match the description Mike Fontaine had given. I thought about showing the image to Rylah to see how she'd react. Something like this, however, surely had the potential to increase the fiend's power, make her more deadly. And even if the sigil was connected to Rylah somehow, what then? I didn't have enough information to do anything but get myself into further danger. Better to keep it to myself for now, I thought, and wait for the right moment to weaponize this data.

I thumbed past more horrors, then came to what I was pinning my hopes on: a padded envelope containing interviews recorded on micro-cassette tapes. I scavenged batteries from the TV remote, then slid the tape marked 'Exorcist Testimony' into the old recorder and pushed 'play.' A soft hiss, some quick rumbling, then a ghost from the past, my own voice, two decades prior, reached through the vanished years to greet me.

"January 14, 1994. Interview with Roman Catholic priest and church-sanctioned exorcist," twenty-nine-year-old Miriam stated crisply. "This session is being conducted on the condition of anonymity, so, henceforth, interview subject will be referred to only as 'Fr. Frank…'"

Chapter Ten
Light Bringer

"If you believe in angels, then by definition you believe in demons, too," Fr. Frank had told me the day I met him. "That's all they are, angels who made a hideous exercise of free will, charred remnants of once-magnificent beings. Angels were designed to be messengers, a conduit between God in Heaven and men on earth. Instead of escorting mortal souls to paradise, fallen angels are determined to drag as many as they're able along with them to Hell. Misery loves company, yes?"

The old priest had spoken those words on a sunny January afternoon as we'd walked the campus of Catholic University. It had been a mild winter in Washington that year, and on the day of our interview, the temperature had reached into the high sixties. The campus was nearly deserted then (a Saturday during Christmas break) except for a few students playing hacky-sack on the quad, and the occasional bike rider crossing the grounds. Father Frank had met me at the C.U. Metro stop and escorted me from there, grateful for an excuse to enjoy a midday stroll. We'd arrived at the library just after three, and sat down to discuss his incredible work.

"Do you mind if I record this?" I'd asked, taking out the cassette recorder. "I'll take notes, too, but this would really help."

He'd smiled and nodded, and asked that I neither use his real name nor acknowledge him in the book to protect the people he had assisted. I agreed, then began recording. After a quick introduction, I asked Fr. Frank about his background and what drew him to this unusual ministry. Twenty years later, I found myself listening to his somber voice once more, this time with desperation rather than curiosity.

"This is a vocation I acquired quite by happenstance. I never set out on this course, never pictured myself an expeller of demons. But I met a most extraordinary fellow at seminary — Declan, let's call him — who had a rare gift for reading souls. We became fast friends. *Good* friends. Brothers. The instructors recognized Declan's ability and had him attending exorcisms by our second year. By graduation he was officially apprenticed to a practicing exorcist. It was arduous work, physically and spiritually, yet Declan was ever the portrait of joy, of peace.

"After we were ordained, we were assigned to parishes in neighboring cities. One night, not long into our postings, I received a call from Declan. He said that he'd been dispatched to the home of a uniquely troubled man, and asked if I might accompany him.

"I hurried over. When I arrived, he told me he might need to perform an exorcism and deputized me, *ad actum*, to assist. 'But first we must go down cellar,' he said. 'There's something I need before we leave.' I followed him down the rough wooden steps to a freezer in the corner, one of those long, low appliances. It resembled a gray metal coffin. I could hear its steady hum as we made our way toward it. Declan grasped the lid with both hands and heaved upwards. A thick layer of hoarfrost lined the underside. He held it open with one hand and reached inside with the other.

"*What's he got in there?* I thought, quite apprehensive. *A preserved animal? Some sacred relic? What formidable implement might he possibly require for such an occasion?* Then Declan produced a pair of frozen fudge pops — the kind tikes buy from an ice cream truck — and handed one to me. 'Trust me, we're going to need these later,' he laughed. We took them upstairs to the fridge-freezer, sharing remembrances of ice cream treats from our boyhood days. One must fast before attempting anything as perilous as exorcism, but knowing we had something sweet to look forward to afterwards worked wonders on my nerves.

"What came next, however, was all the more bitter. Are you aware exorcisms should never be performed alone? Too dangerous, like trying to take down a rampaging drunkard who outweighs you by a hundred pounds. No matter how well-trained and careful you are, odds are you will not emerge unscathed. On that evening I officially became Declan's partner, a reinforcing flank to his frontal assault. This would be the first exorcism I took part in. The first of many, sad to say.

"Declan said that the parishioner — let's call him Aaron — was a pious man who had begun having impure urges regarding his seven-year-old niece. It started with dreams in which Aaron would caress the girl, innocently at first, then in an increasingly troublesome manner. The dreams escalated to visions of carnal violation and extreme violence against the child. Soon Aaron was plagued by these musings while awake. He would push such thoughts away, disgusted, yet sometimes aroused, and still they kept returning. Next came voices encouraging him to perform the acts from his wanton dreams. They grew louder and more insistent, crowding out all other thought. Aaron suspected a demonic presence. What happened next removed all doubt.

"When Declan and I visited him that night, Aaron took us upstairs to his study — he was an illustrator by trade — and revealed an accumulation of pornographic drawings of the girl. They'd been sketched on scraps of paper, in the margins of books, upon the very walls. He had no recollection of creating the images although there were undeniably drawn in his own hand. Aaron said he would come upon such pictures and immediately discard them, only to find two more in each's place. He feared the lecherous spirit was usurping him, intent on defiling — perhaps even extinguishing — the child.

"Words cannot convey the utter depravity of those illustrations. Several depicted him ..."

I stopped the tape. Plenty of disturbing visuals were already skulking through my brain, I did *not* need to add visions of a seven-year-old girl being molested to that inventory. *Not today, Satan.* I fast forwarded a bit before hitting 'play' once again.

"...had not acted yet, but worried it was only a matter of time. Aaron reached out to Declan believing only an exorcism could stop the demon.

"Keep in mind, Miriam, that demonic aggression occurs more frequently than the world imagines. Most often, Satan and his minions work directly through us mortals by our own choice. A demon's role is navigator rather than pilot, yes? Mother Church has methods to dispel wicked spirits, but human will is harder to overcome. Every man must decide which team he'll play for and thereby disavow the other. When we do Satan's bidding willfully, even *thankfully*, we commit a sort of spiritual suicide. What was happening to Aaron was something else entirely."

"So Aaron *was* possessed?" my taped voice inquired.

"He was under assault, yes. Remember those old *Tom & Jerry* cartoons where the mischievous feline has an angel on one shoulder and a devil on the other? Well, some men have devils on *both* shoulders, and they require liberation. Aaron's case was one of demonic 'obsession,' meaning the devil was attacking him from *outside* his body rather than from within. Declan explained the difference between obsession and possession as having 'a brute on your back versus a beast in your belly.' The former is dangerous and troublesome, yes, yet far easier to evict. Aaron was still in control of his faculties, at least partially, but a truly powerful diabolic force was fighting to seize control away.

"Declan and I began praying over him. Immediately, Aaron grew agitated and started perspiring profusely. We sprinkled him with holy water, and he emitted a shriek the likes of which I'd never heard! Every droplet blistered his skin. Aaron lunged at Declan, assailing him with insults, blows, blasphemies. When I tried to intervene, Aaron knocked me to the floor as if I were a ragdoll. Through it all, Declan continued his recitation, undaunted. The struggle went on for hours until at last the malignant fiend was dispelled, departing with a final ghastly howl.

"From that night, I was Declan's on-call assistant. We would officiate two hundred and thirty-seven more rituals together over the next twenty-four years. It's staggering how many people do not believe Satan is real, make sport of him. Well, I have heard the voice of the devil, I have been the object of his wrath, and I have seen his destruction firsthand. He is most assuredly real, and there is nothing remotely humorous about him. One who has seen what I have witnessed would not make jokes.

"Others believe in Satan and demons but think they can defeat evil by outsmarting it. The dark forces know this and use it against us mortals, yes? They saw what happened in Eden — Eve's sin was not biting the apple; it was defying the admonition *not* to. Dangle something attractive in front of us and we roll over like an eager mongrel, convinced that our transgression is not *so* bad, or that perhaps we can redeem ourselves on balance in the end. That, my dear friend, is Satan's foot in the door. Or, should I say, his cloven hoof?"

Fr. Frank had emitted a quick snicker. I recognized the sound even on the crackly tape recording. Twenty years later it made me smile again to remember the man. His voice resumed.

"Ah, but you are here today researching Hell, yes? The realm of the fallen angel and his acolytes, the prison of damned souls. I have seen that as well. During my years with Declan, I suffered lacerations, broken bones, concussions — lost a tooth once during an especially violent encounter! Declan suffered far worse, of course. *Far* worse. And yet the anguish from that brief glimpse of Gehenna left scars I cannot adequately describe. The best I can do is to share the story with you, Miriam; take from it what you can.

"Declan had been called to the bedside of a young boy named Joshua. The child was possessed by an incredibly powerful demon. The scene was as awful as you can imagine: ear-splitting screeches, vulgar insults, insinuations about our sexual proclivities, all from the lips of this dear little boy. I was reciting the rosary as Declan performed the sacred incantations. The confrontation was intensifying when suddenly the room began to rumble as if from an earthquake. Pictures fell from the walls, dresser drawers flung open. The boy's father was holding a wooden crucifix; he clutched it so tightly during the disturbance it left splinters in his hands. We continued our efforts as the vibrations grew stronger, more erratic. A lamp flew across the room and hit me square against the forehead. The next thing I knew, I was regaining consciousness in the back of an ambulance.

"A lovely young nurse with red hair and a rather ample bosom was bandaging my wound as I lay on the gurney. 'Relax, you're going to be fine,' she assured. I felt woozy and my head hurt like the dickens! Then the vehicle hit a bump and the nurse fell on top of me. She tried to get to her feet, but the ambulance kept picking up speed and swerving, making it impossible for her to steady herself.

"I could feel the ambulance careening faster and faster, descending downward and downward, like the steepest hill on a rollercoaster ride. Only there didn't seem to be an end to this incline. My nurse was still atop me. She began to rub herself against me and put her hands where she should *not*. The lass's body remained as it had been, but now she had the head of a roach, with huge black eyes and scabrous pincers. We kept falling, my stomach fluttering wildly; I did not think I could withstand another second of it, not one more *instant*. And then, without warning, we slammed to a stop.

"The ambulance doors flung open; the roach-faced nurse pitched me into a wheelchair then whisked me down a narrow passageway to an underground foundry. The vast cavern was lit only by the flames of crackling forges. An odor of rotting flesh and fetid blood burned my throat and stung my eyes. My nurse pulled me to my feet and brought me to the center of the room to witness the terrible labors underway.

"To my left were diabolic creatures — crimson demons ten feet tall, with faces like rabid wolves — chopping the damned into large pieces, then heaping the fragments into piles. All the while these souls were fully alert, writhing in agony, and shrieking for relief. On my right, another legion of demons, similarly large but of a sour yellow color, went among the piles grabbing various parts and sewing them together using spilled entrails as thread. A head from here, a torso from there, an arm, or perhaps two or three from yon. The monstrosities those fiends created would make Dr. Frankenstein himself weep! There were legless men with female breasts that lactated green bile, a two-headed woman with five arms, faces screaming at each other while the quintet of hands clawed viciously at both, a limbless man with fingers protruding from his eye sockets.

"At least such as those were still recognizable as *somewhat* human. Other abominations were merely assemblages of spare parts. Hands and feet and tongues and innards lashed together, scuttling along in the orange darkness. Forgive my candor, but among the worst was a conglomeration of genitalia covered in pulsating sores, twitching and squirming in an apparent attempt to copulate with itself. Toward its middle a set of eyes — one brown, the other hazel — ogled the spectacle; in disgust or lechery, I could not say.

"While I stood transfixed, the roach-nurse brought in a fresh body for harvest: it was little Joshua, his hands and feet bound. The crimson ogres all stopped their carving and moved towards him, eager to dismember the child. Joshua looked over at me, his eyes the very portrait of terror. From out of the gloom another demon emerged, this one taller still and wearing a silver veil that hid its face. 'Decide which it will be, *sacredo*!' the beast shouted. 'You, or the boy! Sacrifice yourself to me and I shall release him — but you, priest, must stay in this place forever!'

"The demon pulled back the cowl as he spoke. At first, I could discern only a set of black horns rising from his scaly scarlet forehead. Then the fabric slipped away, and I saw a face I knew well. A face I *loved* well. It was Declan's.

"'You have sworn to give your life for this innocent,' he taunted, parroting Declan's voice. 'But what about your *afterlife* for him? It's one thing to die for your fellow-man, will you take his place in eternal Hell?'

"I could not stand to see little Joshua in such torment, and so with a heavy heart I decided to become the boy's savior. I took a step forward and everything began to, to *fade*. How can I explain? My senses, memories, logic, all starting to melt away; my very being was fraying. It felt as if I was being absorbed into a boundless ocean of suffering, a sea of sorrow and pain and loss. I was melting into it, and it was flowing into me. I was losing physicality as well. My limbs were growing numb, my breathing ever-more labored. I hurried toward the boy, worried that if I didn't make quick work of the deed, I wouldn't have the strength to finish.

"The Declan-fiend watched my toil, delighted. It felt as if miles, hours, eons passed before I reached Joshua. The little boy sat quietly as I struggled to loosen his restraints. I fought the urge to look at the Declan-gargoyle. It chided me as I worked to free the boy. 'It's all right,' I told Joshua as I finished. 'This is almost over, and you're soon back with your father.' The child gave no reply.

"I picked Joshua up and placed him in the wheelchair beside the passageway. 'The boy will remain here until your surrender is complete!' Declan's specter shouted. 'Now come and kneel prostrate before me!' His voice was a close match to my friend's, but with an anger and bitterness that could not conceivably have emanated from the true Declan. I staggered towards him; mind full of clouds. I was coming to the end of memory, memory even of myself. The closest sense I could compare it to is being haunted by a dream you cannot quite remember upon waking. A thought just beyond grasp. Another feeling was rushing in to fill its void: the most terrible sense of dread and despair I have even known. That ocean again, ready to drown me.

"I lumbered back to the spot where the beast stood, ready to accept my fate. My limbs so unbearably heavy, and my head pounding with such agony I was sure to collapse. The smell of burning flesh was nauseating, the taste of the rancid air thick on my tongue. Hell's grotesque oddities seemed to be urging me on; one eyeless creature with two torsos attached to a lone head crept up to me raising a fist, the mouth sewn into its armpit vomiting blood.

"My knee was about to bend when a last flicker of memory ran through my mind: the voice of my second-grade teacher, Sister Genevieve. 'Don't try to do God's job for Him,' she would tell us. 'That's where Adam and Eve went wrong. You don't *make* the plan; your job is to follow His.' I let her words reverberate, toiling to hold their meaning. The 'nothingness' began to recede, and the fog in my head started clearing. Suddenly I could picture the dear old nun, her round face smiling at me through gold-rimmed spectacles. In that instant, my course of action was clear.

"Unafraid, I looked up at the demon-Declan and declared, 'Joshua does not need me to rescue him; you have no claim to the child. He was made in the divine image and redeemed through the blood of Christ. He is not yours, never was, and through the grace of God never will be.' I spoke without malice or arrogance, just putting forth the facts. 'Nor do *I* require deliverance from you. Your lies, your manipulations, cannot change that most basic truth.'

"With that, the roach-woman shrieked and clawed her enormous insect-eyes out. Declan's doppelganger howled and increased in size until he burst through the cavern's ceiling, the foundry crumbling to pieces around us, its fires gone suddenly cold. We stood now in a vast wasteland of smoky-blue murk. The sound and the stench of human misery remained overwhelming. Joshua, praise be, was no longer anywhere to be seen. Through the mist I could see Satan's mutilated figures beating, molesting, disemboweling one another — which were human and which demonic I could not say. At intervals I caught sight of a face that seemed familiar, but if I tried to focus, the fog would become more deliberate and cloak it from me. I was praying to the archangel Michael — he had fought the rebel angels, yes? — when a tremendous force grabbed me from behind and plucked me away from the miserable scene.

"In a flash, I was unceremoniously deposited back into my chair in Joshua's bedroom. Declan was standing at the boy's bedside making the sign of the cross. The child smiled weakly as his relieved father sobbed with joy. The demon had been vanquished, and the boy was once again himself.

"I gathered my wits and rose to leave. Declan collected his tools, prayer book, crucifix, holy water, and we readied our departure. Joshua's father thanked us through tears. As we left the room, Joshua called out softly to me, saying, 'I'm glad I didn't have to stay with the bug-lady.' Declan turned and looked from me to the boy and back again, the oddest expression on his face. He said nothing as we exited the home.

"Such work always left us exhausted, so it was not unusual that we drove back to Declan's place in silence. After some hot coffee, he suggested we discuss the day's events while they were fresh in our minds. Compare notes, so to speak. He sounded curt, but I chalked that up to exhaustion. Alas, that was not the case. What followed would ultimately end not just our partnership, but a friendship that had endured since our college days. I didn't know it at the time, but this was to be the last conversation Declan and I would ever have.

"No sooner had we begun than we realized there were huge discrepancies in our accounts. Not to say we couldn't remember what happened. Quite the contrary! Declan and I both had clear, vivid memories of the procedure, but to our dismay they were completely at odds. He insisted we started by blessing the house room by room. I remember going straight up to Joshua's bedroom. Declan recalled the boy's father actively participating in the ritual. In *my* version, the man sat in the background barely uttering a sound. We couldn't even agree on the pattern of the boy's bedspread! He said it was most definitely yellow and orange plaid. I, however, remember a distinct blue floral design. It was as if we had attended the same event but in different universes.

"When it became obvious we would find no common ground, I shrugged. 'Perhaps the devil is playing tricks on our minds,' I said. That, as it happens, was not the thing to say. My old friend looked at me with such wary eyes, assessing me. I realized he had been doing so since before we left the boy's home. 'I need to show you something,' he said, 'in the attic,' and began leading the way. I was following him up the stairs when a voice — *his* voice — called from behind. 'Where are you going?' I turned and there was Declan, still seated in his chair. I looked again at the stairs, and the Declan who *wasn't* had disappeared.

"I tried to explain what I'd seen, but he would have no part of it. 'It's merely an echo,' I stammered, grasping for some explanation. 'The dying gasp of a banished demon.' Declan thought it something else. He believed the fiend had exited Joshua during the exorcism and taken up residence in me, that now, every action I took was part of a scheme to break him, a trap that would ensnare his soul. Declan, I understood too late, had also experienced a terrifying vision during the ritual, and where I had seen *his* face on a diabolic entity, he had surely seen *mine*. When Joshua referred to the 'bug-lady,' the seed was planted that perhaps his was not a vision at all, that whatever he had seen had roots in reality.

"Declan descended into acute paranoia. Everything after that, he believed, was a demonic simulation to test him. He could no longer trust anything, not his eyes, nor his ears, nor his mind. Most of all, he could not trust me. He was certain I was a part of the conspiracy. From that night, Declan could not tolerate my presence in his life, and asked to be reassigned to another city.

"The bishop sent him to a remote monastery by the Italian seaside for what was to be a short respite. I was forbidden from corresponding with him until he recovered. Everyone agreed it was for the best. However the day of his recovery never came. Declan remains cloistered with the monks to this day, if he still lives. He's wandering his own abyss now, I suppose, as I am mine.

"Satan stole my friend from me that day. However I live in hope the victory is temporary. I pray Declan will be restored and we shall be glad companions once more in the world yet to come."

There was a long pause in the recording. *Is this how it's going to be with me and Abby?* I wondered as the seconds ticked by. *Lost to each other for whatever years I have left?* Father Frank's voice brought me out of the gloom, shifting focus away from Rylah and her devastation and back to resolving the problem at hand.

"Evil and madness are kindred parasites, with a fair amount of overlap between them. Not to say those who are troubled in the mind are evil, but rather they suffer torments that rival damnation. Theirs is a world of disorder and dismay. They dare not trust even their own senses. Though very few who are insane are truly malevolent, those who willingly embrace evil have surrendered their sanity along with their soul. Flung it away, yes? That, distilled down to its essence, is the nature of Hell.

"Declan was beset by evil which devolved into lunacy. His faith, however, his heart and his spirit and his fidelity, remained true. After his collapse, no doubt *because* of it, I turned my attentions to those who had become ensnared in diablerie and could not extricate themselves, spellcasters who conjured demons, whether playing at witchcraft, or making a lifelong practice of sorcery. 'Tis a dangerous game, no matter how light-heartedly it's undertaken. Satan does not 'dabble' in humanity. Be assured; he devours it. Many have been hoisted on their own perilous petards, yes? They don't see how far adrift they are until the sea drowns them.

"Then there are those who seek consort with the dead. I do not refer to those who mourn lost loved ones and reach out from a place of desperation. Grief is a cousin of madness, too, and by grace, the bereaved will be requited. But necromancy for sport or profit or power is its own brand of iniquity. Trying to tear through the veil between this world and the next, hoping to snatch from it a prize we have no right to claim. Trust me, the boundary is there not to punish humanity but to protect it. 'None of the dead come back,' John the Divine reminds us, 'but some stay.' Makes sense, yes? Souls in paradise have no cause to return to earth; those in Hell can only bring strife. And any who linger in the gray are a menace to us and to themselves.

"Of course, ghosts and demons are distinct creatures, but sometimes they keep company. An unholy alliance indeed! Lost and prowling spirits, fueled by their envy of the living for whom hope still exists. When such marauders are invited to our plane of existence, no good can come of it, only harm. My mission became the retrieval of lost sheep, of shooing away their ravaging wolves, returning them to the flock. Of course, not all lost lambs want to return. Some would rather shed their skin and become something else."

"How do you mean?" enquired the younger Miriam. Another pause, followed by Fr. Frank's frightening response.

"There exist human souls who traject Hell on earth. Just as saints channel goodness --- Francis of Assisi, Mother Teresa, those who embody God's benevolence in action --- there are people who function as conduits of evil. They are not themselves demons, nor are they 'possessed' in the official sense, they have simply chosen a course of barbarity and destruction. They relish the wreckage they've wrought. Like pyromaniacs, their delight is not in producing ashes, but in watching everything around them burn."

Like Levi, I thought as I listened to the old tape, *with his collection of mutilated animals. And now Rylah who relishes torturing children, and worse.*

"I have encountered only a scant few in my time, praise be, but believe me, that was more than enough for this old curate. I could see the flames of Hell burning in their accursed eyes. Evil would do better to lay low, stay silent, hide itself from adversaries. But Satan and his sycophants can't help themselves — pride trumps prudence. They want credit for their carnage, want to revel in the ruin, want others to see what they've wrought and pay homage. Most of all, they want their detractors to cower before them, petrified. Braggarts and bullies, the entire lot!

"Fortunately, this boldness is oft-times their undoing. No bully can withstand being called to account for his actions. Sinister spirits feed off fear and ignorance, yet quickly wither when the mirror is turned 'round on them. You want to cast out a demon? Make it say its name, reveal its substance. Discover as much about it as you can, then use that information against it. Knowledge is power, yes? So long as we remember from whose quiver that arrow is drawn."

148

The tape went silent once more, this time resuming after a much shorter break.

"My time in Hell taught me one absolute, undeniable truth: that the fiercest enemy any of us will ever face is the darkness lurking in our own heart."

I could still see the pained expression on Fr. Frank's face when he'd made that statement. At the time, I had wondered how his visions might still have been so clear, his pain so raw, through the passage of so many years. Now, with Rylah camped in the next room and Abby's life on the line, I was about to learn firsthand just how deep and pervasive psycho-spiritual scars could be.

Chapter Eleven
Inhabit the Mirror

Sometime during the night I discovered Rylah's power to torment me was not limited to my waking hours.

I woke up in a chair, shards of the Vermicular File slicing through my psyche. Only I wasn't at my house in Charleston, I was in the I.C.U. parents' dorm at Children's National Hospital. Cole, the man whose daughter's appendix had burst sending poison throughout her little body, was sleeping on a sofa across from me. Someone was shaking my arm: the nurse from Dr. Mackey's pediatric neurology team.

"Are you Roman's mother?" she said, sounding detached, disinterested. "Come with me." I followed her down the hall toward intensive care, gliding weightlessly, lulled by the 'blip, blip, blip' of electronic monitors. We had almost reached Roman's bedside when the equipment stopped beeping and began emitting a shrill, steady wail. The nurse pulled back the curtain and there lay my twelve-year-old son, motionless, staring up with empty eyes. Dr. Mackey turned to me and instead of smiling and telling me Roman was going to be okay, shook her head and said, "let's call it."

"Time of death, 3:14 a.m.," the nurse responded, ripping the IV needle from his arm.

"Wait. That's not what happened!" I shouted. "The nurse brought me here because Roman woke up; he was getting better! You said he'd be going home soon! This is NOT what happened!!!"

The nurse, ignoring me, dragged Roman's body onto a gurney and covered it with a white sheet.

"NO!" I sobbed, angry. "Roman doesn't die when he's twelve! He recovers, goes back to school. He's going to get an engineering degree from George Mason University! His college roommates are Alex and Richard. We see them all the time, they're like family! How would I know that?"

I realized I was ranting, not sure if I was trying to convince them or myself.

No response from either woman. The nurse wheeled the gurney toward the morgue as I continued protesting all the way down the long corridor.

"Alex and Roman have been friends since fifth grade, and, and Richard — he's got a crush on Abby and is working up the nerve to ask her out! And Roman has a girlfriend now, Daniela — she's really pretty! They dress up and go to those Cosplay conventions together! Last time Roman was the Terminator and Daniela was Sarah Connor! How would I know that? How could I possibly know ANY of this if we'd lost Roman when he was a still a child?!?"

The nurse pushed open the morgue's door and there stood Rylah, the slim, fierce-eyed blonde I'd seen in Mike's newspaper photo. She was dressed in green scrubs, leaning over another draped table. Grinning, she yanked back the sheet to reveal the cadaver underneath. It was Abigail.

The shock jolted me back to my Charleston bedroom. Pages from the Vermicular File lay spilled across the bed and along the floor. I'd been attempting to shake off the 'dream fog' when the doorbell rang. Rylah was nowhere to be seen as I dashed through the family room and opened the front door, terrified of who might be waiting on the stoop. To my surprise it was Roman, smiling and apologetic.

"Hi, Mom! I know I was supposed to call before I showed up, but my plans changed, and I sort of forgot. Sorry."

A terrifying thought seared through me.

"Oh, God! Abby's not with you, is she?"

"No, I didn't stop by Aunt Ruthie's. Figured I go see her on the way home. Are you okay? You're all sweaty."

"I was having a nightmare."

"Nayhm thorrey, thad's too bayd," he slurred, still smiling.

"Why are you talking like that?"

151

"Nayhk whud?'

Roman's garbled speech sounded exactly like what I'd heard years ago, when the brain lesion had first taken hold of him.

"Stop doing that, Roman." Tears — and terror — were creeping up my throat. "It's not funny."

"Whudz nahd thuhnee?" My son staggered towards me, grabbing the back of his neck. "Mahy hed hurz."

Roman managed one last step before collapsing on the hallway floor. "Nayh jess cayhm to zay gud-bahee. Gud-bahee, Mahlm, nayh luhf yoo." Then his eyes went wide, boring through me.

"No!" I screamed, scooping him up and clutching him tight. His body began convulsing wildly. *Thank God. He's not dead!* When I looked down, I was longer holding my son; the writhing form in my arms was Rylah, cackling hysterically.

"Heard you talkin' to your boy earlier!" she taunted. "Thought you might fancy a little reunion."

I shrieked and pushed her to the ground. She lay there giggling as the doorbell rang.

"Wonder who *that* could be," she smirked.

Before I could take a step, Charles walked in, his nose shedding red drips onto the white tile floor. "Hey, *Madre,* I want to show you something," he said, motioning me onward. "Come see."

I drifted to the door. However instead of our garage, it opened to a narrow hall lined with metal lockers. Kerby Middle School, where Charles had attended seventh grade. As the two of us proceeded along, the beads of blood from Charles' nose became drops then splatters then puddles. I was about to ask my youngest if he felt okay when he stopped in front of an opening between the rows.

"Here we are!"

It was the Boys' restroom beside Charles' Social Studies classroom.

"The sink — you never got to see it," he giggled. "C'mon, I'll show you."

Inside was a row of metal washbasins, the furthest one smeared with bright red blood. A handful of scarlet-stained paper towels lay crumpled on the floor below.

"It's gross, but sort of funny, in a way, I guess," I said in a daze.

"Funny," Charles echoed. His nose was an open spigot; blood poured from his eyes and ears as well. "I should make mature and civilized decisions," he added, smiling. When he opened his mouth again, a thick red waterfall cascaded out.

"Charles, I should've taken this more seriously," I stammered. "Nosebleeds can be dangerous; you need to be careful…"

I grabbed a tissue to try to stem the flow, but when I pressed it against his upper lip, Charles' face caved in like a deflating balloon. The rest of him quickly followed. Within seconds, my boy had been reduced to a red puddle pooled around his clothes. Charles' thick black glasses sat atop the dark red mess.

A loud scream roused me: my own.

Am I really *awake now, or is this just the next round of my nightmare?* The nightstand clock read 8:18 a.m. and morning sunshine was spilling in between the slatted window blinds. I scratched my fingernails against my palms to test whether I was conscious — *does that even work?* — and a stab of pain lit up each hand. The 'Hell box' lay askew on the floor, pages from the Vermicular File scattered all over the bed. Something cold and metallic was pressing against my leg: the cassette recorder. I seized it and hit 'play,' and younger Miriam's voice issued forth, introducing the Fr. Frank interview. I clicked it off, fairly certain I was back to reality.

Through the bedroom door I could hear Rylah. It sounded like she was shuffling around the kitchen. I had no idea why; she obviously didn't need to eat. As soon as I entered the family room she stopped rooting, then peered over at me, holding up the locust husk and the Abby 'doll baby' she'd found hidden in the drawer. Panic bit again as I wondered what new horrors she was preparing to unleash with her vile recovered toys.

"You said you didn't need those anymore," I mumbled, feigning indifference. "Thought they were just for 'mirroring'

153

Abby — which you're already doing."

Rylah sneered, sizing me up. Once more, she couldn't decide which would be more satisfying: watching me agonize over *not* knowing what she was up to, or fretting over the latest torment headed my way. A few seconds lapsed, then her expression warmed, and she held up something else — the photo showing Sophie.

"So, *Mama*, you ready to get your girl back?"

"Why won't you say her name?"

Rylah grimaced.

"Abigail," I continued. "Her name, the person you're mimicking — poorly, I might add — is *Abigail*. Abby. Abs, even. But you don't ever refer to her by any of those; it's always 'your girl,' or 'your daughter.' You say 'Sophie' — no problem. Why can't you say her name, too?"

A storm raged in Rylah's stolen eyes; I felt once more how badly she wanted to rip me apart. Her hatred was rancid perfume, and I could smell it twenty feet away. She wouldn't answer the question, but that was all right. I didn't really care about the specifics, all that mattered was confirming Rylah was subject to rules and limits and restrictions. Her silence told me she wasn't invincible and if I found the right means, I could defeat her. That was all the response I needed. I left Rylah seething and headed out the door, anxious to gather more ammunition to use against her.

The Vermicular File had provided some truly valuable insights. Reviewing it reminded me evil isn't a monolith; it has striations, diversity, varieties, each specimen requiring its own distinct remedy. *Different strokes for different ghosts.* Rylah wasn't Levi, who loved visiting Hell and would commit horrible atrocities to get there; she *belonged* in the abyss but refused to go. Nor was she the Deathless Angel who abused others for pleasure and profit. To Rylah, the infliction of pain was its own reward. Invoking God wouldn't immediately dispel her as it had Fr. Frank's demons, although Rylah did find prayer irritating. I still needed more; I had to find something specific to vanquish a haint of Charleston lowcountry lore.

Bernadette was in the front parlor when I arrived at the Blue Heron. She'd been shelving books in the otherwise-empty room, pausing every now and then to read a back-cover blurb. When she saw me, she put down the stack, surprised I had come to visit on a Friday morning.

"Well hello, Miriam! Your father's not here. He's gone to the market."

I knew that. Friday was 'shopping day' at the Blue Heron, when the 9 a.m. shuttle bus would take residents to the grocery store and then the pharmacy. My dad went every week even if he didn't need anything, simply to get some fresh air and enjoy a change of scenery. I'd waited until the bus left before pulling into the parking lot and coming inside, not wanting him to see me. Dad would certainly ask where Abby was, and I knew I wouldn't be able to hold it together. On this morning, I had to stay absolutely clear-headed and *focus*.

"Oh, that's right," I said, then paused long enough so it wouldn't be obvious I'd actually come to see her before adding, "can you spare a couple minutes to chat?"

"Is everything all right with your father?" Bernadette asked, concerned.

"Oh, it's nothing like that! Dad's fine, loves it here. When I came by other day, you said something about haints — remember? Abby and I were on our way to Bandun Gate, and you said that wasn't such a good idea, the place had a rough reputation."

Bernadette's eyebrows crinkled together. "You didn't go, did you?"

Another pause. I didn't want to lie to her, but also didn't want to set off any alarm bells.

"We *did* go, actually, and you were right, it was creepy. We walked along the outside, didn't stay too long."

Bernadette stared at me. I wasn't able to tell if she felt worried or upset, or perhaps a bit of both.

"It was quite a construction," I continued. "Lots of interesting little tchotchkes attached. Everything painted Haint Blue. I was hoping maybe you could tell me more about those spirits, the haints."

155

Bernadette stepped toward me, surveying the room. "Let's go into my office," she said quietly. "We can talk there."

As we strode past the main desk, I spotted a tray of fruit and pastries. It hit me I'd hardly eaten anything the last two days, so I grabbed a blueberry muffin and a banana, and began nibbling as we walked. When we arrived at Bernadette's office, she made sure to close the door behind her before she began speaking.

"What do you want to know?"

"Well, I already know some of the basics — haints can't cross over water, they're compulsive, they're mean, they prey on the living."

"They *envy* the living," Bernadette corrected. "They don't want to leave this world — don't want to face what's waiting for them on the other side. That's the engine of their villainy."

"So, if they're onto you, how can you outsmart them?"

"Well, there's ways to throw them off your track. When you leave a cemetery, erase your footprints as you go so they can't follow you home. You can distract haints by pasting your windows with newspaper — they're nosy, and will stop to read every word. Sometimes you can pay them off by leaving money on their grave. Coins. Shiny ones work best."

I finished off the muffin as Bernadette spoke, trying not to appear nervous. *I wish all Rylah wanted from me was money — I'd rob every bank in South Carolina to ransom Abby back.*

"What if one comes after you directly, *targets* you and won't let up, what then? Call Ghostbusters?"

"A bottle tree might catch 'em," she said, ignoring my sarcasm. "You put empties on it upside down, and the haints go inside to investigate and can't find their way out again. If that doesn't work and the vexing gets worse, you need help from a root doctor. You want to stop a haint before it gets too close, too powerful. They have ways to make themselves stronger, like paralyzing you with fear or stealing the breath of a sleeping person…"

"… or putting flowers on their own grave?" I uttered, remembering the visit to that desolate burial plot.

Bernadette frowned, suspicious.

"What's going on?" she asked sternly. "Where is your daughter?"

"Abby went to Myrtle Beach for a few days. Dan's sister lives up there."

Unconvinced, Bernadette glowered at me.

"Seriously," I said, trying to smile, "she went to visit her aunt."

I polished off the banana and told Bernadette I should be on my way so she could get back to work. When I hesitated at the door, her expression softened.

"I know a woman, Isata — she does root work, white magic," she offered. "Not far from here. She knows all about haints and conjure. I'm sure she would talk with you."

Bernadette gave me the address, then made a quick phone call telling Isata to expect me. I thanked her and grabbed another muffin on my way out, hoping this next stop would be my last.

Isata lived in a typical Gullah village comprised of small ranch-style homes and spruce trailers set in rows around a large communal garden. The plot was planted with okra, tomatoes, peanuts, sweet potatoes, corn and cantaloupe depending on the season, its harvest shared among the community's families. And, of course, several rows were devoted to traditional Gullah medicinal plants: snakeroot, bitter apple and Helichrysum arenarium, better known as 'Everlasting Flower.' On the far end of the garden a little wooden chapel, or 'praise house,' hosted Sunday worship services as well as Bible studies and prayer meetings throughout the week.

Isata was waiting by the sand-silt road when I arrived. She waved a hearty 'hello.'

"You must be Bernadette's curious buckruh!" she laughed.

"*Buckruh*?"

"White folk."

I reached out to shake hands, but she pulled me in for a hug, cradling me as if we were old friends. The lively woman was short and plump, dressed in a purple dress printed with turquoise elephants, a wide-brimmed straw hat resting on her coiled salt-and-pepper braids. She had a youthful face and easy smile that made it difficult to peg her age. I'd guess she was mid-sixties.

"Gumbo day," Isatat said, breaking her embrace and heading towards the garden. "Tag along, we can talk. Bernadette says you got questions, how to be shed of a haint."

We walked the okra patch, snapping bright green pods from their sun-scorched stalks. As we filled her container, Isata asked me about my background.

"I was born in Washington, D.C., grew up in the Northern Virginia suburbs. Just moved to this area a few months ago. Been vacationing here for years, though. Our family's always loved Charleston."

"Oooh-wee, *Washin'ton!*" Isata chortled, scrunching up her face. "You got a whole different kinda devil up there! Wearin' a suit and carryin' a briefcase instead of a pitchfork!"

We both chuckled as we moved on to collecting orangey-red tomatoes off the summer vines.

"Though I s'pose scoundrels just about everywhere like to hide their true selves, wear different skin. We got that here, too. Haints, plat-eyes, boo hags, slip-skins, all tryin' their best to fool us. Tell me 'bout this haint that's vexin' you."

"It's the spirit of a woman who died in a fire, I'm pretty sure. Name's Rylah. She was cruel, liked to torture children. I think her neighbors killed her and buried her in the woods near her old house."

"How'd she put the root on you?"

"She's after my daughter, actually. Abby. Got into our house in the body of a locust, then made something she calls a 'doll baby' with Abby's fingernails and hair."

"Oh, that's powerful," Isata whispered. "How's she doin', your Abby?"

"Not so good. She's got headaches, like a terrible buzzing in her brain."

"Sound from the locust. Haint put the torment on her, won't stop 'til the bad spirit's gone for good. You got anythin' of hers, this Rylah? Lock a'her hair, her fingernails?"

I shook my head. "Nothing."

"Tools work real well, too," Isata offered, optimistic. "A spoon or comb or the like. Eyeglasses. Lipstick. Somethin' she used, left her imprint on, 'specially if it was right before the end. Or somethin' that was special to her, had particular meanin'. You write her name on a piece a'paper, fold whatever you got inside, then hold it up," Isata thrust a fist into the air, "in front'a her, like this. It'll bend her will to yours. Won't destroy this Rylah, but can make her do what you say."

"I don't have anything like that, either," I replied, searching my mind. "There are chunks of brick and rubble from her house that survived the fire. I could get one of those. Would that work?"

"You sure the house was hers. She the owner?"

I sighed, deflated. I had no idea whose house it really was. For all I knew, Rylah had rented it from some local family, or maybe she'd been squatting in the old shack without the owner even knowing she was there. The place could've sat abandoned for decades before the hateful wretch moved in and ultimately brought about its destruction. If there was time, I could determine the address, track down old property records, discover whose name was on the deed. But time was something I simply didn't have.

I shook my head. "I'm not sure."

"I wouldn't try it then. You go at a haint that way without somethin' powerful and she'll cut you down where you stand. S'prised she hasn't done you in already."

"She can't, I don't think. I'm pretty sure she isn't able to really hurt me at all. I brought her over the waterways …"

Isata's eyes went wide, stopping me mid-sentence.

"Not on purpose!" I clarified. "It was when she was the insect in my daughter's hair; I had no idea Rylah even *existed* then. I brought her to our house, which thank God is surrounded by water — creeks and a culvert, wetlands — so she's stuck there. She can't harm me, and she can't get away, at least for now."

"Or lie to you."

"What?"

"Spirits in your debt cannot lie," Isata explained. "You can't force her to talk to you, but whatever she says gotta be truthful."

Finally, something big I could use against Rylah! No wonder she wouldn't answer uncomfortable questions — I thought she was just being obstinate, but she'd been protecting her secrets. Now that I knew this, even if I couldn't make her answer me, I'd be able to glean a lot from what she'd refuse to say. It wouldn't be as simple as 'hey Rylah, tell me your Achilles heel,' but years of conducting interviews had taught me how to read people, how to interpret silences as well as responses. I was ready for a probing conversation.

First I had to ask Isata the most important question of all. "What if I *can't* get rid of the haint? What happens to Abby if I can't make Rylah go away?"

Isasta shook her head solemnly. "Hag'll ride her 'tll your girl's all spent. Wear her down. The buzzin' in Abby's head will keep gettin' louder and louder, drown everything else out, sapping the life outta her. You gotta get the jump on a haint or it'll just keep on 'till it gets its way, one way or the other."

Her basket brimming with morning harvest, I walked Isata back to her house. When we reached the porch, the woman climbed onto the second step so she could look me in the eye.

"Best advice I got — get this haint off your Abby, *quick.* Longer she's ridin' your girl, worse it's gonna get. And be wary trustin' your eyes — not all is what it seems."

"What do you mean?"

"Just 'cause this Rylah can't fib you, don't mean she won't try an' trick you. She *looks* like Abby but she's not. Other things can look like what they ain't. You ever see a gator after dusk-dark, or a horse looks too big to be real? They're conjure-animals, from the same dark pit Rylah hails from. Lots a'other dangers too. She can make you see things *not* there as well."

Isata was right; Rylah had already demonstrated her mind-scrambling powers over me with those terrible dreams.

A huge crow, shimmering blue-black with wild sable eyes, appeared overhead as Isata finished speaking. It swooped down and landed beside us on the lawn. The bird turned towards me and let out a belligerent squawk.

"Oh my God!" I gasped. "What is *that*?"

Isata stepped down to take a closer look. After examining the winged creature, she put her hand on my shoulder, stood on tiptoe and whispered in my ear, "that, my buckrah gal, is what we a call 'a crow.'"

She burst out laughing as the affronted bird returned to the skies.

Another drive through the mystical marshlands, another session of soul-searching. The lonely road's stoplight turned red to green, to red, and back again, while I sat lost in thought, no one behind me to honk in protest. I wondered whether I should take a right, head home to interrogate Rylah, hoping she might slip and give something up vital, or if I should go left, back to the old ruins and the gravestone with no name to seek some relic of the cruel phantom. It was almost noon; Sophie was due to arrive in less than nine hours, Roman and Charles not far behind her. Whatever I was going to do it had to be done *now* — the clock was quickly ticking down to zero.

Option one: I could be home in a matter of minutes to begin quizzing Rylah. She might reveal some usable tidbit that could lead to her undoing. And even if I failed, at least I'd be on hand when Sophie showed up so I could shield her from Rylah, send her safely away. And I'd also be around to see what Rylah had planned for unsuspecting houseguests; perhaps she'd turn out to be all bark and no bite, unable to do anything more than frighten the living. The downside, of course, was if she *did* harm Sophie or anyone else, I would be the one going to jail, and Abby would remain exposed and vulnerable.

Option two: It would take me at least forty-five minutes to drive to the old shack, if I could even find it again. What then? Break off a piece charred brick, pry a bit of stone from the crumbled chimney, fold the bits up in notepaper bearing Rylah's name, all the while praying the property was officially hers so my talisman would actually work? If I guessed wrong, she'd wipe out everyone I loved and keep her rampage rolling.

Of course, there was another possibility regarding that site. I pictured myself digging up Rylah's grave with some improvised tool, coming upon her skeletal remains and snatching a tuft of brittle hair, or perhaps a fractured bone. I wasn't even certain the body buried behind the ruined house was truly Rylah's; the decaying corpse might simply be another 'skin' she'd 'worn' like Kadisha Fontaine. *Like she was planning to wear Abby.* Rylah could've been prowling the lowcountry for centuries, the wife of one of the Goose Creek Men who repaid kindness with death, or the daughter of a slaver kidnapping African botanists and forcing them into inhuman servitude. Her evil soul might well have been going from one body to another for generations, leaving agony and heartbreak in her brutal wake.

And then there was the metal box. It must've been important; Rylah chose to burn alive rather than leave it behind. Whoever this ghost once was, I had no doubt the container and its contents were inseparably tied to her. How long would it take me to unearth the little trunk and wrestle it from the corpse's grip? And was I prepared for what I might find inside — implements of witchcraft, mementos of terror, the tiny finger bones of Sammy Watkins charred black from the fire. Worse yet, what if I dredged handful after handful of dirt from the gravesite and never found anything at all? The box and the body both vanished without a trace, just like Teresa and her Deathless Angel.

Option three: I didn't want to let myself think about option three. Option three was handing over Sophie to the monster, thus becoming complicit in her demise. That's a burden I would carry forever, no matter how happy I'd be that Abby was spared. Option three took me from being Rylah's accidental familiar to becoming her willing accomplice in murder. It would fundamentally redefine who I am.

The pressure to choose a course of action and commit to it was crushing. I dreaded the thought of this becoming another decision I'd be second-guessing the rest of my life.

I had been at a life-altering crossroads before, though the stakes were nothing so dire. In early 2003, my agent Nina had phoned to tell me a New York City publisher wanted to interview me for a research-staff position. The company specialized in compilation books, and a senior editor had been impressed with *Encyclopedia of Hell* and thought I had potential. Most of the work could be done remotely via computer, so it wouldn't require moving to the Big Apple, though there would be occasional travel involved. I was so excited I'd driven to Dan's office to tell him the good news in person.

"I need to fly up Monday night to meet with them early Tuesday," I'd gushed. "Then I'll sit in on a production meeting Wednesday, get to know everyone. If it looks like it's working out, I'll have a second-round interview Friday with the head of research. Nina says she thinks I'd be a great fit!"

Instead of a big smile, Dan gave me a reluctant stare. "So — you'd be gone all week? Are they paying for your trip up there, and the hotel?"

"Well, no…"

"How 'bout the kids? I've got that trade show in Baltimore next week. We'd need somebody to watch them until I get home."

"I haven't even thought about that…"

Starry-eyed at the prospect of being a full-time writer, I hadn't stopped to consider any of the details: how much the initial trip would cost, who would fill in on the home-front, what sacrifices would be necessary to make this happen. And it wasn't like the disruptions would be limited to the week-long interview, either. If I got the job, the research and editorial work could be done from home, but I'd still be required to go to New York at least a few days a month. Plus I'd be 'on call' pretty much all the time. If the publishers wanted me to do an interview in Chicago or attend an event in Denver, I wouldn't be able to tell them, 'sorry, Charles has basketball practice' or, 'Abby has a dentist appointment that day.' This career move would mean radical changes for our entire family.

It also didn't help that money was really tight back then. Dan and I had recently taken out a second mortgage to convert loft space into a bedroom for Abby, and we'd still had to max out our credit cards to complete it. Nina assured me this job would be a great way to make connections and get noticed, which could lead to a big payday down the road. Until that time, however, my salary would barely cover travel expenses, much less childcare. There was no room in our budget for such a massive hit.

The timing was bad, too. Dan was attending college three nights a week and traveling for business at least once a month. With me away, that would've meant hiring someone to watch Roman, Abby and Charles not just after school, but evenings and weekends as well. My 'big opportunity' was looking more and more like a costly gamble.

"I'm sure we can make this work, if it's really what you want," Dan had said, trying to sound positive. My Catholic guilt pushed back; I felt like I was selling out my husband and children to indulge artistic vanity. And I worried the stress of it all would sour whatever time I would have with Dan and the kids between New York stints.

In the end, it really wasn't a choice. I stayed home and enjoyed being 'Mom,' telling myself I'd get another break in a year or two. The kids would be older then, and our financial situation more solid. Soon it would be my turn to let 'writer Miriam' shine. Meanwhile, Dan's career was fast-tracked, and I went back to freelancing for the local paper and publishing an occasional magazine article or short story.

Before I knew it, more than a decade had slipped by while I was busy with bake sales and community theatre reviews and parent-teacher conferences.

I can't say I regret it, exactly. I loved watching the kids grow up, and I treasured the memories we made together. Still, over the years I've often wondered what might've happened if I had gone to New York when I'd had the chance and tried my luck at being a full-time professional author. Who would I be now if things had been different then? That unanswerable question was its own illusory ghost.

At least *that* decision had an upside. This time there were no good outcomes; I would lose my daughter, or I would lose my soul. The traffic light turned another cycle as I stared at the empty passenger seat where Abby — *my* Abigail — had so recently been riding shotgun. I pressed my forehead against the steering wheel and gazed down at the floor, the air from the vents cool against my cheeks as I held back tears. *Please, God, there has to be an escape from this nightmare — please show me the way.*

By the time I pulled into the garage I had made a decision. Like Mike Fontaine, torn between his love for Didi and his reluctance to resort to extreme measures in her name, I knew exactly what had to be done.

Chapter Twelve
This is Goodbye

I had to proceed with extreme caution. This was my one shot at getting Abby back, and even the smallest mistake could prove fatal. Rylah couldn't lie to me, okay, but did that mean she'd know if I were lying to her? That was a risk I couldn't take. From the moment I returned to the house, every single word I uttered had to be truthful. It was time for me to be nice and play along.

"Rylah? We need to talk!"

No answer, so I went looking for her. She wasn't in the family room or the kitchen, and though I doubted she'd be in my bedroom I checked there, too. Nothing. I walked the backyard, then circled around the house, and still no Rylah. *What if she's gone? Could she have gotten free somehow — is she on her way to Myrtle Beach to finish Abby off?* Heart beating wildly and sweating from the summer heat, I dashed back inside and resumed my search.

"Rylah? Rylah! Where are you? Answer me!"

I was combing the office-nook-turned-Sophie's-guestroom when I heard rustling upstairs and rushed to investigate. As I reached the top of the landing, Rylah stuck her head out of the bathroom.

"No need getting' yourself in a tizzy, Mama," she scoffed. "I'm right here!"

"What are you doing up here?"

She popped back into the bathroom then emerged holding the Abby doll-baby, the locust shell, and the photograph of Sophie.

"Just waitin' on you to decide you're ready to get your girl back."

I had no idea what Rylah meant, but her explanation would

have to wait. For now, the two of us stood in the hallway sizing each other up. We both knew we were playing the same game but by different rules, with Abby's life the grand prize. Driving home, I'd come up with a list of questions for this fiend and decided this was a good time to spring them on her, hoping to catch her off guard.

"Why do you need a real body, Rylah? Isn't this 'mirroring' thing better? Seems like you can still wreak havoc, and you don't have to worry about being hurt or killed."

She gave me that annoyed, impatient glare again. I could tell she was trying to come up with a response that would cause me maximum distress, while yielding nothing I could use against her. *Abby never makes that face — plenty of others when she's miffed — but never that one.* I didn't wait for an answer and moved on.

"Why didn't you kill Mike Fontaine? You had plenty of opportunity — could've done it whenever you wanted. Or you could've taken your time torturing him when it was just the two of you at the house, no one to stop you. But you kept him around, why? What did he have that you wanted? You didn't need him to get past water — you had Kadisha's body and could go wherever you liked."

Still nothing. I adjusted my strategy.

"Mike told me you were always watching him drive when you two were in the car. Learning, maybe, so you could do it by yourself? Why'd you want to drive, Rylah? Where were you planning to go?"

Icy silence, chilling stares.

"You might as well tell me, because until I get some answers, we're not going to talk about Sophie or Bandun Gate or anything you *do* care about. Now *why* did you want to learn to drive?"

"I already knew how to operate a motorcar!" she snapped indignantly. "Just not with all those contraptions!"

Right, that made sense. Rylah's knowledge and experience with technology would've ended in the late 1940s. She'd have known the basics of driving like steering, speeding up, braking, shifting gears, but a modern dashboard with digital readouts, onboard GPS and a dozen light-up indicators would be as confounding as an airplane's cockpit. In any case, Rylah had tacitly admitted she was in fact trying to master the skill. I needed to push to find out where she was headed, although I already had a pretty good idea of her intended destination.

"Was it that metal box?" I said, watching her reaction. "Buried in your grave. Were you planning to drive there, dig it up, reclaim it?"

I braced myself for another 'Rylah's disgusting hands on me' attack. Instead, she gave me that curdled smirk.

"You're clever, *Mama*. But I know what you're doin', and it won't work. That chest doesn't belong to me — never has. *I* belong to *it*."

She knows I've discovered her 'possession' vulnerability.

"How do you know I don't have it already, Rylah? Maybe I went out to your old place, dug it up myself. Maybe I've got it right now, and I'm going to use it to get Abby back and destroy you once and for all."

Rylah let out a shrill laugh that sounded nothing like Abigail's light-hearted chuckling.

"That's quite the picture — you, a grave-robbin' Mama! Course, you wouldn't be standin' here if you'd come anywhere *near* that box!" Her voice became brittle. "I dare say you'd never *stand* again if you'd laid hands on it. Besides, I'd smell it on you if you'd gotten anywhere close. All I smell is the stench of some hoodoo root doctor, for all the good *that* foolishness will do you."

"So what's inside it?"

"Do you *really* wanna know?"

I should have said 'no' and gotten back to my list. Instead, I hesitated, letting my imagination run wild with morbid curiosity. What *was* in that box, I wondered, that cost Rylah her life, first in the housefire then again when she ran out of time waiting to unearth while masquerading as Kadisha Fontaine? A parade of ugly images shambled through mind: vials of clotted blood, decomposing rodent carcasses, the severed bones of children. The box's contents also surely included Rylah's personal grimoire, filled with hexes and incantations, and methods to bring horror and bloodshed to those around her. Souvenirs, too, of past exploits and atrocities…

Rylah interrupted my musings, running a frigid hand along my shoulder.

"Do you really wanna know, Mama?" she repeated.

Before I could respond, Rylah thrust her finger into my mouth, pinching my left cheek. The agonizing sensations returned, only this time, the snake was inside me, slithering from my stomach into my lungs, around my heart, finally doing loops through my skull. Rylah said something but the words were muffled by the viper's coil. As it slid back down my throat I began retching, vomiting the reptile from my body.

When I opened my eyes, I was no longer in the upstairs hallway, but at the foot of Rylah's walled-in grave, watching the long black snake slither into the woods. The ground rumbled, and suddenly the dirt began erupting to the right and left, like Moses parting the Red Sea. This displacement revealed a plain wooden coffin, decayed and blotted with mildew. Its lid flung open, and skeletal arms lifted Rylah's mysterious box towards me. A feverish scratching sound came from inside the dark metal chest, as if some crazed animal was trying to claw its way out. The latch popped loose, and the box opened about an inch or so. Tiny sliced-off fingers, scores of them in every skin tone, crawled from the gap like worms, oozing blood as they fell to the ground and fled.

Rylah spoke again, her voice a distant thunderstorm. I couldn't decipher the message, although I could tell she was laughing. My attention remained fixed on the box, its lid rising slowly as the throng of the butchered fingers inched away. I peered inside. At first the container appeared to be empty, showing me nothing but velvety, seductive blackness.

When you look into the abyss, the abyss looks into you.

Then the ebony void started roiling, swirling, dotted with little gray-green bugs — fleas, maybe, or aphids. As I watched, the churning specks grew larger until I could see they were locusts with human faces, each contorted in a silent scream. The swarm flew off in a buzzing blur until only one

169

remained. The lone monstrosity hovered on the lid's edge, its eyes pleading, aching. The face of this final insect was Abby's.

I turned to run and was back in my upstairs hallway, Rylah no longer touching me.

"Any more questions 'bout that box, Mama?' she snickered. "I didn't think so. Now, where were we? Oh yes, that man — *Fontaine* — ten days was all I needed. Just ten days 'til dark of the moon, then I could retrieve my treasure and dispatch that distasteful little man. I had such plans for his demise!"

"But he beat you to the punch," I whispered, not realizing I'd said it out loud.

Rylah bolted towards me, baring her teeth. I recoiled so quickly I lost my balance and fell backwards against the wall. She was preparing to savage me once more, but in her haste, she dropped the tissue-doll. That stopped her cold. She bent and picked it up gingerly, the phony smile returning to her lips.

"Let's not talk about the past. You and I got business regardin' the future. *Your girl's future*. You don't want her languishin' in her present state, now, do you? We best focus on that."

My mind harkened back to Kristen, locked in that sweltering, stinking trailer as the Deathless Angel abused her. Despite the abysmal conditions, she still had the presence of mind to formulate a plan, to dupe Andromeda and get away. If I wanted to reclaim *my* life, I'd need to tap into that same calm resolve.

"You *owe* it to your girl to get her back," Rylah scolded playfully. "After all, you're the one who lost her. And consider this, Mama. Anythin' bad happens, it'll be her that haunts you, not me. She'll come to you in your dreams. Is that somethin' you can bear the rest of your days?"

Another memory surfaced: Dr. Mackey handing me the card of a grief and loss counselor who'd help me plan Roman's funeral. Rylah knew how to get to me; I'd already faced the possibility of burying a child, and I could not go through that again.

Rylah held up the photo of Sophie and the boys at the Irish Festival. She tore off the sections showing Charles and Ethan and tossed them away, leaving only the image of her requested 'skin.' In the other hand Rylah clutched the tissue doll-baby, rocking it back and forth in a ghostly dance.

"Who's gonna live, Mama? This girl you *detest*, or your own flesh and blood? Who's gonna get to find a beau, walk down the aisle, give her folks grandbabies someday? Which one'll have a future, and which girl will perish this very night? Time for you to choose!"

The world went quiet as the past wrapped itself around me like a blanket. *Hearing the doctor say, 'it's a girl.' Infant Abby's first smile. A green-eyed toddler in a frilly pink dress. Dropping Abby off at kindergarten. My girl and her brothers playing hide and seek in the backyard. Abby looking like a miniature bride in her white communion gown. Dan building sandcastles with his daughter on Isle of Palms. A teenage beauty at prom. Scary Abs in her Zombie High make-up. Abby laughing beside me on the back porch two days ago as we munched barbecue and potato salad.*

I wasn't ready to let the memories end there.

"We'll go to Bandun Gate tonight," I muttered. "Head over when it starts getting dark. I'll make some phone calls and set everything up."

Rylah let out a triumphant *woop!* before scampering to the bathroom. I followed, curious. When I got to the door, she was scratching something onto Sophie's picture, then rubbed the photo furiously against the doll-baby. Both burst into flames as she cradled them in cupped palms. Just before the curling photograph turned black, I caught sight of what she'd etched across Sophie's face — jagged letters spelling out 'Rylah.'

Moving with unnatural speed, she drew a circle on the tile floor with the ashes, adding a few frenzied details. I recognized the candelabrum-looking sigil immediately. Rylah stepped inside, chanting some undecipherable phrase. Her body caught fire and she emitted a thick, feral growl. I couldn't tell if was from agony or joy. The flames abruptly ceased, and Rylah remained unscathed, delighted to see me so unnerved.

171

"What the Hell!?" I shouted, grabbing a towel and rubbing the ashen symbol. "I don't want your demon-scrawl crap in my house!"

"You best be careful with your sass."

"*Really*, Rylah? What are you and your Satan friends gonna do to me worse than threatening my daughter's life? And what's with this little altar thing here? You said whatever transformation you do has to be at Bandun Gate."

"I wasn't 'transformin',' Mama. Just makin' a pledge is all — here, where it started. Don't get your bloomers in a twist."

I pulled a trash bag from under the sink, wadded up the towel and shoved it in.

"Where it started?" I echoed, mulling her statement. "That first night, you mean. Dumping out the bathroom trash. Collecting Abby's used tissues. Your midnight snot-snack when you were a locust."

"A temporary vessel," she protested. "But as I said, why talk about the past when we have such *grand* adventures ahead of us?"

"Just tell me whatever that ritual was — it hasn't hurt Abby."

"No harm done, cross my heart," Rylah said, making an exaggerated 'X' over her chest.

"What about Sophie?"

"She's perfectly fine, too. *For now.*"

I let out a sigh, relieved my daughter was a hundred miles away. I was fairly sure Rylah couldn't do anything else to Abby from such a distance; all the witch had of my girl was a bit of hair, some mucus, a few nail clippings — all of it dead. Enough to commit corporeal identify theft, apparently, but no part of Abby's living soul. Rylah had even less of Sophie, just an old photo with her name scribbled onto Sophie's face. No, the final showdown was still to come.

Although, if I had realized *then* the terrible power of the ceremony I had just witnessed, I would have done *everything* that followed differently.

There was a lot to do before Rylah and I could leave for the marshlands. First, I needed to go online and get directions for Sophie's revised destination, then contact Charles to relay them to her. I told Rylah it would be better if Sophie met us at Bandun Gate rather than come to the house — even someone as self-absorbed as Sophie would sense something was seriously off, and she'd be much less likely to be spotted by anyone else. Rylah agreed, not wanting to scare off her new 'vessel' before the exchange could take place.

Suspicious I might have second thoughts and try backing out of the deal, Rylah hovered close by as I dialed Charles' number. When she heard me tell him there'd been a change of plans and he needed to update Sophie, she gave a satisfied sneer. I retreated to my bedroom and slammed the door before continuing the conversation, away from Rylah's smug snickering. By the time I came out, the *Encyclopedia of Hell* pages that had been decorating the family room were gone and all the scattered photos stacked neatly on the shelf. To all outward appearances, the place appeared normal.

"What did you tell your boy?" Rylah asked when I emerged from my bedroom.

"I told him I had to be somewhere when Sophie was due to arrive, could he give her the re-route information to meet-up."

"And what'd he say?"

"He said he'd call her and give her the directions."

"Well done, Mama."

Rylah's approval was even worse than her scorn; winning that monster's praise made my stomach turn. I saw she still had Abby's Social Distortion shirt on, which sent fresh waves of revulsion through me. Under no circumstances was I going to let Rylah take *anything* of Abby's to Bandun Gate. I fished an old bathrobe with nail polish stains on the sleeve from the garage rag pile for her to wear. Since the garment had been discarded it no longer had an 'owner,' so I figured Rylah couldn't use it to harm any of us.

"Take off Abby's stuff — you can wear this."

"I don't want it," she said flatly. "I'll strip off your girl's clothing if that's vexin' you. I'm fine wearin' nothin' at all."

173

She thinks I'm trying to trick her with a possession — that once she accepts it, I'll use it against her.

"You're just *borrowing* it," I reassured her. "It's not yours. After tonight it goes back in the trash. I can't be driving around Charleston with a naked woman in my van."

Rylah wasn't convinced. "You know, Mama," she snarled, "once I renounce your girl, any deference I extended to you *ends*. You try crossin' me and I will bathe in your blood while you beg for mercy, understand? Then I promise I'll do worse to your man, your boys and ev'ryone else you care about. You got that?"

"I got it." I nodded. "Now put this on. Cross *my* heart, it's not a trap — it's just a bathrobe."

"I don't trust you."

"I don't trust you, either, but I want Abby back, and I want you *gone*. That means getting to the gate without any problems. A nude woman riding shotgun through Charleston is a potential problem. You want me to swear? Okay, I swear on my daughter's life I will NOT try any shenanigans regarding this robe. Happy?"

One last sneer, then Rylah snatched the garment from my hand.

She shed Abby's clothes, and I immediately put them in the washing machine, then poured in half a bottle of detergent and ran it on the hottest setting. Over the following days, I would launder this load three more times, including a vigorous hand-scrubbing using holy water from the font at St. John's Cathedral.

Next, I took a duffle bag from the hall closet to pack for the return to Bandun Gate. I'd been thinking in terms of a couple flashlights and an umbrella since it had been raining on and off all day, but Rylah had a very different idea of what we'd need. At her direction, I added rope, a utility knife, matches, razor blades, pliers, rubbing alcohol and duct tape to our gear. She wanted to include smelling salts, too, but I didn't have any. I didn't ask what plans she had for any of these items. I did not want to know.

As I tossed a pair of latex gloves into the satchel, a term I'd heard on *Criminal Minds* echoed back to me: 'murder kit.' *Only this time, I'm the culprit, amassing components for some illicit act.* The last thing I slipped in before zipping the bag shut was a crystal rosary my sister Mary had brought me from Rome. It felt oddly out of place among the tools of treachery, however I thought it might come in handy — not only had the beads been blessed, their lustrous aqua color was a close match to Haint Blue.

With sundown fast approaching, I finally had everything in place. The house was back in order. Anyone dropping by would have no clue as to macabre drama that had been playing out over the last few days. I'd filled my tank with gas after leaving Isata's, and the duffle bag was stashed behind the passenger seat. Rylah, wearing the frayed white robe with its red-splotched left sleeve, crouched by the front door awaiting our departure. I wish I could say I had made peace with the plan I was about to put into play, but that wasn't the case. The best I could manage was to promise myself that I'd see it through to its conclusion, no matter what.

There was one last task to complete before heading to Bandun Gate, and it would be the most difficult: I had to call Dan. It was 4 p.m. on the west coast, so I knew he might be in a meeting and unable to talk, but that was okay. Reaching his voicemail would be enough. I just wanted to hear his voice again. *Needed* to hear his voice.

I fumbled with the keypad. I had an overwhelming urge to tell him everything about Abby and Rylah and the recent horrors unfolding in our Charleston home. After all, wouldn't I have wanted the opportunity to weigh in on Abby's fate if our roles had been reversed? And didn't he have the right to know he might be losing his only daughter, so at least he'd have a chance to say goodbye? How could I keep such a huge secret from him?

I put the phone down and waited for the feeling to pass. Nothing good could've come from sharing that information with Dan. He would've thought I'd gone crazy, which was still a better alternative to believing Abby was in mortal danger and he was powerless to help. *That* would have crushed him. Or worse, it might lead to a fight over how to handle the situation. Dan wouldn't have time to fly back and stop me from returning to Bandun Gate, but he could've tried pressuring me to abandon my plans. Maybe he'd flat out tell me not to go, then I would've had to defy him. I couldn't bear the thought of proceeding if Dan was actively rooting against me, but my mind was made up. This is what had to be done.

I drew comfort knowing my omission absolved him of any blame. If I'd sold Dan on my proposal for dealing with Rylah and he'd condoned it, that would've made him part of everything about to occur. I didn't need that burden. I was already feeling guilty enough about Abby without having Dan's fate on my conscious, too. He was the person who had shown me, literally *shown* me, that eternity was more than some vague, inscrutable philosophic notion.

In 1988, February 14 fell on a Sunday, which meant Dan and I could spend our first Valentine's Day together. If it had been a Saturday, his band would've been performing, and weekdays were rough all-around schedule-wise, so there's no way we both would've had time off. I worked days, and Dan was on the night shift. He left for his job about an hour before I got home from mine. Our one overlap of free time was Sunday, and we were going to make the most of it this romantic holiday.

We went to The Bayou, an iconic nightclub in Georgetown. It was a cavernous, two-story brick building with interior balconies that overlooked the stage and dancefloor. The venue was famous for hosting live shows featuring up-and-comers (U2 played there when they were still nobodies) as well as rock legends like Kiss, Bon Jovi, Meatloaf, Blue Oyster Cult. In between marquis attractions, entertainment was provided by The Bayou's house band or by a 'VJ' who showed footage from past concerts.

Our Valentine party included Dan's bandmates and their girlfriends. Mike, the drummer and his fiancé Glenda, and lead singer / guitarist Tony and his future-wife Melanie, shared our table. The place was packed, the air was heavy with the blended scent of perfume, aftershave and cigarette smoke, and the vibe was high-energy. We ordered a round of drinks, resorting to hand signals to communicate over the din.

"Big crowd tonight!" Tony noted as we waited for our cocktails.

Mike nodded, extending his hand to Glenda. "C'mon, babe. Let's get out on the dancefloor while there's still room."

The couple, quickly joined by Tony and Melanie, disappeared into the partying throng.

Dan leaned over to me. "We've never danced together, have we?" he said.

"Nope. Every time we're at a club, you're always hugging your B.C. Rich."

"Well, you're in luck! I left my bass home tonight. Just tonight, mind you. Special occasion and all."

"Then what are we waiting for?"

The two of us glided onto the dancefloor as the last notes of the B-52s' *Rock Lobster* faded out. The tech cued up the next video clip, a slow song perfect for lovers on Valentine's Day: *Don't Dream It's Over* recorded during Crowded House's concert the previous spring. Dan wrapped his arms around my waist and pulled me close, and we swayed to the gentle tune. When they came to lyrics about how the journey never ends for lovers traveling together, he leaned in for a tender kiss.

And in that instant, I comprehended something that had eluded me throughout twelve years of Catholic schooling, a truth no book could ever adequately convey — I finally grasped the concept of 'everlasting.' *Felt* it, deep in my soul. Catechism classes and Sunday sermons had given me an intellectual framework for conceptualizing 'eternity,' however it was the difference between listening to someone describe the color orange and seeing sunrise over the ocean. This was vibrant and palpable and alive; I was part of it, and it was part of me. I knew in that moment the love I felt for Dan would never die.

Now, more than a quarter century later, I was dialing his number and steeling myself for a conversation I did *not* want to have.

"Hey, Bunner," Dan said, three thousand miles away. He was smiling, I could hear it in his voice. "What's up?"

"I miss you." Whatever else, I was not going to lie to him tonight, either. "Just wanted to chat a bit. How are things in Seattle?"

"Okay. Had a great lunch today — filet mignon and crab legs. It was fantastic. Top five, definitely. The software demo went great too, I crushed it."

"Sounds like a pretty good day."

A few quiet seconds.

"You all right, Miriam? You sound kinda, I don't know — down."

I waited a beat, choosing my words carefully.

"I was just thinking about that song *Don't Dream It's Over*." I held back captive tears. "Remember that night at the Bayou, our first-ever dance?"

"I remember. Tony and Melanie were there. Mike and Glen, too. You wore that green dress with the ruffly skirt. It was a fantastic night."

"Yeah, it was," I said, my voice cracking a bit. "I love you in that song, Dan. Always have. Still do."

"Oh, Bunner. I love you, too. Hey, Bob's calling. I gotta take this. Want me to call you back in a few?"

"No, it's fine. I know you've got a lot going on. Just wanted to say hello."

"I'm glad you called. Miss you lots. Give Abby a hug for me. Can't wait to see you both again."

I hung up the phone.

Dan loved the boys, but Abby was his heart.

"I'm not coming back without her," I said to no one. "I swear it on my soul."

The Myrtle branches cast long spindly shadows across the front lawn. Our house appeared odd, almost alien, as I pulled out of the driveway, stopping for one last look before heading to Bandun Gate. I reached behind the seat into the duffle bag, retrieved the rosary and put it around my neck.

"You really think those silly beads gonna protect you?" Rylah laughed. "You're way past that now! Time's come to be nice and play along."

"Look — this is how it's going to work. I'm going to drive, and you're going to be quiet until we get there. We have nothing to say to each other. Got it?"

"Whatever you say, Mama."

"Oh, one last thing. Don't call me 'Mama' again — *ever*."

Chapter Thirteen
The Corridors of Abaddon

I was ascending the Ravenel Bridge again, bound for the same eerie marshland destination I had so recently visited, only this time accompanied by a very different passenger. The day's dying light brushed gold fingertips across the Holy City's spires as the crescent moon, pale and slight, floated low in the purpling sky. Below us, the first streetlamps hummed to life, striking a preemptive blow against the darkness. Rylah kept her gaze on the waning moon. In just a few days, lunar conditions would be ripe for a return to her grave and a much-awaited exhumation.

I headed west off the bridge, skirting the city's northern edge and avoiding the downtown crowds. By day, Charleston teemed with souvenir-shoppers and history buffs; nighttime belonged to revelers. I didn't want to contend with giddy partiers packing the cobblestone streets, darting into pubs, dashing off to shows. They were the ghosts now, faceless creatures scuttling along in the shadows, oblivious. I wondered, were all of them what they seemed? Music from a rooftop bar commandeered the wind. I could feel the pounding beat even through my closed windows.

For the most part, Rylah kept quiet as we made our way to Bandun Gate. At one point I was praying under my breath, silently beseeching every saint whose name I could recall, and Rylah made an exaggerated 'sniffing' gesture, then huffed her disgust. Sometime after that, she noticed me repeatedly checking the dashboard and became suspicious.

"What do you keep lookin' at, woman?"

"These red numbers," I replied, tapping the digital clock. "They show the time. It's 8:04 now. I set the rendezvous for 9 p.m. Don't wanna be late."

"We gonna be?"

"No, we're almost there."

A few minutes later we reached the toppled sign marking the dirt road that led into the marshes. I pulled over, and Rylah spoke up again.

"Why we stoppin' here?"

"This turn-off's easy to miss. I need to make it more visible."

Appeased, Rylah sank back into her seat. I got out, opened the back-hatch, and took an LED road flare from the van's emergency kit. The moon had slipped behind drifting clouds, although it would not have provided much light through the thick forest canopy anyway. I clicked on the light and set it alongside the unpaved roadway, just past the intersection. It wasn't much of a marker, but enough that anyone unfamiliar with these roads would slow down for a look. A light rain, hardly more than mist, began to fall as we resumed our journey.

Two flares were left in the pack. I stopped again to mark the trail as we ambled through. Rylah didn't say anything that second time, so I figured she was satisfied I wasn't going to try any last-minute tricks to sabotage her. As I removed my seat belt to set up the final luminary, she grabbed my shoulder and dug her nails in, hard.

"I'm watchin' you," she snarled. "Don't get any ideas, or your girl'll be the one to pay!"

"We don't have time for this!" I shot back, recoiling. Rylah didn't make another sound for the rest of the ride.

Navigating the shaky bridge in pitch darkness was nerve-wracking, every bump and jostle threatening to plunge us into the water below. Much as I dreaded drowning in a snake-infested creek, my primary fear was being sidelined before I could complete my mission. I tried using the van's brights, but all that did was turn the wet air to a shimmery curtain that obscured everything else. I gripped the wheel and inched along until at last we reached the other side.

Bandun Gate was eerily different after nightfall. Its haint blue frame resembled old bones, the odd accents parasites on a scavenged carcass. I drove past it and made the U-turn, parking the van parallel to the archway, pointing in the direction we'd just come. No other cars were in sight; we'd been the first to arrive. My dashboard clock read 8:21.

"Shouldn't be long now," I said, switching the headlights off and the hazards on. A soft orange glow dotted the darkness, illuminating the rain-dampened greenery that surrounded us.

Rylah was so excited she practically sprinted to the gate. In her haste, she'd left the passenger door ajar; I decided to leave it open. The van's interior dome lights would stay on for about fifteen minutes before automatically shutting off, serving as an improvised 'timer.' *With any luck, I'll be done and gone before they go out.*

Luck, as it turned out, would play no part in the events about to transpire.

I cut the engine and got out. Even though I knew it would be hot out — temperatures remained in the eighties well after sundown, and as humid as mid-day — I'd worn a long-sleeved T-shirt and jeans, and sneakers with socks instead of sandals. I wanted to minimize any potential for skin-to-skin contact with Rylah. I took the latex gloves from our 'murder kit,' slipping them on as I listened to Bandun Gate's night song. The evening symphony played deeper than its daytime variant, more guileful, secretive. The insects' hum was subdued, allowing the rushing current of the tidal marshes to come through. Osprey screeches gave way to owl hoots, accompanied by the soft patter of dwindling rain. By the time I'd fished a flashlight and duct tape from the duffle bag, the sprinkling had ceased altogether.

Rylah called out, summoning me. I found the oak sapling near the gate's archway and with a few twists and loops attached the flashlight to the tree's thin trunk, beam aimed at the gate's opening. The meager light only carried a few feet, but that was all I needed, especially with the intermittent glimmer of the van's hazards.

"I promised I'd teach you 'bout the ways of the dead," Rylah teased. She was leaning against the very post where

Abby had unknowingly initiated their fateful connection. "Time to begin your schoolin'."

I approached her cautiously. Rylah wouldn't risk being stranded in the water-locked marshes again, so I didn't think she'd try to hurt me, at least not yet. Still, I kept a safe distance. Rylah gestured upward, toward the top of Bandun Gate's arch, chuckling. I looked up just as the strange mask, alternating gray and orange in the pulsating light, came loose and floated down, attaching itself to my face.

"First lesson — dyin'!" she announced. "Don't you worry now, I'm not *really* gonna kill you. But this is somethin' you gotta do before we can go any further."

Distracted by the mask, I hadn't noticed Rylah sliding up to me. She thrust her hand against the back of my neck, adding, "you wanna know about the hereafter, this is step one."

At her touch, I careened headlong into a swirl of disorientation, confusion, bewilderment. Had she forced me across Bandun Gate's barrier as Mike had done with Didi-Rylah; had I been transported to the other side? Even now, I can't say for sure. I *was* straddling worlds, that much I know for certain, one foot in the land of the living, the other in the realm of the dead. There could be no other explanation for what followed.

Thoughts foggy and muddled, all I could think about was removing that dreadful mask. It was suffocating me, ice-cold and coarse, like frozen sandpaper grinding my flesh. I pulled and tugged as hard as I could, but it would not come loose. As the struggle continued, I realized the thing wasn't stuck *onto* my skin, but rather some overwhelming force was pressing it against my face from the outside. I was uncertain who — *or what* — was orchestrating this torment.

Sapped of strength, I focused my attention outward. Through the mask's eyeholes I could see thousands and thousands of fluorescent bubbles, each containing an animated image that represented a possibility I had envisioned for my future. Some were tiny, like gathering seashells on Capers Island, or watching *Jeopardy* with my dad. Others loomed larger: writing another book, touring castles in Germany, catching up with my friend Tara over Mexican food back in our hometown. Several images were already enormous but continued to grow and develop even as I watched. These were cloudier and had fewer details than the others, however they were easily the most beautiful. The kids' weddings, a grandchild in my lap, dancing with Dan at an anniversary party where we're both old and gray and still very much in love.

My hands fell away from the mask as I lost myself in the gallery. Every animation was dazzling, the way dreams of what awaits in time yet to come must be. Without warning, the bubbles began to burst, one after another, faster and faster. The little ones went first, then the more sizable vanished, leaving the destruction of my grandest visions for the finale. The last to disappear featured my family — myself, Dan, Roman, Abby, Charles, their yet-blurry and undefined spouses and children — playing together on the seashore. A vast, chilling emptiness swept in behind those buoyant images, filling me not with sorrow, but a crushing sense of hopeless resignation. Whatever future I'd once had was gone.

I couldn't bear the blankness and turned away, surprised to discover an equally expansive tableau behind me. Row upon row of moving images, like an auditorium crammed floor to ceiling with video screens, playing back moments from my life. *The field of memory.* Scenes were constantly changing, some dating as far back as my early childhood. My mother handing me an Easter basket, Dad helping me pick apples, playing 'Go Fish' with my brother Paul and sister Mary in our backyard tree-fort. Most memories were of more recent years: times shared with Dan, or my own children's days as toddlers, school children, teens. The brightest playbacks showed moments that had happened mere days ago, when thoughts of death were the furthest thing from my mind. All the pictures suddenly jumbled together, fading in and out in random flashes. I tried to make myself focus on just *one*, hoping it could provide comfort in this unsettling domain. A clip of toddler-Charles cuddling a stuffed tiger appeared and I seized on it. However the brief joy the image provided was immediately eclipsed by the horrible reality that there would never be any new memories of my son, or anything else, for me, ever.

I spun around and faced the void where my future had been. Something moved there in the murk. *An overlooked 'possibility' that hadn't yet been obliterated,* I thought, *persevering in the bitter chasm.* But no, it was something quite different. A yellowy form was shuffling towards me, short and squat, slouching to one side. It looked like a jaundiced grub and smelled like a trashcan full of dirty diapers. Most bizarre, the pathetic creature's face was hidden beneath a mildewed gray mask identical to the one I was still wearing.

The mask! My hands shot up and I grasped mine from both sides. The pupating larva did the same thing, aping my movements exactly. I gave my mask a few tugs then let one hand fall away; my counterpart did likewise. Curious, I touched my chin, saluted, patted the top of my head. The putrid runt mimicked every motion in perfect unison.

"I've been waiting for you," it said, copying me as I resumed tugging the mask. The voice was familiar, but I couldn't place it.

One final yank and my mask came off, as did the sallow grub's. The slug was standing directly before me, close enough for me to take a good, long look.

"Well? Are you ready?" it asked in the voice I suddenly recognized.

I couldn't speak. I couldn't think. All I could do was gawk, open-mouthed.

The miserable creature was *me.*

"We gotta leave that here," grub-Miriam said, waving a stubby finger my way. "We're mirroring for now. From this point on, we wear me."

"*Wear me?*" I echoed, still reeling.

"That body," I/it replied, "it's obsolete now. Nothing but shed skin. I'm the real us."

I didn't need to ask anything further; I understood the creature's meaning. Hadn't every one of my catechism teachers said death strips away the body so only the spirit

185

remains? Well, this was mine. Not deeply corrupt, not a wicked monster capable of true depravity. My essence was merely a crude lump, shabby and unclean. A flood of so many petty, callous, indifferent acts I'd committed over my lifetime rushed back to me, all the opportunities I'd wasted to choose the better path scorched my psyche like molten coals.

"C'mon," the me-thing said, reaching out its palm for me to clasp. Intuitively I knew it wanted me to surrender my body, and if we made contact, the two of us would meld. "Let's go find Mom!"

Up until that instant, I would not have believed a soul could shatter into pieces, its jagged shards slicing against each other in excruciating spasms. But that's exactly what mine did, hearing those words. A whiff of Evening in Paris, my mother's favorite perfume, floated on the wind, and for an instant I was her little girl again. I ached for her embrace in a way so deep and primal I couldn't adequately describe it if I had a thousand years. Yet despite that savage longing to throw my arms around the beloved woman and tell my mother how much I'd missed her over the dozen years she'd been gone, to hear her voice and see her smile again, I knew it would never happen. *Couldn't* ever happen. Seeing her daughter as a rancid, trifling blob would break my mom's heart; I couldn't do it to her. Not even if it meant losing her for all eternity.

"No!" I sobbed, pulling away.

"Fine, then — do it *your* way," the Miriam-imp huffed, melting away like candlewax.

As the creature liquefied, my vanished-future gallery changed, narrowing into the dingy hallway from my almost-told nightmare, only now it was lined with hundreds of doors. I opened the first and found myself in a sweltering trailer that reeked of urine and stale sweat, a blood-stained mattress on the floor. The dungeon of the Deathless Angel. I shut it and continued to the next passageway, where Levi greeted me, grinning.

"This is for you," he said, holding up Swiff, the fluffy white cat I had when the kids were little. That little fur-ball was easily the most beloved pet I'd ever owned, only now he was missing both front legs, had an eye gouged out, and was hemorrhaging from deep gashes all over his quivering body.

"He's in a lot of pain," Levi said with mock concern, squeezing Swiff so hard I could hear bones crack. "You have to decide what to do about this poor guy. Want me to snap his neck and get it over with, or let him keep suffering? Your call."

The next apparition was even worse, a re-enactment of 'Banquet of the Unbaptized,' this time with three infants who looked exactly like my own children had as babies. The knife-wielding maniac gleefully presiding over the ritual was a dead-ringer for Dan. I hurried down the hall searching for an exit, opening door after door to horrors from the Vermicular File. Father Frank's roach-faced nurse eager to slice me into pieces, the *dukun's* exorcised spirits boasting about disemboweling children and skinning victims alive, a pair of perverted 'saints' pawing at each other's naked, decomposing bodies and inviting me to join them.

I had just stumbled into a medieval torture-orgy when a stab at the top of my spine knocked me flat. The sting had propelled me back to the Wadmalaw marshes, where Rylah hunched beside the gate, rubbing her hand furiously. Apparently she'd accidentally brushed her fingers against the rosary while clenching my neck, simultaneously burning herself and breaking her grip on me. My van was still the only vehicle at the roadside, its dome light on; I'd only been 'gone' a short while. Even so, my time was running out.

"Experience truly is the best teacher, don't ya think?" Rylah chided, giving her wounded hand one last shake.

I got to my feet in what must've been the same spot that Mike Fontaine had stood, his hands gripping Kadisha's shoulders as he prepared to shove his counterfeit wife under the archway. Rylah was mere inches away, resting against one of the fence posts as we faced each other, her white robe seeming to throb like a beating heart in the on-again, off-again flicker of the hazard lights. I had to move quickly.

"You ready for more?" the ghoul asked. "Tonight's gonna be a real eye-opener, I promise."

Ignoring her, I reached into my jeans pocket and took out a piece of paper carefully folded around its hidden cache.

"Years ago, I knew someone named Levi — you remind me of him," I told her, diverting attention away from my hand. "You two have a lot in common. Proud of inflicting agony on innocent creatures, wanting to brag about it, expecting to be congratulated for your cruelty. You both deal in the currency of pain."

Stepping towards the flashlight's pale beam, I lifted the paper's top flap uncovering the word 'Rylah' printed in large black letters. She glanced at it, curious but not alarmed.

"What've you got there, woman?"

"Something I made just for you Rylah, for tonight's activities. A talisman, you might say. A good-luck charm. This is actually my second version. I'd written 'Virgilia Jane Hodges' on the first one, then I realized I wasn't sure that's even your name. The root doctor said it wouldn't work if I didn't get the name right. But you wrote 'Rylah' on that picture of Sophie, referring to yourself, right? So I figured *that* name must have power."

The haint's curiosity turned to agitation.

"Any fool can scribble down a name," she spat. "Doesn't mean you got anythin' over me!"

"Oh, I know that. Isata told me the name's only part of it. I also needed something of yours to make this work. The more recent, the more *meaningful*, the better. And I have that, too, Rylah, so you need to do what I say. Get under the archway. Do it *now*."

"You're bluffin'," she scoffed, although she did slide backwards slowly, traversing Bandun Gate's boundary. I wasn't sure if she was toying with me or if the paper/possession gambit was actually working. If it were to fail, the retaliation she would unleash on me would be biblical.

I unfolded the next crease, tipping the page into the light. Rylah peered at the brown-green smudge but stayed put, mulling the streaky smear.

"No, I'm not bluffing. I have something that belongs to you, and I *know* it does because I gave it to you myself. Not to

Abby. Not to Kadisha Fontaine. To *you*, Rylah. You asked me for this, and I obliged. Then you got sloppy yesterday — you left this for me to find. And I found it today while I was driving back from Isata's place."

I opened up the last section. A few crumpled leaves fell to the ground, but I'd taped down three stems to make sure I wouldn't lose them in the darkness.

"Myrtle blossoms to put on your grave."

Rylah stared at the withered sprigs attached to the paper bearing her name. Her bemused smirk dissolved into a furious scowl. She was about to say something when a distant sound distracted her. An approaching vehicle, still off in the woods, was slowly coming towards us. I knew that signaled the end, one way or the other.

Rylah's insipid grin returned.

"So you think you got over on me? That you've bested me with your silly blooms?"

Despite her victorious tone, Rylah remained on the other side of Bandun Gate. *Maybe* she's *the one bluffing, hoping I'll fold.* I had to press on.

"You need to relinquish your hold on Abby. Whatever you're doing to make her ill, it stops *now*. You're done with her, with *all* of us, forever."

"*Am* I?" Rylah said playfully, looking toward the road and the vehicle slowly drawing closer.

"Do it! Let Abby go!"

My hands were shaking so badly I almost ripped the paper in half.

"Now, Rylah! You let Abby go NOW!!!"

Eons passed as I braced myself for whatever might happen next. All possibilities were on the table: Abby is freed from the vile haint, Rylah pulls some lethal countermove, I am annihilated in a pageant of pain. Throughout our tense stand-off, the van's hazards marked time in a steady rhythm of soft orange / darkness / soft orange / darkness / soft orange / darkness. I counted six cycles (it could've been a thousand) before the monster finally responded.

With dizzying speed, Rylah flew backward into the cursed

189

swampland beyond Bandun Gate, stopping just short of the tree line. She raised her arms behind her in a fierce, arching motion, as if flexing invisible wings. Her face was a contorted tableau of rage, contempt and defiance; any resemblance she'd once had to my daughter was gone forever. I continued brandishing the paper as she writhed, illuminated by electronic lightning.

Rylah growled and hissed, her skin turning the color of rancid olives, boiling, churning, sliding over itself. She began convulsing violently. The bathrobe fell away, and I could see her body scabbing over from head to toe. In the blinking light her macabre transformation appeared choppy and stilted, like the jittery flickering of an old black and white film. The sores started to squirm, morphing into locusts like the one she'd used to escape Bandun Gate, until a massive swarm engulfed her. A dark maw formed where her face had been, and the repulsive, bug-encrusted creature shrieked out a single word.

"Aaaahhhhbeeeeee!"

When the hellion screeched my daughter's name, all the locusts fell dead. Once they'd perished, a lone emerald butterfly, the exact color of Abby's eyes, rose from the piled carcasses and winged its way into the night. I watched, entranced, until it disappeared against the darkness.

Rylah, however, remained.

True Rylah now, distilled to her fundamental essence, hovered in the misty wilds of Bandun Gate. The revenant resembled the woman Rylah must've been in life: her naked body lean and lithe, an attractive face with full cheeks and pouty lips, wavy blonde tresses cascading past her shoulders. The demon Andras' sigil — clear now this was the same symbol I'd seen in the grimoire — had been seared onto her fleshy left breast, directly above the heart.

In other aspects, the specter didn't appear remotely human. Rylah's skin was ashen-ivory streaked with plum-colored veins, and her eyes were liquid silver. Her movements had become untethered to gravity, allowing her to drift and glide in a manner that was both fascinating and terrifying. Rylah's pale yellow hair billowed around her like leaves adrift on a brackish pond.

The spirit ebbed towards me, her cold fury pulsing out in piercing waves. I thought I was dead. Rylah stopped just short of the archway, her glowing eyes boring into me. *Why is she still here?* I wondered, petrified. *Why can I still see her? What does this mean?*

"One thing you got right, woman," she said in a hollow monotone, her pallid lips curling. "You shouldn't trust me."

The hum of the approaching car was growing louder as twin headlights picked through the gloom. Something stirred behind Rylah, deep in the swamp. Red fireflies dotted the darkness in pairs as a low grumbling rumbled through the marshes. The wet scent becoming an acrid, revolting stench of burning flesh.

I turned to leave, praying Rylah would remain trapped in the confines of Bandun Gate. The van's dome light had gone out, not that it mattered anymore. I'd wanted to be gone the instant Abby was safe and Rylah was snared, before anyone else might arrive at this wretched place. Now our one-on-one was about to become a trio.

"It's too late!" Rylah bellowed, hearing the approaching vehicle. "Soon as she crosses that bridge, you're done for!"

"What?" I said, making a quick about-face. "What do you mean? Is the bridge going to collapse?"

Rylah sailed closer, yet stayed on the far side of Bandun Gate's mystic boundary.

"You made a bargain with *me*, and I made a bargain with *him*!" the phantom declared, her sallow finger tracing the sigil on her chest. The scar sizzled as Rylah spoke, stinking of scorched meat. "I promised him *you*! The instant Sophie arrives, the Great Marquis and his multitude are gonna tear you to bits and feast on your soul!"

I heard a dull *thud* as the car left the road and started down the old bridge. *Thump! thump! thump!* it plodded over the boards. Suddenly the ceremony Rylah had conducted in the bathroom came back to me. She must've feared I'd renege at the last minute, so Rylah cut a side deal with her allies in Hell. I didn't blame her; I'd been working all this time to outmaneuver her, too.

"From that first time you set foot in these marshes I knew the old ones *despised* you," she spat. "Figured takin' your girl would oblige them to me, but this is *SO MUCH BETTER!* Once you're slaughtered, I'm no longer beholdin' to you. First thing I'm gonna do after takin' Sophie is find your *Abby* (Rylah cackled her name, wielding it like a sword to thrust in my heart) — and slay her at my leisure, make a real *occasion* of it. Then I'll move on to your men. Oh, I do hope they'll be nice and play along! You be sure to picture all that while the Master is ravagin' you!"

The last piece of Rylah's nefarious scheme dropped into place, and I finally understood what was happening. The haint needed a female body, but couldn't capture one without my help; since she was certain I would sell out Sophie to save my daughter, why not profit double from my sin? Rylah's demon overlord would surely reward her handsomely for the tandem sacrifice. Writing her name on Sophie's photo, burning the doll-baby, Andras' sigil scrawled with the ceremonial ashes — that had nothing to do with harming Abby, it was all about acquiring *me.*

"Your demon's pact hinged on my acceptance of doing evil," I said, putting it all together. "I had to lure Sophie here so you could kill her, had to hand her over to be murdered — that offense would damn me."

"That's right, woman! You betrayed innocent blood, forfeitin' your soul. You're no better than me — no escapin' that now! The covenant's been sealed in fire — with *you* deliverin' the maiden sacrifice here to their sacred ground. Hail, Andras, my lord, my liege! Hail the Great Marquis of Hell!"

The car had been drawing ever closer as Rylah spoke. The little blue hatchback ambled off the bridge, its Virginia license plate visible in the van's blinking caution lights. It crept by us slowly, the rain-glistened windows reflecting intermittent orange, then looped around and pulled in behind my van. Rylah spun, gleeful, toward the cloud of red fireflies. I followed her gaze and made an awful discovery: the ruby lights dotting the darkness were *not* lightning bugs, they were eyes. A ghastly demon army had amassed in the marshes behind Bandun Gate.

Rylah's pale arms shot into the air, ready to welcome the advancing forces. The assembled fiends, however, held position, fixed in the swampland. Her silver eyes darted to the car and back, confused by the troops' reticence.

"I haven't delivered a maiden sacrifice," I said flatly. "There's no 'nubile female' coming your way. Now move *back*, Rylah, where you won't be seen, and stay quiet."

She was instantly yanked backward, swallowed by the shadows, and deposited amongst the infernal soldiers.

I took a few steps toward the hatchback as the passenger-side window rolled down. The driver leaned across the seat.

"Hey!" a husky voice called. "That you, Mom?"

No surprise, it was my eldest son, who had defied explicit orders not to come anywhere near Bandun Gate.

"I thought we were supposed to meet at the diner, Roman."

"Figured I'd come by here since it was on the way."

"Uh, it's *not* 'on the way' and besides, I'm about done here," I replied, laboring to sound relaxed. "You go on ahead. I'll see you there."

My son paused, skeptical. "I don't mind waiting."

"No — the restaurant's gonna be slammed on a Friday night, and I'm starving! Go grab us a table. I'll be there. Ten minutes, tops."

Roman gave Bandun Gate a once-over, scanning the darkness where Rylah and the looming demons stood fast. Roman noticed nothing beyond the fence posts but trees.

"You sure?" he said at last.

"Yup! Just gotta get my flashlight, have one last look around. Hey, order me a Diet Coke and some coconut shrimp, okay? I'll see you soon!"

Another pause, another herculean effort to maintain my cool. Then Roman shrugged, gave me a 'thumbs up,' and drove off.

Once he'd gone, Rylah bolted to the mouth of the gate, furious.

"Where's the girl?" she demanded.

"Sophie isn't coming. She never was."

"That's not possible!" Rylah blurted. "You promised to bring her here tonight! I would'a known if you'd been deceivin' me!"

"I never 'promised' to give you Sophie. I said we'd go to Bandun Gate, which we did. That I planned to meet someone at nine — it was Roman, although the meet was *supposed* to be at a restaurant near here. I told you I gave Charles directions to pass on to Sophie — they were how to get from Clemson to Ruth's house in Myrtle Beach, where I sent her to protect her from *you*. And I said I wanted Abby back and you *gone*; we both know that's true, don't we?"

Rylah's rage coursed through her, turning those gleaming eyes a luminous black. I thought of Fr. Frank, how he'd been spot-on about allowing diabolic spirits to believe they had the upper hand while quietly devising a counterstrike. Planning our return to Bandun Gate had been the perfect diversion to outfox Rylah. It had never even occurred to her I wouldn't serve up Sophie, someone I could barely tolerate. In Rylah's world, everyone was disposable. She wouldn't have thought twice about snuffing out someone's life to get what she wanted, and she expected no different from me.

"You speak the language of the dead, Rylah, but you never bothered to learn about connecting with the living. That's why you keep getting *dispatched* — by your neighbors, by Mike Fontaine, and now by me."

The red eyes began drawing closer as the demon army advanced. They were still partially veiled as they came forth from the black, but I could make out monstrous silhouettes: claws, horns, beaks, appendages that squirmed like vipers. One abomination towered above the others, riding a huge wolf and leading the troops. *Andras, Great Marquis of Hell.* He was a shadow against the murk, though in the hazards' splashing light I could clearly see a long metallic object in his right hand. Rylah saw it too: a silver sword pointed directly at her.

She tried to escape, slamming into the invisible boundary beneath Bandun Gate's arch. Rylah banged her vein-riddled fists against the unseen partition like a mad woman frantically beating a glass door. The baby shoe suspended overhead bobbed on its string as she flailed; the serving spoons became wind chimes. Like the haint herself, the dangling items didn't pass from their side of the gate to the other but simply bounced off an imperceptible barricade as the commotion played out.

"You bitch!" she seethed as I gaped at the spectacle. "So proud a'yourself, *you bitch*! You think you're so clever!"

"No, not clever," I replied, backing away. "I just know how to do my research."

It was time to flee. I knew Roman wouldn't go to the restaurant; he'd drive to the main road, find a place to pull over where there was cell service, and call his girlfriend, Daniela. Maybe he'd listen to a few Knife Party tunes while checking the rearview mirror for my van. If I didn't show up within a few minutes, he'd come back looking for me. Roman was never supposed to be at Bandun Gate at all, the last thing I wanted was him making a return trip.

The duped demons were starting to descend on Rylah; that was something I did *not* want to see.

"*You're* the only one who's broken a promise tonight," I told my nemesis as I grabbed the flashlight. "Something tells me this crowd doesn't handle disappointment well. I'll leave you to settle up."

Rylah's diabolic 'liege' came into full view as he dismounted the wolf only a few yards away from where I stood. Andras, the demon whose sigil resembled an ornate candelabrum inside a circle. Great Marquis of Hell. Sower of discord. Commander of thirty legions of odious spirits. Body of an angel with the head of a raven, riding upon an enormous wolf. Master of teaching humans methods of murder and mayhem.

"This isn't over!" Rylah screeched, pummeling the barrier. "I won't forget this! *THEY* won't forget! You can't just walk away! *THIS ISN'T OVER!*"

One more thing I had discovered about her overlord, a citation from the Vermicular File that had proven especially useful. The old grimoire had described Andras as a 'vindictive, unforgiving demon' who would vent his powerful rage on 'the careless conjurer.'

Right before I reached the van, I looked over my shoulder. Rylah's overlord strutted to the edge of the boundary and as he drew closer, the bird-headed beast transformed into the most handsome man I had ever seen. He didn't speak aloud, but I heard his words in my head, a generous invitation:

'This exquisite power can be yours. Swear allegiance to me, and I'll show you delights as you've never known.' The fiend smiled at me, and a tangle of maggots squirmed between his teeth.

An ancient verse echoed inside me, a psalm my geometry teacher was fond of quoting when threatening students with detention: *I abhor the assembly of evildoers and refuse to sit with the wicked.* Rylah was screaming by then, her shrieks rising above the devils' thundering howls. Other voices, formerly-human, had joined the cacophony, laughing, screeching, grunting in revelry. I made the sign of the cross, kissed the crucifix on my rosary, and forced myself to look away as Rylah disappeared into the savage swarm.

Even before I'd buckled my seatbelt, I was questioning the bizarre events I had just witnessed. *Was any of this real? Had Abby ever been in danger, or was she simply suffering a bad headache from too much sun and not enough sleep?* Two decades after hearing about how Fr. Frank's friend Declan, an intelligent, rational man, abruptly lost his grip on reality and descended into madness, the sad story suddenly made perfect sense. So did Mike Fontaine's compulsion to keep re-reading an old newspaper story in order to stave off doubts about what he'd done to his wife. A direct confrontation with preternatural evil is enough to unravel anyone's sanity.

Please, God, don't let that be me.

The last thing I saw before driving off was that ambiguous ethereal mask. It was attached, inexplicably, to Bandun Gate once again, switching gray to orange with the hazards' blinking glow. Its position had changed, though. It was now perched above the place Rylah had been struggling to escape. And a new decoration had been added there, too.

Directly below the mask, a white terrycloth bathrobe with dark red splatters on its left sleeve leapt and danced on the gusting wind.

Chapter Fourteen
Estuary

Everything is different now. *Everything*.

I fled Bandun Gate and set out to meet Roman. Sure enough, he was waiting by the main road where I'd placed the first flare. I stopped long enough to scoop it up then waved him on, and we drove convoy-style to Johns Island. Throughout the short trip I kept checking my rearview mirror, expecting to see Rylah charging through the night, arms outstretched to grab hold of me and send me into tortured oblivion. Or Andras, appearing in his demon guise astride an enormous black wolf, piercing me with ebony raven-eyes. Or maybe just a grimy old mask trailing me in the darkness.

The ride turned out to be uneventful, and we arrived at the diner without incident. I sent Roman inside so I could call Abby. I *needed* to hear her voice and wouldn't be able to focus on anything else until I had. She picked up on the second ring.

"How's your head, Abby?" I asked, holding my breath. "Any improvement?"

"I slept pretty much all day, woke up about an hour ago, felt pretty good until about ten minutes ago. Now I'm sicker than ever."

Panic, devastation. Had Rylah's 'mirror ritual' done permanent damage after all, or maybe even kicked into overdrive when the ghost was ambushed? Vanquishing Rylah had been my last hope for saving Abby. My *only* hope.

"What's the problem?"

"Sophie arrived!" Abby snorted, cackling. I could breathe again. "Just when I was feeling better, *Mahm*, so thanks for that. I'm stuck here with her 'til Sunday — Roman bailed, so I'm Charles' ride back to Charleston."

"Well," I said, savoring the private irony, "I suppose things could always be *a lot* worse."

Abby was indeed herself again, thank God. I indulged a few happy tears, told her to be brave dealing with Sophie, then hurried into the restaurant to have dinner with her big brother.

Roman was sitting at the table with his arms crossed, playfully glaring at me as I took the chair opposite him.

"So, you gonna tell me what's going on?" he asked.

What could I say? What *should* I say? Roman hadn't seen anything at Bandun Gate, which was a huge relief. I didn't know if his car's rain-splashed windows had veiled Rylah and the others from him, or maybe the spectacle could only be viewed by those of us intimately involved. Whatever the reason, I didn't care. I was just glad he'd missed it all, wasn't part of it, and at that point I had neither the energy nor the desire to hash it all out again. Exhausted and unnerved, all I wanted was a basket of shrimp, a bowl of corn fritters and an evening of normalcy. Besides, I was still rather upset with Roman for showing up at Bandun Gate despite my firm admonition to stay clear of the place.

That afternoon, I hadn't been off the phone with Charles two minutes when my cell rang again, this time Roman on the line. When I saw his name on the 'incoming' notification I didn't want to pick up, so I let the call go to voicemail. He'd keep calling, I realized as soon as the ringing ceased, and if I continued ignoring his attempts, he'd eventually reach out to Dan to air his concerns about what was happening in Charleston. *What's with Mom? She's acting really weird, and now she won't take my calls.* That complication would have been exponentially more problematic. I'd begrudgingly dialed Roman back, determined to prevent those dominoes from falling. He launched into his probe without as much as a 'hello.'

"Charles said you just called and told him Sophie should come to Aunt Ruth's — that we should all stay with her for the

199

weekend, not go to Charleston," he said, recapping the conversation I'd had with his brother. "You said you had to be somewhere tonight, wouldn't be home — what's that all about?"

He'll know if I try to play him; be honest but evasive.

"I figured you'd all have more fun in Myrtle Beach," I said, matter-of-factly. "Go to the Sky Wheel, water park, maybe hit the Ripley's Museum. Lots of fun stuff there for you college kids. Ruthie loved the idea when I ran it by her."

Roman stayed quiet, evaluating my input, so I continued.

"And I *am* going out tonight — a place I've been researching. Heard some local legends about it, thought I'd see what it's like after dark."

"Is it that weird gate you took Abby to?"

My stomach flipped somersaults. "How'd you know about that?"

"Abby texted me pictures when you guys went the other day. Looks pretty interesting. How 'bout I come down and go with you tonight? I'd like to see it — and Sophie's a total asshat, wouldn't mind dipping out before she gets to Ruthie's."

"No!" I'd shouted, way too forcefully. Catching myself, I shifted to a more offhanded tone. "I'm not gonna be there that long, and it's way back in the marshes — probably too dark to see much of anything anyway. You'll have a way better time in Myrtle Beach, even with Sophie around."

Silence. The damage had been done; Roman would not be dissuaded from coming to Charleston. After an excruciating pause, I decided it would be best if I charted his course rather than allow him to devise his own itinerary.

"How about this," I'd offered, hoping an invitation would appease him. "There's a seafood place on John's Island — we'd go every summer when you guys were little. Has an animal name, and a big tree out front wrapped in white Christmas lights. Remember?"

"Yeah, I know where you're talking about. It's on the main drag near Angel Oak."

"Yes! That's not too far from where I'm going. If you *really* want to come down tonight, we could meet there, have a late dinner. I should have things wrapped up by, say, 9 o'clock. If I'm late, just get us a table and I'll be along."

"Since when do you eat dinner at nine?" he'd asked. "You're usually getting ready for bed by then."

"Well, it doesn't even start getting dark until after eight," I noted. "I'm making an exception to my schedule to visit that gate."

Another brief interlude, a heavy sigh, then he'd agreed. I wasn't happy about the arrangement, but it was better than Roman storming the area blindly searching for Bandun Gate, likely getting lost in the process. God only knows what else could be lurking in those accursed marshes, ready to snag a wandering stranger. If everything worked out the way I'd planned, I'd be able to make that dinner date. And if it didn't, well, I had prepared for that outcome, too.

Before I left for my bleak errand, I had written a note to leave on my driver's seat at Bandun Gate. It read simply, 'RYLAH - Mike Fontaine can help,' and included Mike's phone number and his firm's website. If Roman made his way to the gate and my vehicle was still there but I wasn't, he'd have to leave to make the call since there was no cell service in the marshes. Putting him in *any* danger was a risk I hadn't wanted to take, but once Roman set his mind on something, there was no talking him down. My best option was to minimize his exposure, and that was what I had tried (and ultimately failed) to do.

"So how'd you find the gate?" I asked my son as we sat in the restaurant.

"GPS coordinates," Roman replied with a cocky smile. "Got 'em off the photo Abby texted me. Plugged 'em into my onboard --- which is a good thing I had, because phone GPS doesn't work out there --- led me to the gate no problem. You weren't kidding about it being out in the boonies."

Should've seen that coming. I hadn't counted on Roman's ingenuity thwarting my safeguard strategy, though in retrospect it was utterly predictable. All three kids had inherited their father's 'computer-genius' abilities, and pulling location data from a digital photo file was mere child's play. Likewise, I should have anticipated my son's need to orchestrate his own resolution to the 'Mom sounds distressed' crisis instead of following my instructions.

From birth, Roman had been perpetually convinced that virtually *everything* would work out better if only he were ceded total control. Crashing Bandun Gate was no exception. It made me queasy thinking how close he'd come to that horde of demons; proximity to Rylah was bad enough. If I'd had the slightest *inkling* of what she had been concocting, of the diabolic battalion she'd summoned to Bandun Gate, I would have done literally *anything* to keep Roman away.

Familiar guilt washed over me; I realized I'd put my child in terrible danger yet again. *What was I thinking?* Suppose I had died there, or been incapacitated — had I really thought Roman would just sit in the diner all night, munching French fries and wondering what was keeping me so long? *Of course* Roman would've come looking for me, one way or another. I'd even left a breadcrumb trail in the form of electronic flares.

I had left something else as well — a 'worst case scenario' backstop for Dan and the kids. I'd written an account of my interactions with Rylah and set it on my nightstand, sealed in an envelope addressed to our parish priest. If I hadn't made it out, I wanted to share my story with someone who might actually believe me, or at least wouldn't reject the tale out of hand. Father Matthew would have done some research, comforted my family, prayed for my eternal soul.

I'd penned one last note before setting out with Rylah: a post-it stuck on Dan's mirror saying, "I'll always be your Bunner."

Roman's menu lay ignored as he awaited an explanation of my conduct. The most incredible aroma — cornbread, crabmeat, a hint of onion — wafted by as our perky waitress set a plate of crab cakes down at the table beside ours. Suddenly I was ravenous; the last real meal I'd had was the take-out barbecue with Abby two days ago.

"Look, I'm *starving*, and I just wanna concentrate on my

dinner order," I informed my son. "Like I already told you, I've been researching Charleston ghost stories and Bandun Gate was a big part of that. For now, let's just leave it there."

Saturday I slept until noon, finally waking to the sound of my son playing Xbox in the family room. It was the first night in I couldn't remember how long that I hadn't dreamed at all. As I stretched and yawned, the phrase 'slept like the dead' came to mind and made me smile. *I'll take it.*

After a big pancake brunch, the two of us spent the afternoon sitting on the back porch watching egrets and playing Jenga. Roman never brought up Bandun Gate or my last-minute changes to Sophie's vacation plans, and I never volunteered any further information. He seemed satisfied that all was right with the world. Why wouldn't he be? His mom was chatting, joking, bantering like a woman who didn't have a care in the world.

Abby and Charles arrived late Sunday, and Dan on Monday afternoon. I'd worried that when everyone got to talking, Dan might notice discrepancies about my time with Abby in Charleston. I'd referenced visiting the old house on Thursday and Abby's weird behavior there, which conflicted with Abby's timeline of going to Myrtle Beach Wednesday night. Fortunately, Dan tended to zone out when he was preoccupied with business and often couldn't recall specifics from our phone calls. And he hadn't seen his daughter in months, so topics like Abby's college classes, future job plans, and budding romance with Roman's friend Richard were much more pressing. To my relief, he never brought up the trip to the ruins or Abby's demeanor, and seemed to have forgotten the conversation entirely.

On Wednesday of our little family reunion, Dan took the kids to Isle of Palms for an afternoon of water skiing. I begged off, encouraging them to enjoy some 'Dad time' since I'd already had the kids all to myself that weekend. The minute they were out the door, I made my way north on route seventeen, toting a gallon of Sherwin-Williams Haint Blue, two pints of holy water (part of the haul from St. John's baptismal font, stealthy collected while visiting Charleston the preceding day,) a paint sprayer and the crystal rosary I'd worn to Bandun Gate. There were still some loose ends I needed to tie up.

After a few wrong turns I eventually found my way back to Rylah's burned out house. I parked by the charred shack and went into the woods, ritual implements in tow. There was a thick layer of leaves, pine needles, and rotted debris on the grave, I cleared it away then splashed the blessed water over every inch of ground inside those little walls. I'd half-expected an eruption, like mixing vinegar with baking soda, or at least wisps of steam rising from the dirt. But no, just wet earth stretching out from the unmarked headstone. I loaded the paint sprayer and topped the area with a thick coat of Haint Blue. *Just try to get your precious box* now*, Rylah. I dare you.*

"My days of 'being nice and playing along' are *over*," I informed her absent ghost.

The breeze picked up, rustling the trees. When I had first started my task, all I'd wanted to do was finish and get away as quickly as possible. But as I emptied the sprayer's last few drops onto the foot of Rylah's grave, a strange feeling swept over me: a sudden impulse to dig up that wretched box. In my mind's eye I could see it, dark metal with a key-lock, the lid emblazoned with Andras' demonic imprint. The vile container was calling me, I could hear it loud and clear, playfully whispering my name, enticing me to claim its hidden prize.

"Miriam! Miri-uhmmmm! It's waiting here for YOU, Miriam!" the elsewhere voice teased. *"Aren't you curious? Don't you want to see what's inside? You've never seen anything like it, promise!!!"*

I went back to purging the remaining paint, reciting the Lord's Prayer aloud for Sammy and Kadisha and Rylah's other victims as I shook out the sprayer. I concluded by asking St. Francis to watch over Otto, and draped the aquamarine rosary around the angel statue alongside Mike Fontaine's wedding ring. The shimmering beads shone the color of a cloudless October sky, Mike's golden band the steadfast sun. By the time I'd finished paying my respects, the urge to loot Rylah's coffin had waned, though I suspected if I lingered too long, it would return with a vengeance.

The rest of the kids' stay was, thankfully, uneventful. We went to the beach and the arcade, had hot dogs at Jack's, and barbecue at Melvin's. On Friday the family went to the Blue Heron for lunch with my Dad, and Bernadette made a point to come over and chat with Abby, making sure all was well. Any nagging doubts I'd had about my daughter harboring a ghost were dispelled that Sunday when Abby attended mass and took communion. No screeching like a banshee, no bursting into flames. Whatever connection she'd had with Rylah was broken.

That afternoon, as the kids packed up to leave, Charles ribbed me about dumping Sophie off on my sister-in-law.

"Impressive job, Madre, washing your hands of Sophie, pretending you were worried she wouldn't have any fun in Charleston," he chided, his blue eyes sparkling.

"Well, *didn't* she have a good time in Myrtle Beach?"

"Sure, just like you hoped. You're *so* thoughtful. Sophie sends her deepest thanks."

"I'll bet she does."

"You know, if you didn't want her around, you could've just said so. You didn't have to go to all that trouble getting rid of her."

"Trust me, Charles, you have *no idea*."

Roman, Abby and Charles left for Virginia that afternoon, and my life went back to normal. Or at least as 'normal' as I could expect.

Dan resumed traveling, jetting off to business meetings and seminars and trade shows around the country. Once again, he was gone more than he was home, and I was alone for long stretches of time. During those first weeks following my encounter with Rylah, I kept questioning the experience; *had any of it actually happened?* Maybe spending so much time on my own had gotten to me; I'd psyched myself out after Bernadette's warning, let my imagination run wild. Rylah and the events at Bandun Gate might simply have been bits of every story I had mentally composed over the years but never put to paper. The ghost I was battling nothing but 'writer Miriam' entombed beneath the trappings of everyday life.

What *did* happen at Bandun Gate, in the shadow of the Holy City? Would I ever be able to say for certain?

That October, Hurricane Matthew blew through Charleston, uprooting a massive oak near our pond. The storm-toppled tree got me thinking about Sammy Watkins, perhaps because it reminded me we're all at the mercy of forces beyond ourselves. He'd be around seventy or so, if he was still alive, his body bearing permanent reminders of Rylah's crimes. What had he told boys in the school locker room about that partially-completed sigil on his back, I wondered. Did he ever have to explain it to lovers who found the scar unsettling? Maybe he'd removed it at some point with skin grafts, or camouflaged it with a tattoo. The missing fingers would be harder to hide, though over the decades he would certainly have learned to make do without them.

We all make adjustments to cope with our traumas.

Not long after the hurricane, I started contemplating my 'box of Hell' again, wondering if it was time to let it go. Once more I came very close to discarding it, once more I ultimately opted to keep it in storage. *Never know when it might come in handy*, especially with its more recent additions.

Following my confrontation with Rylah, I'd placed the never-delivered explanation letter and my note with Mike's phone number in the Vermicular File. It seemed an appropriate home for the mementos. Father Frank and Mike Fontaine, it occurred to me not long after Rylah's demise, were kindred souls; both fought demons despite the dreadful emotional toll, both lost the person closest to them yet continued helping strangers battle dark forces. Together, the two of them saved me from a true 'living Hell.'

Had I done the right thing? Should I have gambled with so many lives? Was some grisly karmic fate awaiting me as punishment for my recklessness?

It's been three years since the extraordinary events at Bandun Gate. Abby is married to Richard now, and Roman is engaged to Daniela. Charles is still in and out of college searching for his calling, still friends with Sophie, who, I have to admit, unwittingly saved Abby's life. If Sophie hadn't been headed to Charleston, Abby never would've left for Myrtle Beach the night Rylah planned to kill her. Dan is away on business more than ever, leaving me plenty of unguarded hours to mull over the choices I made, the events I set in motion.

Every now and then I drive out to those marshes, always in the daylight, always alone, never getting out of the car. There's a peculiar comfort in seeing the bathrobe, (it's in tatters now, mildewed as gray-green as the Spanish moss) dangling down below Bandun Gate's archway. It makes me think I'm not insane.

Last time I went, the weathered mask was gone. I keep imaging I'll wake up one night while Dan's away to find it on the pillow next to me, or that one of the kids will stroll in wearing it, acting so bizarre I'm terrified to look at what's hiding underneath. Maybe one Sunday after I've bowed my head at Eucharist, I'll look up, and Fr. Matthew's face will be cloaked by the hollow-eyed covering as he offers me the Communion wafer.

If I think on it too long, I become convinced the mask is resting atop Rylah's unmarked grave, keeping watch over her abandoned remains, and guarding that curious metal box.

I still visit Isata on occasion, too, to buy fresh tomatoes or okra, or one of her lovely sweetgrass baskets. The first time I saw her after Rylah's departure, Isata greeted me with a simple, "ev'rythin' good now?" and when I nodded, she moved on to talking about the gorgeous autumn weather. We haven't spoken of haints or spells or conjure since.

I never have any contact with Mike Fontaine. He doesn't need to be reminded that I got my beloved girl back, while his is gone forever.

There's one additional habit I've picked up in the post-Rylah era. More and more frequently, I catch myself checking the best-seller lists or reviewing the library's 'Popular New Titles' rack, an uncomfortable mix of jealousy and angst and frustration churning inside me. Immediately following that sensation comes an urge to consult the lunar cycle and see when the next moonless night will be. Whatever's in that enigmatic box would make for a tantalizing tale, I have no doubt. After all, the container is the Vermicular File's separated twin, cradling its own cache of fascinating evils. These days, I'm trying very hard to forget them both.

At times I don't know if I'm back among the damned or finally free of them; if I conquered my demons or traded them for fresh peril. The nightmares have returned but they're different now. Sometimes I'm in Hell looking out, other nights I dream of Rylah and the secrets of the dead entombed in her grave like a bitter buried treasure. When I awaken, I stare for long hours into the darkness remembering her offer to share them with me, and pondering those alluring mysteries just waiting to be unmasked.

'*We can still be friends*,' I hear her whisper from beyond Bandun Gate. '*I'm still here, waiting for you to be nice and play along*'.

And somehow, that's the most terrifying thing of all.

Reality Check

How much of *Bandun Gate* is real? Well, most all of it, at least in some respect. Nearly everything in the story either happened or is rooted in actual events. However not everything contained in these pages happened to *me*, or occurred the same way described in the book. Let's separate fact from fiction.

Encyclopedia of Hell was the first book I wrote, published in 1998. Research started in the early 90s (pre-internet), so information was gathered almost entirely through personal interviews or by reviewing original sources like old books, documents, reports and essays. During that time, I interacted with numerous exorcists, devil worshipers, clerics of various faiths, professors, authors, artists, law enforcement officials, performers and many others who offered their input. And I really did amass a sizable collection of articles, photos, and curios I considered too disturbing to include in the pages of my final manuscript.

From the very beginning, when people learned I was writing about Hell, they'd typically react in one of two ways. Either they found the topic unsavory and quickly changed the subject, or they became intrigued and wanted to discuss the concept in great detail. Many in the latter group eagerly shared personal stories involving the netherworld, telling me about a relative who dabbled in Satanism, a Ouija board experience gone horribly wrong, an acquaintance obsessed with witchcraft and conjuring, etc. This included, among others, a retired government official who had spent a career investigating 'demonic' crimes, a church-sanctioned exorcist, and the father of a girl lost to a religious cult.

The year I started researching *Encyclopedia of Hell*, I also became a mom for the first time. Roman arrived in 1993, and by 1996 he had a sister, Abigail, and a brother, Charles. The combination of inferno investigating and 'three children in three years exhaustion' led to frequent, vivid, gut-wrenching nightmares. Almost all of them involved horrible things being done to my kids, almost always by me. My husband Dan worried I was spreading myself too thin, and a priest warned me that delving into demonology would have terrible, long-lasting repercussions. After the Hell book was published, I moved on to other projects, and the nightmares became less frequent, and less severe.

In early 2006 we almost lost Roman to a mysterious illness. He developed a lesion on his brain stem that the doctors said would likely be fatal, or best-case scenario would leave him profoundly disabled. My son recovered completely, however, with no lasting neurological impact. To this day, there is no medical explanation for what he had, how he contracted it, why it didn't kill him, or how he was healed.

From the time Charles was a toddler, he experienced profuse nosebleeds, which proved especially problematic during the years we lived in Arizona.

In 2015, Dan and I bought a house in the Charleston, South Carolina area to be near to my father in his retirement. We'd been coming to the 'lowcountry' together on family vacations for almost twenty years, and all of us loved the 'Holy City.' Its island beaches, gothic architecture and southern delicacies are beyond exquisite. Dolphins splash in the channels at dawn, and sunset brings flocks of snowy white egrets to the tangerine sky. Charleston truly is a paradise.

But the Holy City has a dark side, too. 'Ghost chasing' is a *huge* industry here; there are so many 'ghost tours' in the area the local media includes the category in its annual 'Best of Charleston' rankings. And even non-believers can find plenty of gloom in the city's bona fide history involving colonist exploitation of native peoples, the slave trade, the Civil War, Reconstruction, and Jim Crow. Specters who cast a shadow over this region run the gamut from legendary miscreants like antebellum call-girl 'Nettie,' to documented scoundrel Lavinia

Fisher, America's first female serial killer who was executed at Charleston's Old City Jail in 1820.

In between are places that emit their own unique uncanny vibe. Dan and I came upon one such site not long after we had moved to the lowcountry. It was a fence and gate back in the overgrown marshes, festooned with scores of bizarre objects, and painted a peculiar shade of light blue. From the moment I saw it, I was simultaneously fascinated and unnerved by the gateway, and adamantly refused to pass under it. I found it so compelling, I took my children, all college age, to see it when they came to visit us. We all figured it was someone's folk art composition. Abby was especially impressed.

I posted a photograph of the structure on a website dedicated to South Carolina scenery. Almost immediately, people started leaving comments that made my jaw drop:

Isn't that place haunted?

I know the family who built this — it's to protect against haints

Wow you're braver than me going there

Intrigued, I started doing some research, beginning with learning what a 'haint' was. According to a Gullah professor I consulted, haints were 'restless, angry spirits of the southern coast,' who returned to menace the living. The term is likely derived from an old European word 'hanter,' meaning to stalk relentlessly. Belief in haints is a staple of the Gullah Geechee ('Gullah' typically refers to the indigenous culture along the Carolinas, 'Geechee' in Georgia and northern Florida), who also teach methods to avoid the spirits and remedies should they attack.

While looking into the origins of the gate, I mentioned to a local woman that I had taken my children there and how much my daughter in particular liked it. The woman was shocked.

"Why would you put your girl in such danger?" she'd asked, dismayed.

"It's okay," I laughed. "Abby's fine. She's back at school in Virginia now."

"How do you *know* she's all right if she's five hundred miles away? How do you know it's even really her anymore?"

Two days later, at 7:30 a.m., my phone rang. I thought it would be Dan, who was away on business, calling to check in. Instead, when I picked up, I heard a woman's frenzied screams followed by a man's voice saying, "I have Abby, and if you want your daughter back alive you better do what I say!"

Stunned, I decided to coax as much information as I could from him.

"How do I know you really have her?" I asked, trying to stay calm. "What's her middle name? Where'd she go to grade school?"

"Tell you what," he replied. "I'm going to cut off her fingers one by one and send them to you. See if they look familiar!"

He hung up, and I immediately dialed Abby's phone. She was usually never without it, but that morning she didn't pick up. No answer at work, either. Her boyfriend's line went straight to voicemail. I talked to Roman and Charles, but neither of them had spoken to Abby since the previous evening. For the next few hours, without success, I tried repeatedly to get ahold of my daughter, and I became increasingly rattled as the day wore on.

I called the local authorities in our hometown, who sent an officer to check on Abby's whereabouts. However they, too, kept hitting dead ends. She seemed to have disappeared. Finally, after a day that felt like a century, we discovered she was attending a class on police tactics, and had been out on the shooting range and then the vehicles course the entire time. Her instructors had strict 'no phones' policies, so students had to leave cellphones in their cars and were not allowed to check them while on site. This left Abby uncharacteristically unreachable.

Her 'kidnapping' ultimately turned out to be part of a shakedown scheme, but it made me realize how powerless I was to help my daughter if she really had been in danger. The Charleston woman's alarm over Abby's recent presence at Bandun Gate only compounded that unease.

Following that incident, and with Dan away for days or weeks on end, I often found myself filling the hours imagining various threats that might imperil the children, especially Abby, both mortal and preternatural.

At the same time, I was still researching the mysterious 'haint' gate. During the course of that investigation, I talked to a man who swore his aunt had been 'displaced' by a malevolent spirit. He claimed that in the mid 1940s, his father's seventeen-year-old sister Elaine went to put flowers on their grandmother's grave, but when she returned, she was 'no longer herself.' The girl who'd come home *looked* like their Laney, but her personality had changed dramatically. Overnight, she went from sweet and friendly to cold and petulant. She refused to interact with anyone and rarely left her room. A few weeks later, 'Lost Laney' announced she was leaving for good, and left with only the clothes on her back, never to be seen again. The family made no attempt to find her, convinced the girl they loved had 'passed on' that day at the cemetery, replaced by a haint.

That story planted a seed; my nightmares started again. I would wake to the sound of someone breathing next to me in the dark, but when I turned on the light, no one was there. Or blaring noise from the TV would jolt me out of bed, yet I'd go out the family room and the set would be off. In one especially disturbing dream, Charles showed up at the door wearing a goat skull and dark robe, then put a concoction on my right hand that made the skin blister and burn, saying he'd gotten the idea from my Hell research. His nose dripped, then gushed, blood as he lingered, smiling.

Other odd incidents occurred, too. By themselves, they would've merely been annoying, but the fact they all happened within such a short timeframe had me rattled. A bird flew into the kitchen window and broke its neck. A day later, a snake appeared on the patio just outside our backdoor. My left pinky finger kept spontaneously becoming dislocated and bruised for no apparent reason, turning blackish-purple from the second knuckle up. I would wake up with puncture marks on my arms and legs, always in tiny pairs, with the exact same distance between them every time and no indication how they got there. Again, nothing earth-shattering, yet still creepy.

That was the genesis of *Bandun Gate*. I started subconsciously weaving what I'd learned about the strange structure with the panic and dread I'd felt over Abby's 'abduction' and the ominous tale of 'Lost Laney.' If my daughter *had* been kidnapped by some thug it would've been awful, but at least I could've paid to get her back. What would be the remedy if some insidious supernatural force snatched her away? The final piece was hearing the true story of Eliza Huger, a woman so wicked no church would allow her body to be buried on its grounds for fear of her curdled spirit.

Eliza Huger was born in the late 1700s to an affluent Charleston family. As a teen, she grew bored with her lowcountry life and ran away to New Orleans. From there, the details of her exploits become sketchy. In some versions, Eliza was a prostitute who murdered her clients. Other stories have her practicing an especially violent form of witchcraft. Most legends agree she died in 1819 when two of her brothers, sent to bring their wayward sister home, found her in bed with a strange man and shot her dead.

The pair returned with Eliza's body, but no cemetery in Charleston would accept it. Eventually the family negotiated a deal with the Old Stone Church in Clemson. Eliza could be buried on the grounds, however her grave had to be walled-in to keep her depraved soul from escaping. Over the decades, despite frequent repairs and reinforcement, the stone wall has crumbled numerous times. Lightning has struck the site so often that only the words "brothers' sorrow" remain readable on Eliza's tombstone.

Rylah is partially based on Eliza Huger, and other characters are based on people I met or consulted about the odd fence and gate. The Gullah root workers are composites of several experts on the culture who introduced me to the fascinating realm of white magic, haints and conjure. Mike Fontaine and the incident involving Kadisha were inspired by the tale of 'lost Laney.'

Father Frank, Levi, the Cult of the Deathless Angel, Hank and other characters and incidents from the Vermicular File all originate from my original research for *Encyclopedia of Hell*.

Fantastic Books
Great Authors

- Gripping Thrillers
- Cosy Mysteries
- Romantic Chick-Lit
- Fascinating Historicals
- Exciting Fantasy
- Young Adult and Children's Adventures
- Non-Fiction

Discover us online
www.darkstroke.com

Find us on instagram:
www.instagram.com/darkstrokebooks